Freeman Wills Crofts was born in Dublin in 1879 and died in 1957. He worked for a Northern Irish railway company as an engineer until 1929, before turning to detective fiction.

His plots reveal his mathematical training and he specialised in the seemingly unbreakable alibi and the intricacies of railway timetables. He also loved ships and trains and they feature in many of his stories.

Crofts' best-known character is Inspector Joseph French. French appears for the first time in *Inspector French's Greatest Case*. He is a detective who achieves his results through dogged persistence.

Raymond Chandler praised Crofts' plots, calling him 'the soundest builder of them all'.

GW00537284

BY THE SAME AUTHOR
ALL PUBLISHED BY HOUSE OF STRATUS

FREEMAN WILLS CROFTS

Silence for the Murderer

HOUSE OF
STRATUS

This edition published in 2000 by House of Stratus, an imprint of Stratus Holdings plc, 24c Old Burlington Street, London, W1X 1RL, UK.

www.houseofstratus.com

Typeset, printed and bound by House of Stratus.

A catalogue record for this book is available from the British Library.

ISBN 1-84232-412-8

CONTENTS

– 1 –

HOMECOMING

Dulcie Heath's step was light and her face eager as on this dull March evening she hastened through the streets of North London. Though buried in her thoughts, subconsciously it seemed to her that the atmosphere was brighter, the houses more attractive, and the people more smiling and friendly than was usually the case. She was bound for Euston, and even the grim old station had a pleasant welcoming air. For Dulcie's mind was full of excited anticipation and her impressions were coloured by her mood.

Though by no means a beauty, yet she was a pleasing enough vision as she hurried along, or rather, she would have been had the streets been sufficiently well lighted to see her clearly. She was short, and if in time she might be stout, this calamity was not yet. Her hair was her best feature, a beautiful rich auburn, and with it went grey eyes and a milky complexion. She was always well dressed, not necessarily in the height of fashion, but daintily and with extreme care. She had brisk movements, a good carriage, and a quiet competent manner which induced confidence.

This was an important moment in her life. She was going to meet her greatest friend, Frank Roscoe, who had arrived in Liverpool a week earlier to be demobbed after six years Army service, mostly in North Africa and Italy. Though

1

they were not formally engaged, there was between them what in her own mind she called an understanding. All through the campaign they had exchanged letters, and she had no doubt whatever that the missing formality would quickly follow his return. In fact she looked forward to an early future in which she would be Mrs Roscoe.

She had been worried when Frank had joined up. He was a dear fellow, so cheery, so good tempered, so good looking and with such delightful manners: lovable in every way. Yet he had a weakness. She hated the thought of it, but she could not hide it from herself: he was not too dependable. He was easily led, and he did not distinguish sufficiently sharply between what belonged to himself and to others. She had been afraid of the effect the Army might have on him. In such strange surroundings there was a real fear that he might make some kind of break.

Fortunately her fears had been groundless, or so she believed from his letters. His promotion to sergeant showed that he had acquitted himself well. Certainly there had been no catastrophe.

It might be wondered why, if she knew of this weakness, she was still ready to marry him. The answer was simple. She loved him, and this small token of human frailty increased rather than diminished her affection.

Though separated from him during these last six years she had had a happy enough life, at least as happy as anyone could have had in London during the War. She had a good job, that of receptionist and secretary to Mr Burt, a Harley Street surgeon. Bartholomew Burt was all, and more than all, that could be desired in an employer: kind, generous and understanding. She had an unbombed flat, which if tiny, was comfortable and convenient. Last, but not least, for her peace of mind, she had given skilled first aid in the blitz, and as she worked among wrecked and burning buildings, she knew that her efforts had helped to save lives and ease the last moments of the less fortunate.

The train was late, and pacing up and down the platform, she thought over her long association with Frank. She had first met him when she was six, their respective fathers being general practitioners in the same quarter of Liverpool. That was four and twenty years ago. Frank was then a precocious boy of nine, inconsequently exasperating, but with a disarming smile and the face of an angel. At that time she had almost worshipped him. He had received her homage as his unquestioned due, treating her with the lofty superiority of his sex and years. Then school had come and only at lengthening intervals had they met.

By a strange freak of fate a somewhat similar disaster later overtook both of them. Frank was in his final year in the Medical School of the London University when his father died suddenly. Instead of the expected comfortable balance, the unhappy man left more debts than assets. Frank threw up his studies and took the only job he could find, that of general clerk to a small firm of builders near Clapham. For five years he drifted from place to place, managing during the process to learn reasonably good shorthand and typing, as well as practically everything that the non-professional can know about cars. So complete was this knowledge that, on joining up he was drafted into the transport section of the Eighth Army as an Air Force motor mechanic. A wound temporarily disqualifying him for this work, he was taken into the Paymaster's office, where practice perfected his shorthand and typing. Again he was wounded as the result of a direct hit on the building. This proved a lengthy business, and it was only after many months in hospital that he was sent home to Liverpool and there demobbed.

Dulcie's history was similar in that while she was training as a nurse, her father also died. He left no debts, but the balance which came to her was small and represented little more than pocket money. She had grown to hate nursing, and as, inspired by Frank's example she had taught herself shorthand and typing, she left the hospital and went to the office of a shipping company. There she worked for some six years, though unhappily, owing to a disagreeable boss. She watched the papers, and when she saw Mr Burt's advertisement for a receptionist and secretary, she answered it. Her knowledge of nursing and the routine of a doctor's house, together with her clerical qualifications, got her the job, and since then she had found herself in clover.

At last the train appeared, moving slowly alongside the platform. Dulcie, a little anxious lest she should miss Frank, took up her position near the engine. Nervous also she was, now that the moment of meeting was upon her. Six years was a long time, and no one could go through Frank's experiences unchanged.

Now the platform was black with people. To her excited imagination there seemed to be no limit to the numbers the train had brought. Hundreds and hundreds: a whole town appeared to be disgorging from it. They poured out past her and across the carriageway and drove off in taxis and private cars: and still no sign of Frank.

The rush was thinning when a tall, rather stooped man hove in sight. He was dressed in shapeless clothes and carried a small suitcase. For a moment Dulcie stared at him doubtfully and then her heart gave a leap. Could it be? This untidy wreck of a man with the pale anxious face and haunted eyes? Could this be Frank?

Then with a gasp of horror she saw that it was. A look of recognition dawned on his features, he waved an arm and moved towards her. She fought down her dismay and tried to smile a real welcome.

"Frank!" she cried. "Oh, Frank!" and careless of publicity and of their somewhat indefinite relations, she flung her arms round his neck and kissed him passionately.

He seemed pleased if slightly surprised by her greeting. "You're a sight for sore eyes, Dulcie," he declared. "My word, but it's good to see you again!"

"Oh, Frank, you've been ill," she went on, holding him off and looking at him more critically. "You look as if you'd been through it."

"Of course I've been ill, honey. That's why I was demobbed. Got a shell splinter in my side. But that's all past. I'm getting on fine now. I don't need to ask about you. You're looking in the pink."

"I am in the pink. But you must be cold and hungry. I've fixed up supper in my flat. I thought we'd be more comfortable there than in a restaurant."

"Sounds good to me."

"I've got a room close by for you as you said in your letter."

"Fine. Good of you, Dulcie, to take so much trouble."

"Don't be silly. Come, let's get on. Stupid of me, I never thought to reserve a taxi and now I'm afraid they're all gone."

"Taxi? You're coming up in the world, old girl. A bus is my limit."

This certainly was a new Frank. He had always been extravagant. Often had scolded him for spending lavishly on some worthless object which had caught his fancy at the moment, regardless of where the money for his next meal was to come from. Now he must be comparatively well off. Even if he had saved none of his pay, his gratuity must be considerable.

She was slightly shocked to find that in the bus they presently boarded, he let her pay. He made a half-hearted attempt to reach his pocket, but obviously delayed till she had handed out the fare. As they ground through the dingy streets he was silent. He replied to her remarks, but he was not bubbling over with conversation as formerly. She noticed that he never once smiled, while in his eyes remained that look of anxiety, almost of fear.

She felt cut to the heart. The war of falling buildings and broken bodies in which she had taken part was bad enough in all conscience, but somehow it seemed almost worse to destroy so fine and upstanding a man as Frank, for that was what had apparently happened.

As he lay in a chair before the fire, lit from Dulcie's slender store of coal to mark a great occasion, and smoked one after another of her hard-won cigarettes, the tension seemed somewhat to leave him. He relaxed and grew drowsy. During the meal they had talked generalities, but she felt increasingly anxious to get down to something more personal. He had written from Liverpool telling her he was coming up to Town to look for a job and asking her to get him a room. What, she wondered, were his plans? Had he a job in view, and if so, what?

"Well," she said presently, "tell me now about things. Did you have a very ghastly time?"

He roused himself. "Not really. There were nasty streaks of course, but on the whole it wasn't too bad. Very decent lot of fellows and all that. I expect you really had it worse here."

"Oh," she said offhandedly, "we got through well enough. But tell me about yourself. Hard luck being wounded."

"I didn't think so. They did us jolly well in the hospitals, and dozing in bed was an easier job than reboring cylinders or moneying out paysheets. Besides, my wound has brought me home."

A slightly baffled feeling was growing up in Dulcie's mind. Though Frank was at last speaking of himself, he seemed at the same time to grow even more impersonal and aloof. A barrier of some kind was shutting him off from her.

"You want a good rest and a bit of feeding up," she declared. "And you won't get it here in London. What about a month in Wales or Cornwall or West Scotland?"

"Sounds good to me," he answered. "I wish I could. But I've got to live. Must get a job at once."

"I thought you wrote that you had an opening with a building firm in Manchester?"

"I thought so too. I went there to see the place after I landed. There was just a heap of rubble where the office had stood. Got a direct hit, they told me."

"Oh, Frank! What hard luck! But won't they open up again?"

"Tom Semple won't: he was the owner and my chum. He was there at the time. They couldn't even find his body."

"How ghastly! But it surely doesn't mean that the firm has come to an end?"

"The firm was Tom Semple. He hadn't floated it as a company or anything. It was his own venture."

"Then that job's gone. Oh, Frank, I *am* sorry. What do you think of doing?"

"Taking anything I can get. Must. I'm stony at the moment."

Dulcie felt completely baffled. On demobilisation these men got quite a tidy sum. Frank had no dependants. He ought to have plenty for a good holiday while he looked about for something suitable.

"But – " she was beginning when he interrupted her.

"You're thinking of my gratuity? You needn't. It's gone. I had some debts that had to be paid."

She gasped. "Oh, surely not all of it? How could – ?"

"Easy enough," he said with a bitter laugh. "In the Army you have to spend money. Then you borrow from people and – it mounts up and – there you are."

"But surely – Frank, dear, don't think I want to pry into your business, but how could so large a sum – ? I mean, I've heard of so many demobbed men and they all had enough to start them in something."

He nodded. "That's right: lucky beggars. But you haven't heard of the thousands of others, like me. Lots of chaps are in the same boat with me. Everything gone." He began to laugh in a nervous uncontrolled way.

"Stop it!" she said sharply. "Pull yourself together! Look here, I'm sorry I haven't a drop of spirits in the place, but the coffee's still hot. Have another cup?"

"No, I'm all right. Sorry and all that."

"I can understand you're worried," she said more gently. "I should be in your place. But let's look at this together. We'll find something before long, don't be afraid."

"It'll need to be before long."

"You don't mean that you're – actually short? Again don't think I'm prying, but how long can you carry on?"

His despairing look returned. "Well," he answered grimly, "if you want to know, I'll tell you. When I paid my fare up to Town and got some sandwiches I had seventeen and fourpence left."

She stared. "Do you mean that that's all the cash you have?"

"Every blessed bean."

Dulcie was so horrified that for the moment she could not speak. A wave of indignation swelled up in her mind. There was more in this, she was positive, than he had told her. His manner was furtive and he would not meet her eyes. He had been up to some of his games. She remembered, during the years before joining up, a number of unfortunate financial episodes. She had believed, though she had never definitely known, that some of these were not unconnected with his frequent change of jobs. How could he have incurred these "debts"?

She felt inclined to ask some pretty searching questions, then as she glanced at him again and saw the misery and fear – yes, fear – in his eyes, her resentment melted and she felt for him only overwhelming pity and love. She was now thankful she had not commented on his remark. Obviously he was in a highly sensitive mood and the wrong word might have done damage. An urgent desire to help him took the place of all other feelings.

"Poor Frank," she murmured softly. "I just can't say how sorry I am. We must look round for something at once. And don't give a thought to how you are to carry on in the meantime. I have a little put by and I can help you till you're able to repay me."

He seemed surprised and rather overwhelmed. His expression lost some of its strain. For a moment he hesitated and she thought he was going to tell her everything. Then he looked away muttering, "You're a good sort, Dulcie. I'll not forget it. If you can see me over a few days I'll pay you back with the first money I get."

It was then that a sudden idea flashed into Dulcie's mind. Graham, Burt's attendant at the Harley Street house, was leaving at the end of the week and his place had not yet been filled. It was not of course the kind of job for Frank, but purely as a temporary measure perhaps it might serve. Burt was an ideal employer, and if Frank were there, Dulcie would have him under her eye and could look after him. She believed, moreover, that on her recommendation Burt would give him a trial.

"Look here," she said, "I've just had a thought. There's a vacancy where I work," and she explained about it. "Of course I know it's not the thing for you, but the question is, would you like to try it purely as a stop gap?"

He looked at her with a sort of despairing hope in his face. "Would I have a chance?" he asked.

Her heart smote her again. What a different Frank! Doubt and humility instead of a careless and condescending superiority!

"Burt would think himself lucky to get you," she returned. "You have both a medical and a clerical training. Then what about your manners and your knowledge of the world? Yes, he'd be lucky."

"Will you speak to him?" Frank's voice was sharp with eagerness.

"You'd take it?"

"Of course I'd take it. Glad to get it. I don't care what the work is or the pay: you can tell him I'd do my best."

Thus came about a move which was to have a profound effect on both their lives. Next morning Dulcie saw Burt, and so skilfully did she conduct the negotiations that the surgeon quickly closed with an obviously advantageous offer. An interview with Frank ended in his appointment, and it was arranged that on the following Monday morning

10

he should take over his new duties. With his usual thoughtful kindness Burt made him an advance on his salary for new clothes.

Mr Bartholomew Burt usually shared the Harley Street house with another specialist, both living in the suburbs and using it only as a place of business. But just then the other rooms were vacant. It was what is sometimes known as a single house, meaning that it had rooms on one side of the staircase only. In front was the common waiting-room, differing from the majority of such places only in the fact that its papers and periodicals were all kept meticulously up to date. Behind, and lit from the back of the house, was Burt's consulting-room, with the usual couch, austere prints and imposing desk. The kitchen would be Frank's sanctum, and Dulcie saw to it that there was a table for his books and an easy chair in which he could lounge. In the return was a sitting-room used by Burt if and when he had a period of relaxation. Beside it Dulcie had her office, and further back were two store rooms filled with old furniture and miscellaneous rubbish. The other doctor, when there was one, had his consulting-room on the second floor, while above was a small laboratory and various other rooms used for technical purposes by both men. A bell from Burt's consulting-room was rung in code to summon receptionist or attendant.

That Frank would give satisfaction was to Dulcie a foregone conclusion. There was nothing he could not do well, if only he would take the necessary trouble. This he would always do in the case of anything new and con-structive or in which for any reason he was specially interested. But with routine work he soon got bored and then his output suffered.

Frank quickly settled down into his new surroundings. The work for a man of his abilities was child's play, and as Dulcie had foreseen, he did it admirably. That Burt was pleased was obvious, though he made no comment. The patients also appeared to like Frank. His quiet politeness pleased them and the fact that he remembered their faces and called them by their names.

As the days passed Dulcie's feelings towards him grew increasingly mixed. She was fonder of him than ever. His indifferent health and strange humility appealed powerfully to her. His manner, though subdued, was pleasanter than she had ever known it. Most evenings he spent at her flat. He seemed content with her company and never suggested going out to shows. Almost he had become domesticated. His health moreover seemed to be slowly improving.

At the same time she was satisfied that he remained miserably unhappy. The look of anxiety rarely left his eyes, and often when he thought he was unobserved, they showed stark terror. What dreadful thing, she wondered, had happened to him while in the Army? Not once, but many times, she tried to find out. But she could not pierce his reserve. Always quietly and pleasantly he put her off.

Then about three weeks after he had started work the load suddenly lifted. The moment her eyes fell on him one morning Dulcie noticed the difference. He was smiling. He held himself more erect. His movements had become more springy and forceful. He called out to her in a voice more like that of the Frank she had known. What was more, he came over to her, picked her up in his arms, swinging her off her feet as if she had been a child, and planted kisses that really were kisses on her face and mouth.

"Frank!" she cried when she could speak, "what has taken you? Let me go! I won't be fit to be seen!"

Almost crying from relief, she made a show of repairing her damaged complexion. "What is it?" she went on eagerly. "Something's happened. You look different."

He grinned with some of his old truculence. "Look different, do I? I feel different. *Well*, you know. Not that ghastly ill feeling I've been having. I feel I could jump over the moon."

"Poor Frank, had you been feeling as badly as that? And you never complained."

"Fat lot of good complaining would have done. But I believe I'm going to be all right now. I haven't felt like this for months."

Whatever the cause, from that moment Frank was a different man. No longer was he content in the evenings to brood over the fire in Dulcie's flat. They must go out. They must get what amusement was possible in post-war London. At last Dulcie was experiencing what she had been looking forward to from the moment she had heard he was returning. She was supremely happy.

The physical change in Frank was equally marked. Energy had come back into his languid frame. The look of despair, of actual fear, had gone from his eyes. Daily his face grew less drawn and his cheeks less hollow. It looked as if complete recovery was a matter of only a short time.

Then as suddenly as the cloud had lifted, it fell again.

On this fateful day the morning had passed as usual and the pair had lunched at one of the small restaurants they now patronised. After lunch Dulcie had returned direct to Harley Street while Frank had gone round to change a book at a twopenny library. During the afternoon she saw him only in the distance. She thought he looked somehow different, but it was not till they met for supper in her flat that she realised what was wrong. All the dreadful signs of misery and depression had returned. The look of fear indeed was more intense than she had ever seen it.

"Frank dear," she said in dismay, "what on earth has happened? You look awful!"

He would not meet her eyes. "I don't somehow feel so well this evening," he muttered. "Don't worry. I'll be all right presently."

"Rubbish!" she retorted. "You needn't try that kind of stuff on me. You've had bad news: what is it?"

For a moment he hesitated. "Oh, nothing," he said then. "A bit of indigestion, I expect."

In spite of her anxiety a wave of anger swept over her. "Don't be a complete ass," she said sharply. "I've put up with this worry about you long enough, knowing something was pretty seriously wrong, but not knowing what it was. I'm going to put up with it no longer. Come, tell me the trouble. I absolutely insist."

He looked more frightened than ever. "But, Dulcie, honey, there's no trouble. I just don't feel – "

Her very love for him gave her courage. "I'll not put up with any more prevarication! You know you're not telling me the truth! Here I've done everything I can to help you, and I think I'm entitled to be treated as something more than a casual acquaintance."

He moved miserably. "Honey, I know what you've done. Don't think I'm not grateful. But – "

"Grateful! That's not what I expect from you. I want ordinary common companionship. If you're in trouble I want you to tell me about it, so that we can fight it together."

That she had made an impression on him she was certain. Once again he hesitated, then he said in a low voice, "I don't think we can do anything about this. I've

14

made a muck of things, and what's worse, I'm afraid you may be involved."

"Tell me, Frank. Tell me."

Then she knew that she had won. He lit a cigarette and began to smoke feverishly. "It wasn't anything at first, you know. I did what anyone might do and there was no harm in it. Then it sort of went from bad to worse. And now it's hopeless. I'm for it and I can't do anything about it."

"Frank, dear, don't talk like that. Nothing's hopeless. Tell me about it and we'll find some way out."

He looked at her as if with a faint fluttering of hope. "You're a good sort, Dulcie," he declared, "as I think I've said before. I know I've felt it often enough. I'll tell you. Indeed it'll be a tremendous relief. I've wanted to tell you and I just couldn't face it."

"There's nothing to face, silly boy. It's only me. Go ahead."

"Well, it began a little time ago when I was getting about again after my second wound. I got a ninety-six hour leave in Rome. There were a lot of the chaps there and we went about and saw things. You know the sort of thing."

She nodded.

"In the evenings we were a bit bored and someone suggested a game. Well, when everyone else was joining in I couldn't stay out. We'd had a few drinks, you understand, and we were all a bit above ourselves. The stakes got higher: you know the way it is."

At all costs she felt she must encourage him. A breath of criticism and he would close up like a clam. "Of course," she agreed, "that's how things happen."

"Well, I had the devil's own luck. You wouldn't believe the way those cards fell. I felt every time they *couldn't* go against me again and plunged higher and higher. But they always did. It was incredible!"

"I know. Luck runs like that. I've often thought there was something devilish in it."

"There was that time. Well, I needn't go into details. When I got back to base I owed sixty-five pounds and I hadn't a bean to pay it with."

"Poor Frank! What did you do?"

"Well, that was the question. The money was fairly lost and if I didn't pay I was finished. I don't mean I could have been arrested or dismissed the Army or anything of that sort, but I just couldn't go on living with the chaps. I couldn't have stood it."

"I know. I do sympathise."

"You can probably guess what's coming. You know I was working in the Paymaster's Department and a lot of money went through my hands. I saw a way I could fix up the books and if it was discovered I could plead a genuine mistake – or at first I thought I could. I needn't tell you how I fought the idea. To make a long story short, I altered some figures and got a false balance. I had to work to an even amount, and at the end of the week I had a hundred pounds of Government money in my pocket."

In spite of having to some extent expected this, Dulcie was horrified. Frank had always been careless about other people's money, but this seemed more deliberate than any of his previous errors, or at least, she told herself bitterly, of any she knew about. Still she must show no criticism: she must have the whole story.

"Poor old Frank!" she murmured. "What a hideous position!"

"It should have been," he answered with rare honesty, "but as a matter of fact I was pleased. I said I had written

16

home for some cash and paid my sixty-five pounds. I had thirty-five pounds in hand and no one was any the worse, for at the rate the Government was squandering its millions, my miserable hundred was the merest drop in the bucket."

"But they – er – discovered the affair?"

"No, they didn't. But I'm not sure that what happened wasn't worse. A man did discover it, a chap called Garnett, a clerk in the same department. But he didn't give me away."

She looked her question.

"He met me one evening and asked me to speak to him in private. He said he had become suspicious about my getting the money from home, for he had handled the letters for our department during the period and he hadn't seen one for me. So then he had looked up the books and at last he had found the faked sheet. He had taken it out and kept it."

"But if he didn't tell the authorities, what was he going to do with it?"

"You'll see. He asked me what it would be worth to me to have the affair kept secret. I tried to bluff, but he said he'd been into the thing carefully, my debts as well as the accounts, and he knew I had thirty-five pounds over. He would take that on account. If I liked to pay, the sheet was safe for the present, if not, he would feel it his duty to report the affair."

Another terrible fear was growing up in Dulcie's mind, but she fought it down. "Could you not have had him for blackmail?"

"I couldn't have proved blackmail without admitting the fraud. That would have been cutting off my nose to spite my face."

"I suppose so. What did you do?"

"What could I do? I paid up. For the time being I heard no more about it, then when it was to be arranged that I was to be demobbed, Garnett turned up again. He said he'd heard I was going Horne and that there'd be a nice tidy sum due me. He said he was very hard up and he wanted it. He'd be glad if I'd make it over to him."

"Oh, Frank! How dreadful for you!"

"I tried to fight him, but I soon saw that if I didn't pay, it would mean that instead of getting home I'd be given perhaps a couple of years in quod. What could I do? I had to pay again."

"But how could you pay what you hadn't received?"

He fixed that up all right. We both went before the Paymaster and I signed a legal document asking for my money to be paid to Garnett. I put up a tale that it was to meet some debts, but I don't think the Paymaster believed it."

"Why?"

"Because he called me back later and asked me was I quite happy about the arrangement and would I like him to look into it. I said of course I was perfectly happy. He looked at me doubtfully but said 'Very well'."

"So that's why you were so hard up when you arrived! Oh, Frank, how you've suffered!"

"But that wasn't the real trouble, Dulcie. I knew I wasn't quit of it. Garnett would be demobbed too, and then he'd come at me again. He'd go on draining me till I was dry. I would have no hope of any kind of a decent life – unless I killed him. I was tempted to do that. Thank God I didn't."

Though that at least was a relief, Dulcie was feeling terribly distressed. Still she believed she should give him only encouragement. "I don't see how he can get you again," she declared. "If he waits too long that sheet will become valueless."

"Not on your life. As long as there's a Paymaster's Department in the Army, it could send me to quod."

"But he'd convict himself. He couldn't explain how it came into his possession. If he got it in Italy, why didn't he report it at once? I can see he had you in his power, but I don't see how he can keep you in it."

"You'll see the position when you've heard the end of my story. Now I've started let me go on: if you can stand any more."

"Frank, dear, don't talk like that."

"Well, I paid up and came home, and the first thing that wasn't black despair was meeting you. You got me this job with Burt, and everything would have been fine only for Garnett. I was always expecting to hear from him with some new demand. Then about five weeks ago I got a piece of the most marvellous news. I thought I was free."

Dulcie remembered that period when Frank seemed to have shed his trouble. She listened almost breathlessly.

"I saw Garnett's name in a list of those missing from a home-bound transport which went ashore on the Burlings. It seemed like stepping back into the world after having lived for months in hell. Now, I thought, everything will be all right. I'll have a chance to get properly fit, and when I've paid Dulcie back what she lent me and put a few pounds together, I'll look for a job that would suit me better. Though, mind you, Dulcie, I'm very content with Burt."

"But something went wrong?"

"I'll say so: only today. Everything was all right till I left you after lunch. Then the very worst happened. I met Garnett."

"Then the list was wrong! Oh, Frank!"

"He stopped me. 'Well, if this isn't a coincidence,' he said. 'You're just the man I've been trying to find. I was adrift in a boat and got picked up after that trouble we had on the way home – you may have seen about it. I've just been demobbed and I wanted to see you.' 'Well,' I said, 'you're seeing me. What is it?' "

Frank paused as if finding the story difficult. Then with an obvious effort he continued: "I needn't go through all our conversation, though it was short and pithy enough. What he had to tell me was that he'd been offered a really good job if he could put down two hundred pounds. He hadn't it, but if I could find it for him he'd sell me the doctored sheet."

"More blackmail!"

"Of course it was blackmail, but it would be for the last time. If I could get hold of that sheet I'd be free. Neither he nor anyone else would have anything on me. It was a proper draw, I can tell you."

"But if you hadn't the money how could you buy it?"

"That's all right. But just remember what I'd have got: freedom and a chance to go ahead and have a normal life: everything I thought I'd lost."

"Oh yes, Frank, I do understand. You must have been nearly frantic."

"I'll say I was frantic. I thought, here's my whole life at stake. If I can get that paper, everything's okay. I wanted a little time to think it over, so I said that before I could do anything I'd have to be sure the paper was genuine and could he let me see it? He looked at me and said he wasn't that kind of a fool; he hadn't it on him. But he would hand it over if I could put up the money. He gave me his address."

"Well, you couldn't. So that was the end of that."

Frank remained silent and his manner was so hangdog that Dulcie suddenly panicked. "What have you done, Frank?" she cried. "You've done something, I can see it in your face. What is it?"

He made two efforts before he could speak. Then he said thickly, "I got the money."

"You got it? Where?"

Again he paused, then began, "I'm afraid you'll b – "

"Oh, stop it!" she interrupted urgently. "Where did you get it? Tell me at once."

He looked at her sadly. "From Burt."

This certainly was unexpected. For a moment she did not understand. "From Burt? Do you mean to say he advanced you two hundred pounds merely on the strength of that story?"

Frank shook his head. "He doesn't know," he muttered.

There was a terrible pause. Dulcie looked as if she could not believe her ears. "Do you mean that you've – *stolen* it?"

"No, no," he spoke hurriedly, "only borrowed it. I'll pay it back directly I can. You do believe that, don't you, Dulcie?"

Dulcie felt she was in the grip of a nightmare. This horror could not be real. "But how did you do it?" she insisted. "Where did you find two hundred pounds?"

"It really was an accident," he returned more eagerly. "The thing came on me suddenly: so quickly I hadn't time to think. I saw the money and I took it. Then it was too late to put it back."

"But two hundred pounds doesn't lie about waiting to be picked up. Where did you get it?"

"Well, it was this way. This afternoon after Mrs Redlake had gone out I heard Burt go up to his laboratory. So I went into his room to make up the fire, as I would normally do. Then as it happened I saw – "

"Yes? Go on."

"I saw his keys hanging in his safe. Suddenly it came over me that he must have a lot of money from patients who pay in cash. It was just a sudden thought, you understand."

Dulcie felt as if an icy weight was slowly pressing down on her heart. "Go on," she repeated faintly.

"I didn't wait to think. If I had waited to think I wouldn't have done it. But there was the money, or so I believed. And Burt might come down any minute. So there was no time to think. I opened the safe and in the drawer I found scores of notes of all values. I counted out two hundred singles: I had time because I could have heard him coming overhead. Then I closed up the safe again and – and – that was all."

Dulcie groaned. "Oh, Frank I just couldn't have believed it of you! To *steal* from Burt! You can't do it! You must put the money back at once! I'll find a way of getting it into the safe. I sometimes have to open it for papers."

He looked at her queerly. "But I can't. It's gone. I've given it to Garnett and got the paper."

Dulcie could not speak. Slowly she turned her back. Her head went down into her hands and presently she was sobbing as if her heart would break.

– 2 –

THE SCHEME

It was a long time before normal relations between Dulcie and Frank were re-established.

When he saw her distress he was undoubtedly penitent, though whether because of irritation at her weeping or of sorrow for his crime she did not know. But he did try to comfort her.

"Now, honey, don't take on like that," he begged. "It's not so bad as you think. It's not a theft, only a loan. Burt'll not know anything about it and I'll pay it back and it'll be all right."

Dulcie was not mollified. "It's not so simple as that," she reminded him when at last her tears had ceased and she could speak normally. "You say you'll pay him back. But how? Where's the money coming from?"

"I can live on very little. I should be able to clear it off within the year."

"A year! But he'll miss the money immediately; perhaps tomorrow."

"Not necessarily. There are still a lot of notes left."

"Of course he'll miss it. He's not altogether a fool."

He glanced at her appraisingly. "You think so? Well look, Dulcie, you'll have to help me out. If you don't, I'm afraid I'm finished."

Once again her heart sank. What further demand would she have to meet? "I don't understand," she said dully.

"You clear that drawer out every now and then, don't you? Lodge the cash in the bank?"

"Yes, but only when he tells me to."

"Well look here," Frank repeated and then stopped. He seemed to have a difficulty in putting his suggestion into words. "Could you not – I mean, if you would just help me out in this, all our troubles would be over."

"I asked you how," she insisted.

"What I wondered was – I mean, could you not, for example, pretend you had paid it in to the bank? That's only an idea of course, but – could you not?"

She stared. "I do think, Frank, you've gone out of your mind."

"Listen," he implored. "It would be easy. All you'd have to do would be to say to him that you'd noticed that a lot of cash had accumulated and you supposed he'd forgotten to mention it to you. So you'd taken the liberty of lodging two hundred and you hoped that was all right."

She swung round in her chair. "You *have* gone out of your mind! Don't you see that that would bring me in too: make me a thief also?"

"Now, honey, don't take that view. You couldn't be a thief and no one could ever imagine it. What I suggest is quite simple. Just a casual phrase and the thing's done."

"Oh, is it? And where would be the bank receipt for the two hundred?"

"You could let it be understood that it would be among the next lot of bank papers you brought him."

"I see. I'm to become a liar for you as well as a thief. Think again, Frank Roscoe! I'm not such a fool as you take me for."

"Then you won't?" he said appealingly. "You could do it so easily if only you would."

"I don't know how you can even think of such a thing."

He sighed. "No, I see you're right. Of course you couldn't do that. I'm sorry for asking."

"But what will you do?"

"What can I do? I'll confess the thing and take my medicine."

"But they'll send you to prison."

"I know, but again what can I do? I've taken the money and there's no way of hiding it."

A long silence reigned while a furious battle raged in Dulcie's mind. Frank was incorrigible! The present was all he thought of, the easy way out for the moment. The morrow's reckoning could look after itself, or rather, someone else could stand the racket. She did not suppose he deliberately intended to involve others, but it was what always happened. How many times in their childhood had he done the damage and she paid the penalty!

But this was not a childish scrape. This was serious. Easily it might ruin both their lives. If she refused to help him he would go to prison. Would she be justified in refusing? More than justified! Most moralists indeed would hold that the very strength of the temptation to save him would be no more than a test of her principles. Dulcie was swayed backwards and forwards. Nothing could make theft and falsehood right, and apart from the penalty they might involve, she loathed the idea of both. On the other hand, should she not sacrifice herself, even to the extent of doing what was wrong, for the sake of Frank?

In the end it was no balancing of abstract right and wrong which brought her to a decision. When she saw Frank so humbled and broken she realised that her own conduct had never been in question. She loved him. That was what mattered. Under no conceivable circumstances could she leave him in the lurch. She must share his trouble, share every last drop no matter how bitter the draught might prove. To do so would indeed be her joy. Better to suffer with Frank than to have all the glories of Solomon without him. The fact that he was to blame made no difference whatever.

But he must not be too sure of her nor take her help for granted. She would not now tell him her decision. A night's uncertainty would be salutary. Slowly she turned to him.

"I just can't tell you, Frank, what I think about this. So I won't say anything. Our happiness may be gone and we've got to face it. I don't see how, even if I wanted to, I could prevent Burt finding out. I believe after all that your best plan would be to go to him in the morning and make a clean breast of the whole thing. There's just the off-chance that he might not prosecute."

"A precious small one."

She shrugged without replying.

"Hang it all, Dulcie," he went on, "I know I did wrong. It was what I told you: I had to decide on the spur of the moment, and then it was too late to undo it. Look here, you might see some way out. Do think it over."

"Am I likely to do anything else? You can come in to breakfast in the morning and if a scheme has occurred to me I'll let you know. But it's unlikely one will."

Her detachment had obviously given him a nasty jar, but he seemed afraid of making matters worse, and agreed without hesitation. Next morning he was still in a chastened mood, and as Dulcie was distracted with fear and loathing of what faced her, the meal was somewhat of an ordeal to both.

When an hour later she had gone through the letters with Burt and had stood up to leave the room, she took a tight hold on herself and made the plunge.

"I should have told you, Mr Burt, that I took two hundred pounds in notes out of the drawer yesterday to lodge with the cheques. I thought it was scarcely safe so much being there, and that you'd forgotten to tell me. It leaves plenty to carry on with."

"Oh, quite right," he answered as he picked up the telephone and began to dial. "Probably I've been keeping too much."

Dulcie tottered rather than walked from the room, but Burt was intent on his call and she did not think he had noticed anything. She was in a cold sweat when she dropped on to the chair in her room. She had done it! She was now herself a thief, and till that money was paid back life would be hell. If it ever was paid back! All she had done might well be merely to postpone for a day the dreadful reckoning. Tomorrow she would be slap up against it. Tomorrow she would have to put before Burt her bi-weekly financial statement, with which she always included the bank paying-in book with the relevant receipted items on its counterfoils. If Burt remembered the £200 she was sunk. He might or he might not. He was shrewd enough, but his whole thought was for the technical side of his work, and the attention he gave to finance was perfunctory. Besides, and this hurt Dulcie till she could scarcely keep back the tears, he trusted her. He seldom did more than glance at what she put before him.

As, physically sick from distress, she pondered her position, Frank appeared. His face was alight with eagerness. "Well?" he whispered, "have you pulled it off?"

A sudden revulsion of feeling swept over Dulcie. Here was the cause of all her suffering, and looking as if he had not a care in the world. It was the last straw. "Get out of my sight!" she hissed fiercely. "If you come near me I'll kill you!"

Had she been normal she must have laughed at his ludicrous deflation. His jaw dropped and he stared as if he could not believe eyes or ears. Before she could speak again he was gone.

In the end it was fate that stepped in to save Dulcie. Next day shortly before the time came for her to present her accounts a close friend of Burt's, another surgeon, rang him up to ask his experience on some involved technical point. It was a matter in which Burt was keenly interested, and when Dulcie entered he was intently looking up his case notes.

"I was just going," Dulcie explained. "Is it convenient for you to look through the statement?"

"Yes, yes, of course," Burt answered, though keeping his finger between the pages of his book. "Let me see the figures."

He glanced at the return even more casually than usual, read off the total and said that it was about what he expected, and turned back to his work. Once again Dulcie found her legs would scarcely carry her out.

They were safe for the moment, but well she knew that it was for the moment only. The first time Burt opened his money drawer he would remember what she had said. Whether he would further remember that the £200 had not figured in her return was on the lap of the gods. There was a reasonable chance that he might not, because unless he specially asked for it, he would not again see the paying-in

THE SCHEME

book with its vital counterfoil. She had taken it away with her, as she customarily kept it in her own desk.

When at last she told Frank what she had done, he made a great show of gratitude and sorrow for the trouble he had brought upon her. But he could not keep the jubilation out of his manner. Once again he had made the breach and someone else had stepped into it.

As day succeeded day and Burt made no reference to his loss, Dulcie began to think that the immediate danger was past. Of course as she had seen, all they had gained was time. At the end of each year Burt had a complete stocktaking and personally compared all his calculated balances with the bank's figures. From this inquisition a loss of £200 could not possibly be hidden. But until then it was unlikely that the discovery would be made. That gave them over eight months to replace the money.

But the relief which this conclusion brought Dulcie soon became tempered by a new anxiety. Was Frank going to be able to replace the money in the time? She did not see how he could support himself and pay more than a pound a week, and that would amount to less than forty pounds. By skimping herself dreadfully – perhaps by giving up her beloved flat she might put up another pound a week, and she had a small nest egg of £60 in the bank. But this would only mean £90 or with Frank's £40, £130 altogether. Even were she willing to cook Burt's accounts, which she was not, she did not believe that the loss of so large a sum as £70 could be hidden.

The position indeed was worse than this, for the time began to pass without bringing in from Frank his promised weekly offering. Always there was a good reason why he could not pay. Always he needed something without which he could not possibly carry on at Burt's, and as he did not fail to point out, if he lost his job they would be worse off than ever. They were all right for the moment and obviously he was not worrying, but to Dulcie the position was a nightmare. They seemed to be heading straight for disaster.

It was about a month after the affair, at one of their many conferences on the situation, that to the astonishment of both of them Dulcie's self-control suddenly snapped and she let Frank have it full in the face in a burst of concentrated venom. Then before he could recover himself she hurled at him an ultimatum. If he did not quickly suggest something and put it into operation, she would go to Burt and confess the whole thing and they could take whatever came to them.

She saw, indeed rather to her surprise, that she had at last impressed him.

"Look, honey," he implored, "don't do that. Wait a little longer. I'm not such a hopeless fool as you imagine. I've been thinking over this thing and I've got an idea. I believe it'll bring us in all the money we want."

"What is it?" she asked dully.

"It isn't ready yet. That's why I haven't mentioned it. Give me a bit more time and I'll get it perfect."

Her outburst had relieved her feelings and she thought this over dispassionately. Was it genuine or only another excuse? She believed him ingenious enough to devise plans to meet any situation, if only he would take the trouble. Then as she looked at him, he seemed so earnest and so woebegone that her love for him once again overwhelmed everything and she felt ashamed of her doubts.

"Oh, Frank!" she cried, and she was very near tears, "if only you would!"

"Give me a week," he went on. "Just one week. Then I'll put before you a scheme that I honestly believe will do the trick. You'd have to help me with it, but you'd do that."

Dulcie could only agree. With a cynicism which slightly horrified her she wondered what new sacrifices would be demanded of her. But all she said was: "Very well, this night week you'll tell me, and till then we'll say no more about it."

But before the week was out he was ready with his proposal. When he came to her flat on the Sunday morning she saw that he was bubbling over with something.

"Well," she said smiling, "what is it?"

"It's that scheme, Dulcie. We weren't to talk about it till Tuesday, but it's ready now."

"Good," she answered. "I'll be glad to get a move on. What is it?"

He seemed to find it hard to begin. "I don't know that you'll like it very much," he said doubtfully. "It's all right really, but it may not be exactly what you'd have chosen."

"I'd know that better if you told me what it was," she pointed out.

"Just what I'm doing," he declared. "You see, what I thought was that we're in an ugly jam. It is pretty bad, isn't it?"

"We've said that about fifteen thousand times in the last month."

"That's right. Well, to meet a desperate situation you need a desperate remedy, as someone has said. You agree?"

"Never mind abstract propositions. What's the great idea?"

"That's what I'm coming to. What I mean is, that what we do must be drastic: perhaps not exactly what we should do if everything was normal."

Dulcie's heart again was sinking. An overture in this key was ominous. "Go on," she said shortly.

"I don't like the plan very much myself. But it really is the only way. And that's the thing to think of in case you don't like it much either."

She swung round on him. "For heaven's sake, Frank, stop that twaddle and say what you've got to say!"

"Well," he paused, then having apparently screwed up the necessary courage he added, "we could get it – from the patients."

She stared. "From the patients? What on earth are you talking about?"

"I mean from certain of the patients. Most of them are ordinary people, well off but not rich. I don't include any of these. But others are just wallowing in oof. People come to Burt who think as little of a thousand pounds as you or I do of half a crown. I suggest that we might get a little from them: that is, from people who absolutely couldn't feel the loss."

To Dulcie this sounded completely mad. "I really don't know what you're talking about, Frank. How could we get money from the patients?"

"Well," he moved uneasily on his chair, "easily enough, only – don't fly off the handle till you've heard the whole story." He paused, then as she did not reply, went on: "What I really mean is if we overcharged them a bit."

Still Dulcie did not understand, though all her evil premonitions returned to her. "You'll have to do better than that," she told him. "It's about as clear as pea soup."

"Suppose we take an actual case." Having taken the plunge, he was now speaking eagerly. "Suppose some old Croesus has an operation. Suppose Burt tells you to send in a bill for 120 guineas. Suppose you send in one for 130 and we keep the extra ten."

Dulcie was appalled. The scheme was simply deliberate, premeditated theft! Stealing, just as directly as if they put their hands in the patients' pockets. And Burt, who had been so good to her and who trusted her, was to be repaid with deceit and fraud! She could hardly trust herself to answer.

"Really, Frank, I couldn't have believed you'd propose such a plan. The kindest thing I can do for you is to forget it."

"I know. That's one's natural first reaction. It was mine. Then when I thought it over, I saw it wasn't so bad."

"I don't see how it could be worse."

"It could be a lot worse. It would be if we did nothing. Look how we stand now. We've stolen from Burt. I know *you* didn't do it, honey: it was only your goodness to me that involved you. All the same, though I hate to say it, you *are* involved. When you told Burt you had put the two hundred in the bank you became involved: I mean of course in the eyes of the law."

It was true. Dulcie had never deceived herself. She had become a thief. But she had done it hastily to meet a sudden emergency. This was different. If she went into this, she would do it deliberately and with her eyes open. There would be no excuse whatever.

"I don't want to hear any more about it," she told him. "How could you have thought I'd do such a thing? You may put the idea right out of your mind."

He nodded, but continued. "Yes, honey, but look at it this way. We're both in this thing and what do we both most want? Why, to be out of it. Isn't that right?"

"Of course it's right. But going in deeper won't help that."

"You haven't got the idea. As we are now, we can't get out. We can't pay off what we've taken before Burt's stocktaking. Then he'll discover it and we'll be for it."

Again it was true. This was what Dulcie had been telling herself for some time past, though she had not believed that Frank had also realised it.

"If so, we're finished," she answered dully.

"No, that's just it," he retorted. "This scheme gives us a way out. No, no," he went on as she would have spoken, "let me finish. We want to get out, and we can only get out by repaying Burt. Besides, we *want* to repay Burt."

"At least that's true."

"Of course it's true. And so is the next step. We can only repay Burt by getting it from the patients."

"Oh, no, no, no! I won't think of it!"

"Look, Dulcie," and his manner had grown unusually firm. "This is not a question of stealing money or of not stealing it. That's been done. We have stolen money and nothing we can do can alter it. This is a question of dealing with the consequences. If we don't take this chance, the thing comes out and we're sacked and probably go to prison. If we do it, nothing more happens. Burt is repaid and the thing ends."

"But we'll then have stolen from the patients."

"Yes, but that's different. We'll hate and regret it, I know, but it will do no harm. We won't hurt anyone. We wouldn't take a penny from anyone who could possibly feel the loss."

"It would be so deliberate."

"I'll put it in a nutshell. Why shouldn't we transfer our theft from where it would hurt to where it wouldn't?"

Dulcie was silent. This was Frank all over. He could prove that black was white and leave you wondering why you had not seen it for yourself. Her determination wavered slightly.

"It scarcely matters what we think," she said presently. "Even if we wanted to do it, we couldn't. It's quite impossible."

He must have known he was winning, but he showed no signs of elation. "That's a different matter," he returned quietly. "My job is to work out a method and I'll guarantee to do it. Your job is to say whether we adopt it."

"But how could we? The patients know what they're going to be charged. If we sent them a bill for more they'd immediately write to Burt."

"No, they wouldn't. You'd have to trust me about details. Look here. Nine patients out of ten want to know what their operation is going to cost them, and with those of course we could do nothing. But a small proportion of the very rich don't ask. It may be that they really are so rich they don't care, or it may be swank: to show they could meet anything without feeling it. You know that as well as I do."

"I suppose that's true," she admitted.

"Very well. We'd only act in such cases. These patients' secretaries would write their cheques and they'd sign them without bothering about the amounts. If they did think Burt's fee was rather high they'd say nothing. They'd consider it *infra dig.*"

Plausible as ever! As ever his case looked as if it were true.

"But how could we know that Burt hadn't told them the fee?"

Frank was now evidently fighting down his delight. "Leave that to your Frank, old girl," he urged, "it's a detail. But I'll tell you all the same. I have an old stethoscope and I'll make an end to fit the keyhole of the consulting-room. In the case of likely patients it will be my job to listen to the interview. Only if no mention of the fee is made can we take action."

This again revolted her, but he met her objections with the in-for-a-penny-in-for-a-pound argument. Then she foresaw difficulties about the carrying out of the plan: the bank returns, the getting of the cash, the balance for Burt. But for all he had an answer. Obviously he had thought the matter out carefully.

In the end, sick at heart and desperately worried, she gave way. Frank's scheme, hateful as it was, presented a way of escape from certain ruin, and morally it was no worse than what they had already done. She loathed the whole idea, but as she told herself, the choice was not between good and evil. It was merely taking the lesser of two evils.

Frank certainly had tact. Not the slightest trace of triumph appeared in his manner. He showed only regret for her distress and gratitude for her self-sacrifice. He said that though all the details were worked out, he had to procure some special articles, and they would have to wait for a few days before beginning operations. Thankful for the respite, Dulcie asked no more questions.

During the next week Frank was busy on mysterious ploys, the details of which he kept to himself. Then once more he reverted to the subject.

"I want the loan of twenty pounds, old girl," he said calmly, "or thirty if you can spare it. You needn't be frightened: I'm not going to spend it, only to open an account in the bank."

When she pressed him for his reasons he answered equally casually: "When we start you'll want an extra cheque book. This is the safest way to get it." On the in-for-a-penny-in-for-a-pound principle which he had already invoked, she gave him the money. Not till afterwards did she learn that he had opened the account in Burt's branch, giving his private address only and saying that he was a demobbed soldier who had not yet taken a job.

Three days later he announced that the preliminaries were complete and that they were ready to begin. Dulcie was so miserable about the whole thing that action only slightly added to her worry. Like an automaton she did what he asked her.

They began by examining the case cards of those patients who were calling on the following day. None of those listed for the first day, Frank thought, would suit their purpose, and so it happened for four days. But on the fifth a certain Sir Cloudesley Ridgewell was due for a final consultation, which would settle whether or not he must undergo a major operation. After looking him up in various reference books, Frank decided he was a likely subject. He was a self-made man of great wealth and might well exhibit the desired trait.

Next day he duly arrived and Frank showed him in to Burt. Frank then walked away with his usual step, immediately tip-toeing back to the consulting-room door. He had put rubbers on the soles of his shoes but not on the heels, so that he could walk noisily or silently as he considered desirable. At the door he listened with his stethoscope and when the patient left he reported to Dulcie. The operation was to take place and no reference to fees had been made.

As it would be some time before the bill would go in, Frank continued his activities. Every three or four days a likely patient called and Frank listened to the interview. With most of them he lost his time, for a fee was mentioned, but very slowly the number of possibles mounted. In six weeks he had added seven names to his list.

At long last the time came to send out an account to the first of these: it happened to be Sir Cloudesley Ridgewell. Burt had told Dulcie the fee was to be 150 guineas and with a piteous expression she passed the news on to Frank.

"Don't look so worried, old thing," he told her. "You'll find what you have to do simplicity itself. Look, I'll help you. Send Sir Cloudesley his account exactly as you would have done, only make it for 180 guineas instead of 150."

Dulcie was aghast. "Oh," she protested, "not such a tremendous difference as that! He'll spot it at once."

"Not on your life! Now," he shook his finger at her, "you've got to do what you're told in this: that's our bargain. There's no use in taking all this trouble for a pound or two. This one haul will bring us in thirty guineas."

"I never thought of anything like that. It takes my breath away."

"You'll get it back. Don't be an owl, Dulcie. Make out the account and send it off. But don't forget that your counterfoil must show 150 guineas, not 180."

"It's horrible!"

"Yes, I don't like it myself. But it's our only hope." For two days Dulcie lived in a state of absolute dread, which she hid only by the exercise of all her willpower. Then the next morning's post brought in a cheque for the full amount, without any query or adverse comment. She could scarcely believe it. Relief that the blow had not yet fallen began to tinge her fear that sooner or later it must.

Frank took the payment as a matter of course. "I told you it would come," he pointed out. "Don't be so scared. You'll find that everything will work out quite smoothly."

Now for Dulcie the proceedings became complicated, and she could never have carried out the plan but for Frank's presence and help at every point.

"The first thing is Ridgewell's receipt," he explained. "You've got to fill that in carefully. The receipt portion which you send to Ridgewell will be for 180 guineas, but the counterfoil which you retain will show 150 guineas."

"I *hate* this!"

"Old girl, it's the price we've got to pay for safety."

"Suppose Ridgewell mentions the figure to Burt?"

"In that case you'll have made a regrettable error which you'll immediately correct. But he won't. Think of it and you'll see it's the last thing he'd do."

"I suppose you're right."

"Of course I'm right. After the thing was settled, that type of man – the type who didn't inquire about the fee – would think it beneath him to raise the question."

"Very well, that finishes about the receipt. But I don't see what happens next. Surely there'll be a snag at the bank? I've got a cheque for 180 guineas, whereas it should be for 150. Won't that show in the bank return?"

"Not the way we'll work it. To follow this let's first go over just what you do with the cheques now. You endorse and pay in all of them, and with them you hand the cashier a paying-in book in which you've entered these cheques and their total. The cashier checks, rubber stamps, initials the counterfoil and returns the book to you. This is your proof that the money has been lodged."

"Well? I still don't follow."

"You will in a moment. Now Burt will want to see the receipted counterfoil as proof that his cheques have been lodged. You do show it to him, don't you?"

"Yes, it makes part of my bi-weekly statement."

"Very well. Now this counterfoil shows 180 guineas, so you can't show it to him. Therefore you will have to keep two paying-in books, one for the bank and the other for Burt. The one you use at the bank will show the total of the cheques actually received, in this case 180 guineas, the one you show to Burt will show the fee he said, in this case 150 guineas. He therefore will know nothing about the extra thirty guineas."

"Oh, Frank, how horrible! It's all crooked! And I still don't see how it'll work. That counterfoil I put before Burt won't have the bank receipt on it."

Frank grinned at her. "Not such a fool as she looks," he mocked. "But you must trust your Frank, old girl. He foresaw the difficulty and dealt with it. After superhuman efforts he made a rubber stamp like the bank's. Further, his well-known skill with the pen can accomplish the initials. Then hey, presto! your counterfoil will have the required bank receipt."

"It's horrible, Frank," she said again, but with less conviction. In spite of her distress a sneaking admiration for Frank's resource had crept into her mind.

"I know, honey," he said softly, "but you've gone too far to draw back. To stop now would be immediate ruin. To follow the thing through will mean complete safety."

He was right! Frank was always right! She felt herself trapped.

"Oh, well, I suppose I can do nothing else," she said, trying once again to concentrate on the details. "But still I don't understand it. How shall we get the thirty guineas?"

"Now you're talking. Let's go into that. Tell me, in the ordinary course doesn't Burt sometimes want you to get him cash from the bank?"

"Often. He gives me a note of how much and I get it and leave it on his desk."

"Exactly. And just how do you get it?"

"How? I fill in a cheque for cash and sign it for him 'per pro', you know."

"Quite. I knew that for I've seen the counterfoils in your cheque book. Well, in the case of our scheme you'll do exactly the same. When you pay in an increased fee, you at the same time cash a cheque for the increase. This cheque you must fill in from a duplicate cheque book. And that's where my account comes in. If you asked for a second cheque book a question might arise. You'll use mine."

She had no more to say. He had an answer for everything. Sick at heart, she entered among others in her "bank" paying-in book the 180 guinea cheque. At the same time she filled in a cheque for thirty guineas cash from Frank's book. Then she screwed up her courage and went to the bank. Trying to speak as normally as possible, she handed all across the counter. The cashier took the cheques to be lodged, compared them with the paying-in book, and stamped and initialled the counterfoil, making polite remarks on the weather the while. He examined the cheque for thirty guineas cash and without the slightest hesitation handed her the money. When she left she was satisfied that he had suspected nothing. How indeed could he?

On returning to Harley Street she filled in "Burt's" paying-in book so as to show Sir Cloudesley's cheque as 150 guineas. Frank then borrowed the book, returning it presently receipted with the authentic bank stamp and initials.

"Oh, Frank!" she whispered intensely, relief from her bank experiences mingling with admiration for his skill, "how did you do it? Wherever did you get the stamp?"

"I admit," he answered, trying to hide his exultation, "it wasn't easy. I ordered a lot of stamps from different firms. One had a frame of the right size and shape. The others contained words or letters in the right type. All these stamps, you understand, referred to matters remote from banks. Then I cut them up and fitted the pieces I wanted into the new stamp."

"It's horrible, but rather marvellous. I don't know how you did it."

"Nor I," he grunted. "By the way, don't keep your duplicate books in your desk in case someone has a look round. Can you hide them anywhere?"

She looked about the room. "In here behind my bookcase," she said. "They'll never be seen."

"Fine. Then don't forget the one point: you needn't have any qualms about this scheme. Everything with both Burt and the bank is absolutely straight. It's only a few semi-millionaires who'll lose something so tiny that they won't even notice it."

"I hate and loathe the whole thing. However we needn't speak of that. I'm in it now."

"Thirty guineas," he reminded her. "Nearly a sixth of what we want. Stick it, Dulcie, and we'll soon be clear."

So Frank's scheme was inaugurated.

– 3 –

BOAT BURNING

For some time after this first essay of Dulcie's into crime she remained acutely unhappy, oscillating between distress at the wrong she had done and terror as to its possible consequences. But as day succeeded day and events continued to pursue the even tenor of their course, her emotions became dulled. After all, their fault had not been so great. What Frank had said was true. The real mischief had been done in those few seconds by the safe in Burt's consulting-room, and this later development in no way increased the guilt. As for her own conduct, it had been purely unselfish. All she had done had been for Frank, and she had gained no material advantage for herself; nothing but anxiety and misery and fear.

On the other hand the success of Frank's scheme staggered her. If they could get thirty guineas in one haul, they would have to alter only a very few accounts to obtain the total they required. This would make discovery much less likely than if operations were continuous. Success or failure obviously hinged on the careful selection of the victims, and the fact that so few patients need be chosen would greatly minimise the danger.

All the same accidents did happen, and only the slightest suspicion would be necessary to bring the entire affair into the open. Well, she could but hope for the best.

Then another point struck her. Every now and then the bank sent in the machine-filled statement sheets which recorded all transactions in Burt's current account. These would give away the fraud! She put the matter to Frank at the first opportunity.

"I know," he answered. "I've thought about that and I admit I don't see any way out of it. I had hoped to alter the sheets to suit our figures, but it was just too big a job. I couldn't manage it."

"Then what's to be done when they come in?"

"Nothing. File them away without showing them to Burt. He's unlikely to ask for them, because the receipted counterfoils he gets will give him all the information he wants. Don't ever forget that the totals your counterfoils show will be correct: corresponding sums will actually be in the bank."

Dulcie was not convinced. "But if he does ask for them?" she insisted.

"If he does, give him only those that are at least six months old. Say the later ones haven't come in. Put him off somehow."

"They'll be wanted when he does his income tax."

"Well, *you* prepare his return," Frank retorted irritably. "Hang it all, Dulcie, don't crab everything. There's always a way out if you'll only look for it."

"You seem pretty sure."

"Of course I'm sure. The first plank in the scheme is that Burt's keen on the scientific side of his job and bored with finance. So unless he suspects, he won't look into things. And he won't suspect."

Dulcie was relieved by Frank's arguments, if not entirely convinced. But as time passed and all went well, her conscience became dulled and her confidence grew. The scheme certainly functioned marvellously. Every couple of weeks some twenty to thirty guineas were added to their balance, and she believed that in three or four months they would have the whole sum.

During this period another development was taking place which filled Dulcie with profound joy. Frank was improving in health. He was losing his frightened drawn look and putting on flesh. His manner was more normal and his dreadful fits of depression were almost things of the past. She began to think, what for some time she had doubted, that complete recovery would be only a matter of time. With returning health came also energy and grip. Daily he became more an experienced man of the world, who beneath his suave manners knew his own mind and could stand on his own feet.

The one thing that worried her about him was that nothing had been settled as to their engagement. It was understood that their marriage was waiting only till he was earning enough to provide a home. Dulcie understood so at least, though it had never actually been put into words. He should make a proper formal proposal, she told herself with exasperation, but he gave no signs of any such purpose.

At last one evening she did herself broach the question, though not exactly deliberately. They were dining together at a small restaurant and had been discussing their prospects.

"Oh, Frank," she suddenly said, rather to her own surprise, "I'm sick of this way of living! These horrible restaurants! I want to settle down. A little house or even a flat; a place of our own. Could we not begin to look out for something?"

"Don't speak of it, honey," he returned. "You make me sick with longing. Money! Money! Money! That's the trouble! With all this bombing and destruction, where could we get anything for what we could pay?"

She murmured an agreement and he went on: "I've been thinking about it a lot and I see I must get another job, something that will bring in more. But I don't want to do that till Burt has been repaid."

This was horse sense and again she fully agreed. "Of course you can't leave till that's done. But I wondered if we need wait so long." Momentarily she hesitated, then took the plunge. "I mean, could we not be married and each of us still carry on our jobs?"

"I've thought of that too," he returned. "It's immensely alluring, but should we be any the better off? The form of marriage would neither increase our income nor find us a place to live. If your flat was bigger it would be a different matter, but we couldn't possibly both squeeze in. Besides, Dulcie," he swung round and faced her and his manner grew more serious, "I can't pretend that I would like my wife to have to support herself. When I'm married I want to offer my wife a home, as other men do. I know cases where the wife runs an office job and it's sheer hell. She can't run the house properly and everything's strained and it leads to friction and quarrelling. My wife must be able not only to run our house, but also to have reasonable time to herself."

It was all true. A house and an office job were in a way incompatible, except perhaps for a very gifted woman. Both could scarcely be done properly, and to retain the office one, the house would have to suffer. Small cheap restaurants were undoubtedly unpleasant, but at least the food was ready. She pictured herself arriving home tired and damp on wet and stormy nights, and finding the house cold and nothing prepared for a meal. Frank as usual was right! It would lead to frayed tempers and unhappiness.

Though she was disappointed that their marriage seemed no nearer than before, she was at least glad that he had taken its accomplishment for granted. She was thankful too that money was the only barrier. She repeated that as soon as Burt was repaid Frank must look out for a new place. Not only for the extra money, but because that of attendant to a Harley Street surgeon was no job for a man of his abilities.

Some thirteen weeks after putting Frank's scheme into operation there came a great day for the partners. A cheque came in which brought the balance they had accumulated to £204 0s. 0d., all and more than they wanted. Frank insisted on a small celebration at one of the better class Soho restaurants.

"Oh, Frank," Dulcie declared when they had returned to her flat, "I just can't say how thankful I am that that's over! Now we must begin to save to pay back the patients."

"Well, honey, that's very nice of you, but I don't know how you're going to do it."

She looked at him. "What's the difficulty?"

He shrugged. "Have you thought it out? We've had, let us say, £30 from X. What would you say to X, when you sent it back?"

She was silent. Once again Frank was right: she had not stopped to think. Now she saw that any return of the money would give them away. Even if they sent it anonymously the letter might be traced. She had read enough detective stories to believe that investigators could find out *anything*. And curiosity might cause some of these rich men to have a search made. She had hoped that she might get rid of the weight of the theft from her conscience. Now that didn't seem possible.

"It's rather a blow," she answered regretfully. "I had hoped we could get out square, but I'm afraid you're right. Oh, well, we've only two things to do and I think we may forget the whole ghastly nightmare."

"What two things do you mean?"

"Why, the return of the money to Burt and the fixing up of his income tax statement."

"But, honey, we've settled about both those. Why raise difficulties over them now?"

"We haven't dealt with them and you needn't pretend there's not a risk."

"We'll do what we settled," he declared firmly. "You'll wait till the next time Burt gives you cash to lodge and you'll pay in £200 more than he's given you."

"He may notice the increased figure on the paying-in counterfoil."

"Well, we dealt with that too. If he does, you've got to be all sorry and upset. You'll own up to a grave fault. You'll remind him that you took £200 out of his safe to lodge, and you'll say that through an error you can't understand, the notes got hidden behind some papers in your desk. You have just found them and paid them in. He may wonder about it, but he can't say anything."

"I'll be happier when it's done."

"No doubt." Frank's voice was dry. "Then the income tax. We also settled about that. You tell him you can do it, or better still, tell him I'm an expert and would be glad to do it for a small fee. If you put it nicely he couldn't refuse you."

As usual Frank had an answer to all her questions, and as usual, she gave way to him. But now, though she did not know it, she was coming to one of the great struggles of her life, one of the most far-reaching and fateful decisions with which she had ever been confronted.

The campaign was opened on that same evening when for the second time she declared her satisfaction that the fraud was at an end. This time Frank did not reply, but looked at her quizzically. "But is it?" he asked softly.

She stared in her turn. "What do you mean?" she demanded. "Don't you know it is?"

"You've just said so. But are you right?"

"What's taken you? We wanted the two hundred and we've got it. What more do you want?"

He swung round and faced her. "Look, honey," he said, lowering his voice impressively, "do you know what that scheme's been bringing us in? Something like eight hundred a year! *Eight hundred!*"

"It brought us in two hundred in three months. Yes, I've been able to work out what that means per year. I can do simple arithmetic."

"We've got two hundred, but that's not ours. It's Burt's, and it must be paid back to him. But – Can't you see what I mean, Dulcie?"

Even then for a moment she did not understand, but as he sat silently looking at her his incredible meaning flashed devastatingly into her mind. At first she simply could not move.

"I see you don't like the idea," he went on, "but don't get on your hind legs about it. Listen. We want to set up house. We can't do it because we haven't enough money. Eight hundred a year added to what we make – You see, don't you?"

She found her voice. "Frank! It's horrible! How can you suggest it?"

"Honey, you've got it wrong," he declared. "I'm not asking you to hurt anyone. Here's money to be had for the picking up: why should we not have it? It's not as if the patients wanted it. They've got so much they couldn't miss it. Dulcie, old girl, there's no need for you to get upset. It's not as bad as you think."

She was on the verge of tears. "But I am upset. It's just hateful!"

"Look, Dulcie," he went on and his voice was so caressing that it pierced her heart. "It's not really wrong. It's only what all governments do and all laws allow: taking a little from the over-rich and giving it to the poor. That's a well-established principle and no one could object to it."

Now the great struggle raged in Dulcie's mind, an even more bitter one than when Frank first put up his idea. For a long time the battle swayed backwards and forwards. At first horror and loathing of the theft were in the ascendant, then the alluring picture of what with money their lives might become, drew her overwhelmingly. Why, she thought again, should they not take the money? It was not as if the question was a clear cut right or wrong. Nothing in this life was clear cut; everything was a balance of conflicting issues. Here were she and Frank, and their lives were slipping away and they were not able to enjoy those simple elementary advantages that everyone was entitled to, simply because they had not enough money. And here was money, ample money as it were flowing past them, and they had only to put out their hands and pick a little up. That small effort and their problems would be solved and their lives would be full of satisfaction and happiness! It was so easy. The plan worked so well. It hurt no one. Besides, she would be doing it with Frank...It will be seen that Dulcie's moral standards had suffered through what she had done!

She could not have told at what precise point the die was cast, but she suddenly knew that she had reached her decision. Frank, marriage, a home, all that she wanted in life held out to her. And against it there was only a little outmoded conscientious scruple. Who could hesitate?

Once again Frank took it without elation. He kissed her and told her how good she was to sacrifice her feelings for him, for the building of a home was the one thing he most desired in life. Then he made no further reference to the matter, but next morning looked up the histories of the day's likely patients as if no break in the scheme had been mooted.

For the following week he seemed preoccupied and then with disarming deprecation he referred again to the subject.

"There's one snag in our scheme," he told her. "It's worried me every day since we began, but I haven't seen how to get over it. Now I do."

She looked her question.

"It's the listening at the consulting-room door," he went on. "It's not satisfactory. First, there's a danger that I might be seen. One of the patients might feel ill or something and come out of the waiting-room. The fat would be in the fire all right then."

"If we touch pitch," she began dolefully.

"It's a risk and we shouldn't take it," he interrupted. "But that's not the worst. With that stethoscope affair I can't really hear properly. Often I've not been absolutely sure that the fee wasn't mentioned."

Dulcie was genuinely horrified. "Oh, Frank! How could you? We might have been ruined."

"Well, the risk had to be taken or we'd never have got anywhere. But I've got a scheme now that'll make it completely safe."

Dulcie was surprised to find how since she had taken her decision, her reactions towards the affair had changed. While she still disliked and feared it, moral considerations had receded into the background and profits had become the vital need. She could now almost welcome Frank's suggestion that he was going to make its operation safer.

"What's your plan?" she demanded.

Frank had obviously expected uncompromising obstruction. When it did not materialise he was elated.

"Did you ever hear," he grinned delightedly, "of a mike, or more politely, of a microphone?"

"Well?"

"I've spent a hectic week making one and now we're going to Harley Street to fix it. When it's there you'll hear every word of Burt's interviews in complete safety."

"I will?"

"Yes, the speaker'll be under your desk."

"Oh." Dulcie thought over this. "But that's putting more of it on to me."

"Old girl, there's nowhere else it could go."

"I don't like it, Frank. It gets more and more deliberate."

"You mean, safer and safer. Put on your things, honey, and we'll go now. I have everything in a bag in my room and we'll pick it up on our way."

Worried and rather unhappy, she agreed.

In Burt's consulting-room they closed the old-fashioned shutters so as to be able to switch on the lights without fear of being seen. Frank sat down at the desk and pushed back the lid. It was never locked because it contained nothing of special value. Then he took from his bag a small paper parcel and carefully unrolled it.

"Behold!" he exclaimed dramatically as he showed the contents to Dulcie.

It was an electric bell push, quite ordinary at the top or push-button end, but twice as deep as usual.

"The mike?" asked Dulcie wonderingly.

"The mike! Look here."

As has been mentioned, there was a bell from the desk to the passage, with a code for calling either Dulcie or Frank. The push operating it was screwed to the side of the desk upon which the roll-top slid, so that Burt could ring without leaving his seat. A flex connected the desk with the wall. Frank now laid his push beside that of the bell.

"Both the same!" Dulcie exclaimed.

"The same and yet not the same," Frank answered consequentially. "Identical in front, so that Burt won't notice the change. But different at the back. So different that mine won't fit as things are. I'll have to gouge out a hollow in the wood to house it."

"That'll be a job, surely?"

"No, it's easy. What wasn't easy was to make the back of the push small enough to be hid in the thickness of the wood. But I've managed it."

Dulcie's interest was overcoming her distress. "How does it work?" she asked.

"It's a brainy gadget, though I say it myself," Frank returned. "You wouldn't believe the trouble it gave. I had to stew up books and experiment with mikes till I thought I'd go dotty. I stuck it till I got it."

"That doesn't tell me how it works."

"Wrong entry, you owl. The correct line on that one is 'Frank! How utterly marvellous you are!'"

"Well, it's true, but not in the sense you mean. Your equal in conceit I've never met."

"Now, honey, that's below the belt." When Frank indulged in mild badinage it meant that he was enjoying himself. He was an artist to the extent that he loved creating. This push-microphone was his creation, and so long as he was occupied with it and it was functioning satisfactorily, he would be happy. "Well, see," he went on, "here's how it works. The mike is hidden in the base and there's a rather complicated switch attached to the button. When the button is normal, I mean fully out, the mike is switched in. Normally then, everything spoken at the desk will be picked up by the mike. But if the button is pushed, the mike is first switched out, and then the bell is switched in and rings normally. There'll be nothing to suggest to Burt that the thing has been tampered with."

"That sounds all right."

"All right! It's far more than all right! It's masterly!"

She took no notice of this. "But look here," she went on. "I don't know much about electricity, but I should have thought four wires would be wanted, two for the mike circuit and two for the bell."

Frank scrutinised her with his head on one side. "Well, well, well," he said in a tone of surprise. "I declare she's not such a fool as she looks. That right enough was a snag. Four wires would have been easier, but we just couldn't get an extra pair through the wall. But I've got that fixed too. I worked till I got the battery the right strength, and this is what happens. The bell circuit is unaltered, but new wires are attached to it at the bell and carried on to the phone in your room. We'll fix that later. Now when this mike here on Burt's desk is switched in, there's enough current to work your speaker, but not enough to work the bell. When the bell's switched in more current comes on and rings the bell. Got it now?"

"I'll hand it to you, Frank. I hate the whole thing, but that does sound pretty smart."

While they were talking Frank had removed the old push and wires, and was chipping out a hollow in the wood to take the enlarged base. Nearly an hour passed before the new push was in place and connected up. There was as yet no way of testing the mike, but the bell shrilled as of yore.

They spent another couple of hours running the extension wires from the bell to Dulcie's desk, their great endeavour being to keep them invisible. When two o'clock struck they knocked off for the night. Next evening they met again and completed the installation, fixing the speaker to the bottom of Dulcie's desk. It worked perfectly. Every word spoken by Frank at Burt's desk was clearly heard by Dulcie at her own.

They now began to work the scheme more intensively than ever. Dulcie found that she could not only hear everything that Burt said, but could also judge from the tone of the conversation how promising a victim was the selected patient. Satisfied on this point, she sent out her cooked accounts with more confidence. Money began coming in more quickly.

With much trepidation she had overcome one difficulty. When Burt had instructed her to pay in some cash from his safe, she had added the "borrowed" £200. By showing Burt the papers quickly and speaking casually, she had managed to get the receipt past him without his noticing its swollen amount. Once again she tottered rather than walked out of the room.

So a number of weeks went uneventfully by while their bank balances swelled and Dulcie's conscientious qualms gave her less and less trouble. Then one Sunday evening when they were sitting in her flat after supper, Frank made an unsettling remark.

"Look here, old girl, I've been worrying a bit lately. I don't think we're getting anywhere, fixed as we are. I think we'll have to make a change."

Dulcie stared. "Not getting anywhere? Why, I thought you'd be satisfied. We're making a thousand a year above our salaries. What more do you want?"

"I don't mean money. It's coming in fine, better than we could have hoped. But money isn't everything. I want position. I don't want my wife to have a doctor's attendant for a husband."

"Well, that sounds sense. What do you propose to do about it?"

"I must get another job."

"And leave me to work the scheme alone? I *don't* think!"

"I didn't contemplate going to Patagonia or Tibet. If I got a job here in Town I'd help with the scheme just the same."

Dulcie considered this. Oh, if they could only give up the scheme altogether! She loathed it, but the lure of the money had grown irresistible. As to Frank's position, she did not feel it keenly. Not as it concerned herself: she would have married him if he had been a professional beggar. But a change was desirable on his own account. He should be doing work more satisfying to his self-respect. On the other hand, she could scarcely bring herself to think of what Harley Street would be like without him. "I should miss you horribly," she told him, "but of course we can't consider that. Had you any special job in mind?"

He grinned. "You mean, what would I choose?" He shook his head. "It won't work out that way, honey. More like taking anything I can get and being thankful."

"Well, what are you good at? Consider it in the way you do consider things. Systematically, I mean."

"Anything to oblige. Well, here is Frank Roscoe, a highly-gifted and qualified man whom any employer would be lucky to get. Assets: a good appearance, excellent manners, and sufficient knowledge of the world to enable him to hold his own in any circle. That correct?"

"Noted most of all for modesty. Yes? Go ahead."

"Splendid mixer. Bridge, billiards and tennis, can do. Rowing and swimming a speciality. Reasonably well educated. First class shorthand, typing, filing and so forth. Excellent mechanic and second to none in the handling and maintenance of cars."

"Plausible as the devil and would do his best friend in the eye for sixpence."

"That's what I call dirty."

"Very well, what job would suit so superb a lord of creation?"

"I've thought that I could sell cars," Frank went on seriously, "or perhaps get a decent job with the RAC or the AA. Something to do with cars would suit. Secretary to an MP would be a promising line. I don't know. I'll just have to keep a good look out."

To do him justice, he did take real trouble to find something. He began by buying good clothes and necessary etceteras such as a cigarette case and lighter. Then indefatigably he answered advertisements and asked for interviews. The car salesman idea proved a dud. Persons who already had an assured social position were, he gathered, more desirable. Partnerships of various kinds he looked for, but any worth having required more money than he was prepared to spend, while of those into which he would have been welcomed, he doubted the *bona fides*.

One evening after some weeks of frustrated effort he bought a *Times* and began somewhat hopelessly to scan its advertisement columns. He read about chauffeurs and nursemaids, managers of small businesses and general servants, gardeners and ladies who for a home would be willing to undertake light duties. Then his eye became glued to the page and he reread the following:

WANTED. Private Secretary. Man of good education required to live in. Treated as member of family. All technical qualifications. Apply in writing to Sir Roland Chatterton, Jasmine Lodge, near Staines, Middlesex.

Frank whistled inaudibly. Man of good education: he was that. Required to live in and treated as one of the family: might not that lead to the very things he really wanted: money, security, social position and perhaps power? All technical qualifications. Well, that was a bit vague, but with the help of some judicious bluff he believed he could put it over. It might be worth trying.

Without losing time he took the paper in to Dulcie. She thought for a moment. "Try for it, Frank!" she advised. "It sounds the thing. Write off at once."

"I'll find out something about the old boy first," he returned, and hurried off to Harley Street.

There was quite a long paragraph in *Who's Who* about Sir Roland Chatterton. He had been born in 1877, making him now sixty-nine. On leaving Oxford he had gone into the Foreign Office, then serving for many years in West Africa. After that he had been transferred to India, where he had held positions of increasing importance. Then he had returned to West Africa as Governor of an area twenty times the size of England. At the age of fifty-nine he had retired owing to ill health and had settled at Jasmine Lodge. He had married twice, having two children by his first wife, of whom Juliet, the daughter, survived, the son having been killed in a motor accident while at Sandhurst.

All this seemed promising and he returned to Dulcie with the information. She was impressed. "I don't think you should hesitate," she declared. "What about writing an application now?"

His letter, when after revision it was complete, was a model of what, between gentlemen, such a communication should be. Without bemoaning his hard luck, he explained that a serious loss of income had made it imperative that he should earn his own living. He sketched his parents' position and his own education, saying that while he had been at London University financial embarrassment had compelled him to leave before actually taking his degree. He added an approximately truthful account of his subsequent activities, not minimising his war service, and ended up: "As to my technical qualifications, I am proficient in shorthand, typewriting, filing and business methods, and I understand cars, both as a mechanic and a driver. But perhaps you would like to test my work for yourself? If so, and if you should consider me otherwise suitable, I should be glad to go to you for a probationary period." As references he gave the rector of his father's parish and some of his Army commanders, saying that none of the others for whom he had worked knew anything of his secretarial abilities.

He copied the letter in his best hand on to good quality paper. By 2 a.m. it was posted.

To his astonishment two days later there was an answer fixing an appointment for 3 p.m. on the following afternoon. He had suggested pleading a chill to Burt and asking for leave to go home, but Dulcie insisted on his telling the surgeon the exact truth. He did so and Burt, recognising that he could not keep so highly qualified an attendant for ever, gave him leave with a good grace, wishing him luck.

An hour later, immaculately turned out, Frank took a train for Staines.

– 4 –

JASMINE LODGE

" 'Found it advisable,' " said Juliet Chatterton, only daughter of Sir Roland Chatterton, KCB, KBE, of Jasmine Lodge, near Staines in the County of Middlesex. " 'The admiral found it advisable – ' You know, Daddy, I feel like the duck in *Alice in Wonderland* – or was it the duck? I want to ask what 'it' means? What did the admiral find?"

"You put me out, girl," her father said with resignation. "The admiral found it advisable to stop the leave of the entire ship's company during the rest – no, remainder – of their stay."

" 'Remainder of their stay,' " repeated the young woman, scribbling furiously. "Wouldn't 'cancel' be better than 'stop'? I mean, if leave had already been granted – "

They were seated, father and daughter, in the former's library. Sir Roland was reclining on his chaise longue before the fire. In his day he had been a fine upstanding figure of a man, and still his face showed strength, with its high and wide forehead, steady intelligent eyes and firm mouth and jaw. But now he was crippled with rheumatism and had to spend most of his time lying down. He could hobble short distances with the aid of two sticks, but for any more extended journeys he required an arm, usually that of his attendant, Arthur Boone.

But his stiffened limbs had in no way impaired the almost youthful keenness and vigour of his mind. He was now engaged in writing his autobiography. It was for this that he required a secretary, for with his twisted fingers he found sustained writing impossible. Since his former secretary, Troughton, had had to leave unexpectedly owing to his father's sudden death, Juliet and her stepmother had helped him. Their intentions had been of the best, but Juliet suspected that their ministrations had powerfully increased his longing for professional aid.

Juliet was ensconced in a low chair at the other side of the fire, her writing pad on her knee. She looked rather charming as she sat waiting for the episode of the admiral to develop. She was small and (dark like her late mother, a complete contrast to Sir Roland. Her expression was pleasant and good natured, though a certain lack about the lower part of her face suggested that great strength of character need not be looked for. Though slightly in awe of her father, who was stern and inclined to be unyielding, she was really fond of him. She felt his illness was a tragedy. At least dimly she realised how bitterly so proud and active a man must feel his helplessness and dependence on others. Certainly he was good about it! He never complained and always tried to be cheerful and consider those who attended on him. It was a pleasure to her to help him with his book, but she regretted her ignorance of shorthand and typing, which made that help so ineffective.

Juliet loved their little estate on the Thames and she thought that the view from this library window was the best thing about it. She had noticed that her father never tired of looking at it, though now in mid-March it was too cold for him to leave the fire. Indeed he had often said that it was this view which had determined him to buy the house.

Directly outside were lawns and flower beds with a path to the river going straight through their centre. To the left stood three magnificent beeches, enormous and stately trees which had been growing there since long before Napoleon left Corsica. Behind them was a tennis ground leading back to a belt of tall shrubs, which sheltered the garden from the north and east. To the right the grounds were bounded by the Merrow, a fair-sized stream which here entered the Thames, the lawn sloping gently down to both rivers. Placed in the angle between the rivers was what looked like a clump of evergreen shrubs. This was actually a great deal more. It was a sun trap which Sir Roland had had made for himself, and it was the joy of his heart. Planted thickly on the north-west, north, east and south-east sides, the bushes made a complete screen and windbreak. Only the south-west corner was open to sun and water. In the centre stood a giant oak, and beneath its branches during fine periods in the summer the old man would have his chair placed. Sometimes he would sit there surrounded by his books and papers for the entire day.

His *Times* advertisement, drawn up by Juliet, had been answered by forty-seven applicants, of whom he had arranged to see four. Three of these had already called, and though he thought that all might suit, he had not greatly taken to any one of them. Now he was waiting for the fourth, Frank Roscoe. This man's letter had been the most promising of the lot – the others had been too humble – and he was looking forward to meeting him with some eagerness. He had on the previous day rung up the clergyman and one of the officers given as references. The former he found had retired and was not available, but the latter's report was reasonably good.

The affair of the admiral having reached its appointed denouement, Juliet looked at the clock. "Five minutes to three," she observed. "Your next applicant should soon be putting in an appearance. I think I'll make myself scarce."

"No, Juliet, don't go," her father returned. "I should like you to see him. This so far is the promising one, and if he's to live in the house we must all like him."

"Oh, all right. Then of course I'll stay." She got up and put away her pad. "I do hope this one will be better than the last. Poor Mr Troughton was really a good sort, but he was terribly heavy on the hand. He had absolutely no conversation, but he was the best person I've ever known for bringing other people's efforts to a standstill."

"He wasn't so bad."

"Oh, Daddy, you know he couldn't have been worse! Someone would make a remark hopefully, thinking the subject might be good for at least five minutes, and with one devastating remark it was dead beyond possibility of recovery."

Sir Roland smiled grimly. "I grant you he wasn't a chatterbox."

"I'm all for understatement myself. You remind me of the Irishman who had to drown some cats. He described their reactions by the remark that they weren't too well pleased about it."

On the stroke of three Boone, Sir Roland's saturnine attendant, threw open the library door with the words, "Mr Roscoe to see you, sir."

Juliet looked keenly at the tall, good looking and well-dressed man who came forward and spoke with easy though respectful manners. This was much more the type she had been hoping for. Her interest grew.

She could see her father was pleased by his punctuality, as he held out his hand. "Excuse my not getting up, Mr Roscoe," he said, "but unfortunately I am an invalid. Let me introduce you to my daughter, Miss Chatterton."

Juliet liked the young man's restrained smile and his handshake, neither flabby nor too cordial. "Ex-officer," she said to herself, shrewdly if mistakenly.

"Won't you sit down," went on Sir Roland. "You'll find cigarettes in the box on the table."

Having offered the box to Juliet and given her a light, Frank took a cigarette. Sir Roland also took one and with some difficulty lit it. This, Juliet knew, was one of a series of tiny tests, and she watched with amused interest the newcomer's reaction. He acquitted himself with distinction. The other three applicants had sprung up to help, a thing Sir Roland hated because of the attention it directed to his infirmity. But Frank apparently did not see his host's difficulties, but kept his eyes on the window. Leaning back he said easily: "What a completely charming place you have here. In summer it must be just perfect."

"It's not bad," admitted Sir Roland. "It's a lot better since I had it. I made the tennis court and that shrubbery you see."

"Dad's very ingenious, Mr Roscoe," put in Juliet, "though he never blows his own trumpet. That shrubbery place, as he calls it, is his own idea. It's really a sun trap, sheltered from the north and east and open only to the river."

Frank smiled. "I can scarcely imagine anything more delightful. But I'm fond of all this country. It's fine in itself and of course the river absolutely makes it."

Further subtle flattery of her father? Juliet wondered. Then she thought she was wrong and that the caller had really meant what he said.

They talked for a little, and Juliet believed her father was favourably impressed. At least he presently turned to business.

"Well," he said with a smile, "I realise that it wasn't to discuss scenery and local history that you called. Let me tell you what I want done and then you can say, first, whether you'll like the job and second, whether you have the necessary qualifications."

Frank laughed. "Unless, sir," he declared, "you've got some perfectly frightful requirements, I can reply to your first point at once. I should like nothing better than to come. However, your second will naturally be the deciding factor."

"Then I'll tell you what I want," and Sir Roland went on to describe general secretarial work. "None of that would require a high order of technical skill, but it would need confidence on my part and tact and good humour on yours."

"I would try to meet those conditions."

"I'm sure you would. Then as I have spent my life in the Government service, you would have to get out facts and figures from books of reference or from various Government offices or other sources. You would have to keep a detailed index of all that was written, so as to be able to look up in a few seconds what I had previously said on any point. You see, my book is more than a mere biography. I examine certain questions and advocate policies. I mean really that you'd have to *help*, no matter what was the precise nature of the work."

"I'm afraid, sir," Frank said diplomatically, "a good deal of that would be new to me. All the same I believe I could do it. I can at least assure you of my willingness to help in every way possible."

"Very well, that's all I could expect. Now there's what may seem to you a snag, due, let us say, to a sick man's whim. I can't work regular hours. If I feel ill I can't do anything: if I feel well I shall want to work at the most unsuitable times. Perhaps I should do nothing all day and then set to work after dinner and go on into the night. Could you stand that?"

"Oh yes, of course I could," Frank answered, "but it does raise a point. Should I be guaranteed any free time? I mean, if I wanted to run up to Town to meet someone, should I be able to keep an appointment?"

"Certainly, you'd have to be. You would definitely have Sundays and one free afternoon in the week. But I should rather have our relations such that each would try to suit the other's convenience as far as was reasonably possible. If you wanted to go to Town you would say so, and I would arrange your leave unless there was some special reason to prevent it. If I particularly wanted something done on your regular afternoon off, you would change it for another unless this would cause some special inconvenience. With good will on both sides such adjustments become easy."

"It's the way I should like to have it," Frank assured him.

"You would have plenty of free time," Sir Roland continued. "You would be treated as a member of the family, and subject to my reasonable requirements, would be able to play tennis, boat, and do whatever else you liked. Subject to the same requirements, you could order your day as you liked. If, for example, there was typing to be done and you wanted to play tennis, you could play provided you did the typing at another time. You would have liberty, but I should have to feel I could trust you not to make it licence."

"Are you a tennis player?" inquired Juliet.

"I was at one time, Miss Chatterton. But I'm rather badly out of practice."

Sir Roland looked as if he thought this was progressing somewhat rapidly. "Well," he said, "arrangements about work and leisure would sort themselves out during the month's probation which I should require. Now with regard to finances I have here – "

Juliet got up. "I think I'll leave you and Mr Roscoe to talk over your business," she began, but her father interrupted her.

"Just a moment, if you don't mind." He turned back to Frank. "I was saying that I have here a note of my financial proposals. Just glance over it and see if you consider it satisfactory?"

Frank read the paper carefully, then handed it back. "I should consider that handsome, sir."

"All right," Sir Roland answered, "let us consider the matter settled. You come for a month, and at the end of it we can discuss the matter again. Now there remains only one question: when can you start?"

"This is Friday," said Frank. "I fear I must give Mr Burt a week's notice. Would it suit you if I came down on Sunday night week, so as to be ready to start work on Monday morning?"

"Admirably." Sir Roland turned to his daughter. "I wonder, Juliet, would you show Mr Roscoe round the place? Then bring him back and we'll have tea."

Juliet was more interested than she would have admitted in the arrival of this prepossessing stranger. He seemed in many ways her ideal of what a man should be. Reasonably good looking and well turned out, he was obviously a man of the world, with his polished manners which could be respectful without the slightest approach to ob-sequiousness. A glance at his face showed that he was highly intelligent. Yet with it all he had a sort of boyish simplicity, almost puckish, which she found strangely attractive.

"We've had to rearrange the rooms," she began when he had closed the door behind them. "That room was always the library, but we've had to take the old drawing-room for my father's bedroom; he can't manage the stairs, you know. That means that the sitting-room is upstairs: I'll show you. But first, here's the room you'll work in, the old morning-room. I'm afraid there's not much view, but probably you won't mind."

"If I'm to type and look up references, a view would be a handicap," he pointed out.

"Well, in here you won't be tempted."

It was in fact a pleasant enough room with plenty of light and a quite passable outlook on the drive and trees behind it. Everything was very modern, from the typing table to the four-drawer steel filing cabinet which stood against the wall opposite the window. It was a place where work should be easy.

"I don't see why you should have apologised for it," Frank observed. "I think it's fine, view included."

"Oh well, if you stay you'll see plenty of it. Now come and I'll show you your own room."

On both ground and first floors a wide corridor ran down the middle of the house from end to end. Juliet pointed out the various doors. Like the workroom, Frank's room faced to the back, so the view here also was poor. But it was a good room, comfortably fitted up as a bed-sitting-room, and Juliet thought he ought to be pleased with it. He certainly seemed so.

"Why, Miss Chatterton," he exclaimed, "this is luxury. I shouldn't have expected anything like it. This room is worse than a view where I work. I shall be tempted never to leave it."

They went out and strolled down to the river. "We're lucky that the tow path's on the other side so that the place goes right down to the water's edge," Juliet explained. "Are you fond of boating?"

Frank loved boating, but unhappily he had never done any punting.

"Well, you can practice it here if you like. There's a large and a small boat and a punt in the boathouse." She led the way past the little structure to the clump of bushes to the right of the grounds. "Here's Dad's sun trap. It's not much of a sun trap now, but on a hot August day it really is rather delightful."

She thought she had never shown anything to a more appreciative visitor. Frank appeared immensely impressed. Indeed she had to admit to herself, not without reason, the situation and layout of the place was certainly charming, and a seat beneath the big oak tree in the sun trap on a fine day, with its shade and view, would have been hard to beat.

When they had seen everything they returned to the library. There after tea and a short further chat Juliet rang for Boone to show Frank out.

"Well," Sir Roland asked when the door had closed, "what do you think of him?"

"Much the best we've had yet. If he's good at tennis and bridge he might be quite an acquisition. Poor Mr Troughton couldn't play either for nuts."

"That certainly is the important point. I appreciate that it doesn't matter whether he's any good as a secretary."

"I expect he'll be all right," Juliet returned lightly. "He couldn't be worse than some you've had."

"Miss Juliet Chatterton, for example? Perhaps you're right, though I shouldn't have ventured to say it myself."

"You know, Dad, we have to do something to keep you out of mischief. Well, would you like to go on about the admiral?"

They had not much more than resumed work when there was another interruption. Sounds of an approaching vehicle were heard, followed by steps and the murmur of voices in the hall. Then the door opened and a tall fine-looking woman entered the room. While by no means a beauty, she had good features, with a calm dependable face and a kindly expression. She wore an expensive fur coat and walked with an almost regal carriage. Everything about her gave an impression of competence and good sense.

"Ah, Sylvia, nice to see you so soon," Sir Roland greeted her. "We weren't expecting you for another hour."

Lady Chatterton advanced towards the fire. "I had a good day," she announced in a deep contralto. "I got what I wanted in the first shops I went to and there were no queues. Rather wonderful."

"Not one's usual experience," said Juliet. "What about tea? Have you had it?"

"No, that was the one thing I couldn't get. I should like some."

"I'll see about it." Juliet moved to the door, then paused. "Daddy's got a new man. He's just gone. Seems promising."

"Oh." Lady Chatterton turned towards her husband. "I hope he's better than the last?"

Juliet gave a hoot of laughter. "*Poor* Mr Troughton," she murmured as she vanished.

"Juliet has decided he's satisfactory," Sir Roland asserted. "It seems he plays tennis and bridge."

"Not necessarily an asset," Lady Chatterton remarked dubiously. "Are you pleased with him, or is he only the usual best of a bad bunch?"

"I think he's all right. I can't tell till I work with him. But he's quite presentable, if that's what you mean."

"That's at least a mercy. Mr Troughton was the best intentioned creature, but I don't think I could have stood him much longer. When's the new one coming?"

"Sunday week. He has to give a week's notice. He's with Burt, you know: Bartholomew Burt, the surgeon."

"Oh yes, I've met him. A charming person. If your man takes after him, he'll do."

Juliet reappeared. "Tea's just coming, Sylvia. I'll bring over this table, and you can have it at the fire."

"Thank you, my dear."

Though there was twenty-one years between them – Sylvia's forty-seven to Juliet's twenty-six – they were more like sisters than stepmother and stepdaughter. Sylvia had been tactful and had never tried to assert her authority, and once Juliet found that she was neither going to be bossed nor forcibly ousted from her position as mistress of the house, she ceased to feel resentment at the newcomer and voluntarily handed over the reins of government. Now they were the best of friends, more than that indeed, they were deeply attached to one another.

While in the library the talk focussed on the new secretary, the same subject was being discussed in what had formerly been the butler's pantry, but was now "Mr Boone's room". Boone himself was there and with him was Maggie Green, the housemaid.

Arthur Boone had been Sir Roland's attendant for some nine years. After a short apprenticeship in an engineering works, he had been persuaded by an uncle who had influence to train as a male nurse. The uncle had got him a job in a large mental home, and had pushed him on till he was earning quite good wages. But he had never liked the work, and when he saw Sir Roland's advertisement for an attendant, he applied. This job he had found almost ideal and he had done his best to make himself indispensable. As far as such a thing is possible in this world, he had succeeded. Sir Roland would have been lost without him. He scarcely ever needed to tell him what to do, so completely had Boone learnt his ways.

With the other members of the staff Boone was on friendly, if not exactly cordial terms. He was too reserved to be really popular. An exception was Maggie Green, who had joined the establishment some five years after he had. He had liked Maggie and she had seemed to like him. But otherwise than as a friend he had never given her a thought. He believed that if he set himself to win her he would succeed, but he was not, he told himself, a marrying man, and in any case he was scarcely in a position to support a wife. It was a condition of his employment that part of his salary came in board and lodging. And marriage with both of them remaining in their existing jobs did not appeal to him.

For eight of the nine years he had carried on, satisfied with his surroundings and not worrying a great deal about the future. Then an event had happened which had completely changed his outlook and brought a new factor into his life.

One afternoon during the early summer when Troughton was with Sir Roland and he was off duty, he had asked for the use of a boat. Maggie Green's sister, the wife of a publican in an adjoining village, had come to see her, and Boone invited them both out on the river. They had landed on an island and were about to make tea when a thunderstorm of almost tropical severity suddenly came down. They were soaked in a few moments and their expedition was completely spoiled. A miserable return journey faced them, but Maggie had been so cheery and helpful that it passed off almost pleasantly.

This had made Boone think of her in a new way, and as a result an intimacy grew up between them which eventually ripened into love. In due course they became engaged.

Then it was that a chance of marriage seemed to offer. Maggie's brother-in-law, Joe Barlow the publican, became ill with a slow complaint which could only end in one way. Apart from his own fate, this made the outlook for his wife Agnes very dark. They would have to leave the public house, as she could not run it alone. They had saved enough money to live for a few months, but this was likely to be consumed during Joe's lifetime, leaving nothing for Agnes after his death.

Then an idea struck Agnes. If Maggie were going to marry this man Boone, would the two of them join her in the pub? She mooted the idea and both instantly fell for it.

Unfortunately there were two rather serious snags. The first was that neither Boone nor Maggie had experience of the work. Agnes, however, believed that she could teach them all that was necessary. The second snag was that a considerable sum of money would be needed. The Barlows had rented the property, but now the owner had decided to sell. He was not a grasping man and they believed he would only want a fair price. But at least £1,200 would be needed, and they hadn't it. Agnes could contribute nothing. Boone had accumulated £500 and Maggie some £200, leaving them about £500 short.

So matters stood when Frank Roscoe paid his first visit to Jasmine Lodge. Arthur Boone and Maggie were now discussing him. Frank's personality might make a good deal of difference to Boone, for he and the secretary came into contact quite a lot. Boone had a special reason for anxiety as to the personality of anyone with whom he came into professional contact, and this anxiety Maggie shared.

"How much did you see of him?" Maggie was asking.

"Not very much," the attendant answered. "I let him in and took his hat and showed him to the library – which you should have done, only you weren't there."

"I like that," retorted Maggie. "You know very well it's my afternoon off and I was getting ready to go out."

"Very well, don't get on your hind legs."

"Was that all you saw?"

"No, I brought in tea, again in your absence. He was talking to Sir Roland with Miss Juliet putting in her oar the way she does. Then afterwards I showed him out."

"Was he civil?"

"Yes, he was. I must give him that. His manner was correct enough for his position."

"Well, you should be able to form some impression of him after that."

"I should, and I did. He's no fool, is this Mr Frank Roscoe, or I'm a Dutchman. Got the proper old school tie manner and all that, but his eye is as sharp as they make them."

"Would he be inquisitive?"

"He might or he might not: I wouldn't know. But I'm darned sure he'd be observant. And as far as we are concerned there wouldn't be much difference."

"He might be sharp enough and yet mind his own business."

"A lot would depend on what he considered his business."

"I don't like it, Arthur."

"I don't like it either, my girl, but neither you nor I can alter it. He's definitely engaged, so Miss Juliet said. We've got to accept it."

"A pity that old Trout went. He was just ideal for the job."

"Aye. You could have exploded a cracker in front of his nose and he wouldn't have seen it. But we can't expect luck like that all the time."

"What will you do?"

"Just carry on. But I'll have to be more careful. It's a darned nuisance, but there it is."

As may be deduced from this conversation, neither Arthur Boone nor Maggie Green had the impeccable characters their employer presumably imagined. Both were convinced that their wages were not in real accord with the amount of devoted service each contributed, and as Sir Roland unhappily failed to see eye to eye with them on the point, they felt it was up to them to rectify the defect by other means. It was Boone who took the actual steps, Maggie confining her assistance to encouragement and advice.

Boone had indeed not told her exactly what he was doing. He doubted whether she would have stood for quite such deliberate methods. He was in fact systematically robbing Sir Roland. Through his training and association with the mental hospital he knew something about drugs, and one night he had put a small amount of dope in Sir Roland's whisky. Having made sure the potion had been drunk, he had entered the old man's room during the night, abstracted his keys and taken wax impressions. He was sufficiently skilful to cut keys to fit, using Sir Roland's well-equipped workshop, which, since the old man had become more crippled, was seldom entered.

With the keys he was able to open his employer's desk and safe. In this way actual money occasionally changed owners. But what he really wanted was to get hold of and alter accounts. He did a good many messages for Sir Roland in the village shops, paying for certain items and settling various small accounts. These usually cost Sir Roland more than the shopkeepers realised, and quite a healthy balance went into Boone's pocket.

An observant secretary would thus be a most inconvenient innovation. Boone looked forward with a good deal of apprehension to what might be coming.

– 5 –

AMATORY COMPLEXITIES

On that Friday of Frank's visit to Jasmine Lodge, Dulcie had had an arduous day at Harley Street. To facilitate Frank's leave, she had assured Burt that she could do his work as well as her own. She had managed it, but it had proved a heavier job than she had anticipated. She had not finished at her usual time, so after a snack in a restaurant, she had gone back for a couple of hours to finish up the correspondence.

Worse than tiring, the day had been horribly lonely. For months she had been accustomed to seeing Frank at odd moments, or if she did not, she at least knew that he was there in the house. These meetings had been a constant excitement and delight. Today his absence took the joy out of life and made everything seem flat and dull. Indeed she began to wonder how, if he got this job, she could carry on without him.

The pleasure therefore was the greater when, reaching her flat, she found him waiting for her.

"I guessed you might have to work late, old girl," he greeted her, "but I was afraid if I went to Harley Street I might miss you."

"Oh, Frank, what about the job?" she asked urgently.

"Got it!" he grinned. She could see he was delighted.

"Oh, my dear! I am glad! And sorry! Tell me about it."

"Looks all right. Fine house on the river and all that. No shortage of cash. Old boy's semi-paralysed from rheumatism. Writing a book and wants help."

She snorted. "If you imagine you're going to get off with that, you've another thought coming to you. I want to know everything. Begin properly at the beginning and tell me."

He grew more serious. "Look here," he demanded, "have you had supper?"

"Not a proper one, no. Have you?"

"No, and something within is calling out about it. I tell you, come to the Red Lizard and we'll celebrate."

Over the meal Frank gave a detailed account of his day. Jasmine Lodge was comfortable, the people seemed all right, and he believed he could do the job to the old boy's satisfaction.

"And Miss Chatterton?" went on Dulcie. Frank's account of her had been sketchy. "I want details. I warn you, if you merely say she's all right, I'll scream."

"If you really feel you ought to scream, go right ahead," he told her. "As a matter of fact, she does seem all right. What else do you want me to say?"

"What's she like?"

"Oh, ordinary. On the small side, if anything. Nothing remarkable about her one way or another."

"What did she talk about?"

"Just what was going. Went all tactful when the question of my salary came up: wanted to go and leave us to it. But Sir Roland wouldn't let her. He had all the terms written out and he handed the paper to me. I accepted. Most high toned. There was no discussion."

Dulcie felt slightly dissatisfied about Juliet Chatterton. She knew how Frank ran after a pretty face and she could not but wonder whether the lady really could be so nondescript as he made out. Was he not protesting too little? Then she chid herself. She knew jealousy was one of her weaknesses and she told herself she must fight against it.

"What are the terms?" she asked, switching off Juliet.

"Not too bad, I think."

"You mean, all right?"

"Well, yes, I do. I'm to live as a member of the family, so I'll be all right as to board and lodging. That'll count of course as quite a bit of the salary: more than I like, because the living will be better than is necessary. After that I get five pounds a week."

"Oh, Frank, I think that's good! You'll be able to save most of it."

"I should think so," he returned without enthusiasm. "But the old boy particularly said that to 'keep up my position as a member of the household some special outlay would be needed,' those were his words. So perhaps I'll not be able to save as much as I'd like."

"I think it's fine." She hesitated, then continued. "But look here, Frank, there's a snag. When we talked about a job you said you'd get one in London and could help me with the scheme. Your taking this at Staines means we'll have to give up the scheme and lose the extra money."

He made an emphatic gesture. "Not on your life! I've thought about that and there's no reason why you shouldn't carry on by yourself. If so, of course you'd get all the profits. If I wasn't working it with you I couldn't expect half."

This was a new idea. She remained silent.

"A thousand a year," he followed up, "would be quite a help when it came to setting up house."

"But I couldn't work it without you," she said hesitatingly. Dulcie's standpoint had moved a good deal since Frank had first suggested the plan.

"Of course you could," Frank answered with conviction. "You do nine-tenths of the work as it is, and the rest you'd find as easy as wink. See, all I do is to stamp and initial your paying-in counterfoils when you've filled them in. I would give you the stamp. The only thing you'd have to do would be to copy the cashier's initials, and they're written so carelessly that it wouldn't matter much what you put down."

Dulcie still looked doubtful. "I don't like it," she muttered.

"You can't make a thousand a year without taking *some* trouble. Don't be silly, Dulcie. Just remember the initials must be written quickly. It doesn't matter if they're not very like the original. But don't ever attempt to copy them slowly. That makes a shaky line and it's spotted immediately."

At this a wave of distaste and remorse did sweep over Dulcie, but she soon crushed it down. "Oh, well, I'll try. Look, Frank, I'm *terribly* glad about your good luck. But I'll miss you horribly. When shall I see you?"

He seemed relieved. "I'll have Sundays and one other afternoon a week. The afternoon doesn't seem a great catch, unless by chance it's a Saturday. But Sundays we should have together. I'd come up by an early train and go back by a late one and we'd have the whole day."

"That won't be so bad, I suppose. But the weeks will be long without you. It's been just ideal working together, so to speak, in the same job."

"But, honey, I'm not going to Jasmine Lodge for the rest of my life. The job won't last long."

"Not last? What do you mean? I thought it was permanent."

"Not on your life! I've taken it only as a stepping-stone. Do you think I'd maroon myself in the depths of the country for ever? No, I'll be back in Town soon, as secretary to an MP or some big pot at the War Office."

"But how will this job help you to anything like that?"

"I've got to do research for the old boy: visit Government offices and Army people and all that. Facts for his book. You can trust your Frank to make contacts."

Next day he gave his formal notice to Burt, who was characteristically pleasant about it, wishing Frank good luck and handing him an excellent testimonial. Then Burt told Dulcie to insert an advertisement for a successor in the half-dozen papers she thought most suitable. As a result they had a visit from a quiet, inoffensive-looking man named John Rider, a former cloakroom attendant on one of the railways. Burt left it to Dulcie to interview him and she thought him suitable. She finally engaged him because he could start on the Thursday, which would give Frank three days to instruct him in his duties.

The following Sunday Dulcie and Frank spent together, and in the late afternoon she saw him off for Staines. As she returned to her solitary supper she felt as lonely as if he had gone to the North Pole. Firmly she told herself that she was being a fool. She determined to carry on and make the best of things, but she found it by no means easy.

During this week the thoughts of Juliet Chatterton had turned quite often to the new secretary. She could not hide from herself that the coming of this good-looking and accomplished young man might be an interesting addition to her somewhat dull life. Her life, she knew, should not be dull, but the fact remained that it was. She was ready enough to admit that the fault was her own, but that did not in itself help matters.

The truth was she had no real companion in the household. Her father, besides being rather unapproachable, was wrapped up in his book and the involved questions he discussed in it. Her stepmother was kindly and friendly, but was much occupied in running the place and in certain post-war social work. No one else in her own station lived in the house, though they had many friends and visitors. But these visitors were interested either in the particular Service they graced, or in peacetime in hunting and shooting, or polo when they could get it.

Juliet didn't care tuppence for her father's political problems nor for the running of the house, though she helped her stepmother to some extent. Blood sports she loathed, thinking them cruel and wicked. She was therefore more or less permanently out of touch with those with whom she came in contact. It was primarily for this reason that she was inclined to give Frank's arrival more importance than it normally would have received.

The death of her only brother in a motor accident had been a great shock to her. It had another result also. She had in effect become her father's heir. Lady Chatterton would of course be left well off, but the bulk of her father's considerable fortune was now to go to Juliet. So he had said more than once. The news, she told herself with, for her, unusual cynicism, must have become general property, for she immediately found herself more sought after by eligible young men. But so far she had met no one with whom she could contemplate marriage.

On Sunday afternoon they had a number of visitors and it was not until just before dinner that she became aware of

Frank's arrival. Since the War they had not dressed, and in his well-cut dark blue lounge suit and spotless linen he looked positively distinguished. Shortly before the meal he appeared in the lounge, where she happened to be alone. She advanced with outstretched hand.

"Oh," she greeted him, "I didn't know you had come. When did you turn up?"

"About an hour ago," he told her. "I've been upstairs settling in."

"Everything all right up there?"

He smiled. "Palatial! My goodness, when I think of some of the places I've been in, I wonder if it can be the same world."

They began to discuss the North African campaign, she from the personal point of view, he as a strategic and tactical operation. Then Sylvia and Sir Roland came in and the conversation became general.

That evening and the next day passed without incident until in the afternoon Juliet went as usual to the library for tea. Her father and stepmother were there alone.

"Hullo, Daddy," she began, "you look worried. The new amanuensis shaping badly?"

"Nonsense, child," Sir Roland retorted, "I'm not in the least worried and I'm sure I don't look it."

"Well, not exactly careworn. Perhaps I should have said thoughtful."

"What about Mr Roscoe?" put in Sylvia. "Do you think he's going to suit?"

"A bit early to say, but he seems satisfactory so far."

"Did you do much work today?" Juliet went on, speaking from a semi-professional point of view.

"None till after lunch. I didn't get up. I gave him a few letters, not dictating them, you know, but just indicating what was to be said. I must admit they were admirably done, both in phraseology and setting out."

"That's promising," Sylvia considered.

"Then we worked at the book after lunch. He took everything down in shorthand, but whether he can read it again remains to be seen."

"The confirmed optimist," Juliet commented. She was proceeding to develop her theme, but just then Frank walked in and the conversation took another turn.

Towards the end of tea Sylvia turned to him. "Are you a billiard player, Mr Roscoe?"

"I played at home, Lady Chatterton," he answered, "but I'm afraid that's rather a long time ago. Except for a few games during a leave in Rome while I was convalescing, I haven't had a cue in my hand since."

"Then what about a game after tea?" Juliet put in. "Get your hand in again."

"Thank you so much, if you can put up with a poor performance, I'd like nothing better," he declared, then glancing towards Sir Roland, "but shall you not want me?"

"I don't feel like doing any more today," the old man answered. "The typing of what we've done will be wanted tomorrow morning, but if you like to do it after dinner, that will be quite satisfactory."

They played three games, with immense apparent pleasure to Frank and certainly no boredom on Juliet's part. He was rusty, but occasional strokes revealed his old form. Juliet was by no means brilliant, but by her steadiness she contrived to beat him in all three.

"You've been pretty good," she said as they put away their cues. "I can see that. A little practice and you will be again."

They played at different times during that first week, and at the end of it Frank was just able to hold his own.

Then on a Saturday afternoon some people called and there was bridge. Juliet invited him to join in. She noticed that if he did not cover himself with distinction, he at least did not disgrace himself.

Through these games and other occasional meetings Juliet grew more and more interested in Frank. She thought him somewhat mysterious. She imagined him as a man who had had experiences, who had drunk deeply of life, and whose knowledge of the world was profound. She believed he had character and force: a man who would get his own way against odds. This being a faculty in which she herself was deficient, she admired him the more.

His manner towards her also had been perfect. He treated her with just the right blend of deference and familiarity. He paid her small attentions, listened courteously to remarks which she herself felt were inane, and gave weight to her views. And though they were increasingly together, he had never once suggested by word or look an interest in her more than that of a good companion. She enjoyed his society and was glad he had come.

During the whole of her six-and-twenty years Juliet Chatterton had lived a sheltered life. Only two real sorrows had entered into it. The first was when at the age of twelve she had lost her mother, the second, as already stated, when her brother was killed. A third trouble was in a different category.

All her life she had been keen on acting and had wanted to go on the stage. But her father had objected, pointing out what a hard life an actress led and how few there were who reached the upper ranks. All the same, she had defeated him on her twenty-first birthday. Rather unwisely he had asked her if there was any one thing which she would like as a present. She had answered, "Your help to go on the stage." Like Herod of old when cornered by an incalculable daughter, he felt he could not go back on the implications of his question, and he used his influence to get her tuition and tests. They came to nothing. She was in fact tried out by four separate managers, but she was unable to satisfy any one of them.

Bitterly disappointed, she had settled down at Jasmine Lodge in a Micawberish sort of way, hoping against hope that something would turn up to give her an interest or a mission in life. Now she wondered whether the coming of this new secretary was going to make a difference. A really sympathetic friend would be marvellous, particularly one who was so distinguished-looking and so accomplished.

One afternoon they had a conversation which intensified her feeling. During lunch the talk had turned on archaeological remains and a ruined castle in the neighbourhood had been mentioned. Sir Roland was not feeling fit enough to work, so Frank was free. He had asked Juliet if she would care to walk with him to the ruin to investigate some of the things which had been discussed. On the way she mentioned the stage and Frank asked if she was interested.

"Interested?" she returned, "I should just think so! But unhappily it's rather a sore subject," and she told him what had occurred.

Frank made commiserating sounds. "That's pretty hard luck," he declared. "I know how heart-breaking it is in the case of a job, when you're turned down by employer after employer. With you it was not your bread and butter that was at stake, but all the same I'm sure it meant a lot to you."

"How nice of you not to laugh in a superior way, as most of my friends do," she went on. "They think that because I'll have a lot of Dad's money and won't have to work, that my wanting to act is only silly nonsense. Till now no one has shown any sympathy."

"I'm sympathetic because I'm interested in the stage myself," Frank explained. "I don't mean that I've ever done anything on it, except amateur stuff when I was young. But I'd like to try. Particularly I should like to try writing a play."

"Oh!" she seemed thrilled. "I've wanted to do that too. But I haven't known how to set about it. Have you written any so far?"

He shook his head. "It's only been a sort of dream. One has a lot of them. Things you'd like to do, but which you don't suppose you ever will. I've never really settled down to make a serious attempt. Never had time, for one thing."

"Just the same with me except that I didn't have your excuse about time. Tell me, have you a plot?"

"Not exactly. I've thought of what might make one, but I've never tried to work it out in detail."

"I'm sure you could make a good one. What's the general idea?"

"Well, I'm afraid it's rather vague. It's about displaced persons. I saw some of them in Italy, though the problem's not really bad there. The play would show what an absolutely ghastly position they're in and how comparatively easily they could be given new nationality. I think something might be made of it."

Juliet was enthusiastic. This was the kind of thing she liked! "It sounds a splendid subject," she declared warmly. "It could be tremendously dramatic."

"Dramatically I think it would be all right, but an audience mightn't stand for anything so miserable."

"That would depend on how it was handled, wouldn't it?"

"I suppose so. One would have to think that out."

"It might be really worth doing. If it helped to bring home to the public these poor peoples' plight, it might lead to something being done." Juliet's enthusiasm grew. "Why not work at it, Mr Roscoe, now you're here? You'd have time, wouldn't you?"

"It's rather an alluring idea," Frank confessed slowly. "All the same I don't know that I could. I'm not very good at dialogue, I'm afraid."

Juliet had a sudden brainwave. "I suppose," she said rather hesitatingly, "I couldn't help you? I couldn't do a plot for nuts, but I think I could make a shot at dialogue."

He looked at her and for the first time she thought she saw admiration in his eyes. "It's a marvellous idea," he declared warmly. "Nothing I should like better!"

Juliet was surprised to find her heart beating rapidly with excitement. "Then let's try!" she cried. "It would be grand. Don't let's say anything about it and then they can't laugh at us."

So were laid the foundations of a rapidly-growing intimacy, the possible consequences of which she by no means realised. Frank was as good as his word and after some days showed her his suggested plot. She was delighted. It seemed extremely promising. They discussed and altered some details. Then he wrote a full synopsis. It was now up to her to clothe it with words. On the day on which she wrote across the top of a sheet of ruled quarto paper, "Act I. The Waiting Room of a Mid-European Railway Station," she obtained one of the greatest thrills of her life.

With such a common interest it was not surprising that their friendship should grow apace. Before long they were Frank and Juliet to one another. But both were careful to keep their relations secret. It was not only a fear of having their incursion into drama ridiculed. Though neither mentioned it, both feared that such an intimacy would be frowned on by the powers that were, and that a compelling reason for Frank's departure would materialise.

The collaboration for some time went with great smoothness and then to Juliet's profound regret there came a break. This was the arrival for a fortnight's visit of a relative, a Captain Firmore. Juliet did not much like him, but apparently he liked her, for he had on various occasions intimated that he might be prepared to consider matrimony. "Me or my money?" she felt inclined to ask him on these occasions, but being well brought up, she had never done so.

Firmore was a big bony-faced young man with a thick neck and an aggressive manner. Presuming on his connection with Sir Roland, he acted as if the house belonged to him, ordering the servants about and treating Juliet as if she was a plaything. He was patronising to Frank, and Juliet could see that Frank hated him at sight.

Under the circumstances it was not unnatural that Juliet found herself monopolised by Firmore, with Frank excluded from their tennis and boating and other pursuits. She would have liked to invite Frank to join them, but she had sense enough to see the unwisdom of this. All the same, she took care not to be cut off altogether from Frank's society. When she knew that the Captain was otherwise engaged she would meet him and they would exchange rapid confidences.

The difference between the two men was brought specially home to her when the latter's visit was nearly at an end. One evening at dinner when Firmore was boasting of his achievements in the hunting field Juliet happened to glance at Frank. She could see from his expression that the recital disgusted him. On the next opportunity she skilfully introduced the subject.

"I don't know why," Frank declared when they had discussed it for some moments, "but I always feel ashamed to admit my real feelings about it. It seems weak-minded and silly, but there it is, I can't help it."

"What feelings?" she asked curiously.

"Well, to be truthful, I loathe it. I don't judge anyone, because people feel differently about these things, but I personally think that all amusements which depend on the suffering of animals are vile."

She was thrilled. "Oh!" she cried, "how glad I am to hear you say that! It's exactly what I think. My cousin and I have had some heated exchanges about it. He despises anyone who isn't keen. He says they don't hunt because they're cowards and afraid of being thrown."

"People who support it have to say something," Frank pointed out. "Of course," he went on, "one must remember that many of the kindest people, people who are fond of animals too, are hunting people. One therefore can't condemn it dogmatically."

"How fair you are!" she exclaimed. "I've noticed that too and it has puzzled me. How can they do it?"

"Want of imagination, I expect. They accept what is generally accepted and don't think of it from the victim's point of view."

Juliet was slightly horrified when she realised her own relief on Deryk Firmore's departure, which took place a day or two later. It was not so much that she disliked the young man as that his presence prevented her from seeing so much of Frank. She honestly believed that this was due to her desire to discuss the play, but actually Frank himself was taking a growing place in her thoughts. She felt sure, moreover, that his interest in her was increasing. The idea of marrying him had not yet occurred to her, but she felt that it was very pleasant having him at Jasmine Lodge.

Three days after Firmore left an event occurred which took her off her guard and brought matters sharply to a head. She and Frank had formed the habit of meeting when possible in the afternoons to discuss the play, which was increasing at least in length. For fear of ridicule Juliet still wished to keep the work secret, though in this she had no conscious desire to deceive her people. Frank had agreed with her. While therefore they would sometimes discuss a walk or a row at lunch and afterwards start off together, more often they said nothing and went separately to the chosen rendezvous.

One afternoon they had gone to the ruined castle already mentioned and it was while climbing to what looked like a sheltered nook that the affair happened. As they mounted, Juliet put her foot on a loose stone. It turned and for a moment she swayed dangerously over a drop. It was not very deep, only about ten feet, but there was jagged crumbling masonry at the bottom and a fall might have been serious. Frank was just behind her, and springing forward, he caught her in his arms. While desperately trying to keep his balance he held her tight.

That did it. Before either of them knew what was happening, her arms were round his neck and he was pressing burning kisses on her face and mouth.

"Oh, Frank!" she breathed as she clung to him.

He suddenly moved and began pushing her back. "No, no," he cried brokenly, "we mustn't! It's not right! We can never marry. My darling, my precious darling, we mustn't do it!"

"Why not?" she answered with a reckless laugh. "Of course we must and we will! How can you say we mustn't?"

"We mustn't," he repeated, and she could feel his tense emotion. "I could never marry you."

It was at this point that Frank made his fundamental mistake. One reference to Dulcie would have cleared up the position, but for the moment he funked it – and was lost.

Now a storm raged in his mind which dwarfed even that with which Dulcie had greeted the idea of the fraud. In a way he was committed to Dulcie. True there had been no formal engagement, but an engagement had been under-stood. He could not go back on her. She had been good to him, and though he did not love her, he was sure she loved him. He stood screwing up courage to tell Juliet the truth, but he found that every moment's delay was making it harder. Then gradually he began asking himself, did he really want to tell her the truth? Within his reach was a prize, a prize that till a few moments ago would have seemed no less out of reach than the job of Prime Minister. He could have it if only he put out his hand and took it. Money, position, security, even power! Once married to Juliet...

While he hesitated, she made his decision still harder. "Dear Frank!" she murmured, clinging to him more tightly, "I can't believe it! I didn't know there was such happiness in the world. You can't leave me now! I'll never give you up! Never as long as life lasts!"

Increasingly he felt that a mention of Dulcie was beyond his power. "Darling, there's no hope," he went on, still struggling to tell her the truth. "What would we live on? I have no position, no money, nothing to offer you."

"Except yourself! Oh, my own, don't talk like that! Money will be no bar. I already have enough to live on: a legacy from an aunt. And of course I'll have most of Dad's. I'll have plenty for us both."

Frank's struggles became weaker. "But you don't imagine, darling, that I could live on my wife! There are some things a man cannot do, and that's one of them."

She smiled at him. "Silly boy! That's one of the barriers between people who don't love one another. With our love things like that will be swept away. The money's there. What does it matter where it comes from?"

"It's sweet beyond words of you, Juliet, but a man has his proper pride."

"No, he hasn't," she retorted. "If he's a poor sort of worm he may love his own superiority more than his wife: not like my Frank!"

Then suddenly something snapped in him. Again he drew her to him passionately. "My darling!" he breathed. "Almost you would persuade me." He kissed her once more, then released her. "But, dearest, we mustn't deceive ourselves. Think of your father. What would he say to such an idea?"

"He'd oppose it at first of course," she answered. "Parents always do. But he'd get accustomed to it in time."

"It's no good. We may as well face it. It's too lovely a dream to be true."

"Nonsense! Let's go home and tell them now."

He kissed her again. "Darling, we must recognise facts. Your father would simply turn me out of the house. You know he would."

She paused in thought. "He might at first, but when he saw I was in earnest he'd invite you back."

"No, he wouldn't. As things are, nothing would induce him to give his consent."

She would have none of it. At length she wore Frank down. He changed his position. "If we could think of such a thing," he said at last, "and I absolutely can't realise it, but if we *could* think of it, we'd have to keep it to ourselves for the present."

"I don't want to seem anxious to hide it."

"Of course not. But don't you see, dearest, if you married me now, it would be in the face of your father's bitter opposition. It would mean a complete break with him. You don't want that, I know. If we can consider the matter at all, we must wait till we can get him to look at our marriage with favour."

For a long time they continued their discussion, then at last they reached a conclusion. They were engaged, there was and could be, no doubt about that fundamental fact. But for the time being it was to be their secret. They would consult together as to the most favourable moment for breaking it to Sir Roland. And until he knew it, everyone else must naturally be left in complete ignorance.

And Dulcie? Frank preferred not to think of her. In any case a fence could not be taken till it was reached.

– 6 –

FEMININE REACTIONS

When Juliet was alone she could scarcely refrain from singing aloud. She was filled with an ecstatic bliss greater than anything she had ever before experienced. Love had so often approached and then passed her by, that she was beginning to feel she had missed it for good. Visions of loneliness had begun to haunt her, of a life which would grow lonelier and more shut in as the years passed. Now all these fears were gone! Now love had come to her! No more dread of loneliness or the slow decay of her best faculties! Frank had changed all that. Dear Frank! Just to think of him made her smile happily: his goodness and kindness and uprightness, his very proper – though misguided – feeling about the money, his desire that her father's consent should be obtained, his fear that as his wife she might not have all she was accustomed to: no wonder she smiled! The fact was, Frank was a *gentleman*, in the good old-fashioned sense. Her good fortune almost frightened her.

While Frank so completely fulfilled her ideals in these essentials, he was also just as she would have wished him in lesser matters. His mind was not fixed, like most of the men in her own set, on amusements. He did not hunt or shoot or even fish. He played games, but they were not the be-all and end-all of his existence. His desires lay, like her own, in

96

the direction of the intellect and the arts. Dear Frank! Had there ever been anyone like him?

All the same there were difficulties ahead. Frank was entirely right when he said that they should not marry against her father's wishes. But would her father give his consent? Even though Juliet was a confirmed wishful thinker, she could not visualise his approval. She could hear the very tones of his voice as he would say, "Nonsense, my dear, you can't marry a penniless nobody," and if after a long battle his position was somewhat shaken, the most that could be hoped for would be, "Well, let him go and make some money to support you properly, and then I'll think of it."

The more Juliet considered this aspect of the affair, the more worried she grew. Suppose her father's refusal were adamant, what should they do? It was easy to say she was of age and could marry as she chose. She knew her father. He was just and kind according to his lights, but she could not hide from herself that he was hard. If he once decided that the marriage should not take place, he would stop at nothing to prevent it. He would even, she believed, cut her out of his will, rather than appear to countenance what he disapproved.

But if she lost her inheritance, she could not live. What she had told Frank about her aunt's bequest was scarcely the whole truth. Actually she had had such a legacy, but it was too small to make any appreciable difference. No, until their play brought in wealth, as of course it would, they could only marry on her money, and if they married, that money might well become non-existent.

Perplexed, and with the first keen edge gone from her joy, Juliet felt driven back to her Micawberish attitude.

There appeared to be nothing for it but to wait to see what might turn up.

She would have been still less easy in her mind had she overheard two conversations which by a strange freak of fate took place about the same time on the very afternoon of the engagement.

The first was between her father and stepmother. Sir Roland had worked with Frank during the morning and was now taking a rest. He was reading in the library before tea, the book held before him on an ingenious stand. Lady Chatterton was seeking relaxation from her post-war activities with an elaborate piece of knitting employing many needles and coloured wools. For some time silence had reigned and then Sir Roland broke it.

"By the way, Sylvia, I'm sending Roscoe up to Town tomorrow. I want some information from the Colonial Office. I heard you say you wanted a parcel taken up. He could probably do it for you."

"I dare say he could," she answered and they went on to discuss the suggestion. Then seeing her husband did not wish to continue reading, she added: "Tell me about Mr Roscoe. He has been here now some time and you should have made your mind up about him. How is he doing?"

"He's the most efficient secretary I've ever had," Sir Roland answered slowly, "except perhaps Hopkins. I'm not sure that he's not even better than Hopkins."

"That's high praise, for Mr Hopkins was very good. But I didn't mean so much about his work as about himself. How do you like him personally?"

Sir Roland glanced at her keenly but for some moments did not reply. "That's not such an easy question as it sounds," he said at last. "He's extremely careful and well conducted: polite and respectful and anxious to help. He's pretty reserved about himself, but of course he's none the worse for that. I have every reason to like him."

Lady Chatterton laughed. "Which means that you don't. Why not? I'm interested."

"Oh, come now, Sylvia, that's not fair. I never indicated that I didn't like him. To say such a thing would be grossly unfair to a man who is obviously doing his best."

"I really am interested," Lady Chatterton repeated, ignoring this. "Quite clearly you don't like him personally and I'd like to know why."

"Do you like him?" Sir Roland countered.

"If you must know, not particularly. I admit his good qualities, and he has certainly tried to fit in and not be a nuisance in the house. More than that, he's always ready to help in anything he can."

"Then what's wrong?"

"That's what I'm asking you. Like you, I hesitate to say it, but somehow I never feel that I can trust him. I hope that's not very unkind."

"It's rarely unkind to tell the truth. Well, you've put your finger right on the spot. I have the same feeling. It's only right to add that I've watched him very closely and I've never found the slightest indication of anything not perfectly straight."

"I'm glad of that."

"You are, are you? You needn't think you're going to get off with it like that. It's clear you have something in your mind."

"I know nothing against him either."

"Then what is it? I'll turn the tables on you, my lady."

"You always do, you old humbug," Sylvia smiled. "As a matter of fact, I have been a little worried. Nothing crooked, you know, or remotely dishonourable, but just a little disquieting."

"Well?"

"Well, not to beat about the bush, I'm rather afraid for Juliet."

"Juliet?" Surprise was clear in the old man's tone.

"I'm just a little afraid she may be getting fond of him."

Sir Roland frowned. "My dear, I hope you're wrong. That would be a disaster. What reason have you for thinking so?"

"Nothing very tangible, and yet it's suggestive. They're a good deal together. That of course is inevitable when one considers the basis on which Mr Roscoe lives here, and in reason there's no objection. But I've seen them together once or twice when they didn't think they were observed. I wasn't spying on them, you know."

"Weren't you?" Sir Roland grinned. "Glad to know."

"I was sitting in the window of my workroom and they were getting out a boat. There was absolutely nothing that anyone could object to, and yet their every movement shouted out that they were extremely good friends."

"At that distance you might have been mistaken."

"I might, but I don't think I was. Then you can see the way she looks at him and hangs on his words, even at dinner. And you can see also that she suddenly remembers and looks pointedly away."

"Imagination."

"Not altogether. I don't think it's serious, you know Roland, but I think it might easily become so."

There was another silence, again broken by Sir Roland. "This is damnable. I'm being well served after a string of useless apes, and now if you're right I'll have to get rid of

Roscoe. It's the last thing I want to do, but I couldn't let Juliet make a mistake of that sort."

"He probably means nothing. Could you not give him a hint?"

"I could," Sir Roland said grimly, "and I will."

The second conversation might have sounded even more ominous to Juliet, had she been present. It was in progress in Mr Boone's room, and Arthur Boone and Maggie Green were the speakers.

"I'm not so sure," Boone was saying, and his face wore an anxious frown. "I don't *think* he's tumbled to anything, but he's too darned efficient for my taste."

"Could he find anything if he did look?"

"I'm not so sure," the attendant repeated. "He might if he made a proper investigation."

"He'd never do that."

"Wouldn't he? If he thought there was anything wrong his long nose would be into it like a bird after a worm. Kudos with the old man, you know."

"There's something in that. Could you not carry on more secretly?"

Boone shrugged. "Easy to say that. Can you suggest how?"

"Not me, I can't. Not my job."

"Well not me, I can't neither, as you would put it. And it's as much your job as mine. You're ready enough to take the profits anyhow."

"He's going to make changes here, is Mr Roscoe. There'll be a pretty dust up before we're much older or I'll eat my hat."

"What do you mean?"

"I've seen something. There's more going on here than meets the eye. And when the master finds out there'll be the devil to pay."

"What the hell are you talking about?"

"It was yesterday," Maggie answered importantly. "I generally go into Staines on my half-day, as you know, but yesterday there was nothing I wanted to do, so I thought I'd just walk up the river and have some tea at that little Ivy place. You know it?"

Boone nodded.

"I'd seen Mr Roscoe and Miss Juliet going out in the boat an hour or more before I started, and as I walked I kept an eye on the river. Not that I cared where they went or anything of that sort. Just a sort of mild curiosity."

"Well, well," he put in irritably, "get on with the story, can't you?"

"That's what I'm doing, isn't it? How can you understand if I don't explain?"

"Oh, all right. Have it your own way. Only go ahead."

Maggie glanced at him resentfully, then went on. "I'd got to that place about half a mile on this side of the Ivy where the road runs close to the river and you can see down on it over a wall."

"I know."

"The stream divides there and there's a small island."

"I know that too."

"I saw a boat at the island that looked like ours, and then I looked along the island and I saw them, not very clearly for they were partly hidden by shrubs. They were sitting under a tree and she seemed to be reading to him. I recognised the book."

"Good for you. You read its title a hundred and fifty yards away?"

"Don't be so almighty sharp, Arthur Boone," she advised, "or you'll cut yourself. It was a big fat book and I'd seen it in her room. She finished reading and closed it while I was looking, and I saw it's colour."

"Well?"

"Then they began talking sort of eager: you know, leaning over and making gestures and that. And they opened the book again and turned up some pages and talked about it. Thick as thieves, they were. I haven't seen Miss Juliet so interested in anything since I came to the place."

"Pretty good for a hundred and fifty yards."

"You may sneer, but I know what I saw. I can tell you there's something going on between those two."

"Why shouldn't they go out in the boat if they want to?"

"I don't know anyone that can be thicker than you when you're in a crooked twist," Maggie declared spitefully. "I never said they shouldn't go out in the boat. I said there was something between them. And what's more, I know what it is."

He made an impatient gesture. "Hang it all, Maggie, you're enough to make a saint swear. Why can't you go on and tell the blessed story and be done with it?"

"If you'd listen without interrupting you'd know. When I was doing the rooms this morning I had a look round Miss Juliet's. The red cover wasn't there, so I opened one or two of the drawers. I found it presently."

"Yes? Go on, for heaven's sake."

"It was hidden under her clothes in one of the drawers. I slipped it out and had a look at it. What do you think it was?"

"You're telling the story, Maggie, not me."

"It was a play."

"A play?"

"Yes. Most of it was typed, but there were some loose sheets in the cover in her writing. Looks as if they were doing it together."

Boone moved impatiently. "Very interesting story and all that. But what exactly is it to us?"

"I sometimes think you're half-witted. When two young good-looking people of the opposite sex get together over a thing like that, something's going to happen. Use your wits, man, if you have any."

Boone looked at her quizzically. "It's happened already," he declared.

For a moment Maggie could find no adequate rejoinder. She stared open-mouthed. "How do you know?" she asked at last.

"I may be half-witted," Boone said bitterly, "but at least I have my eyesight. And what's more, I sometimes use it. In that way I see things. Strange, isn't it?"

"You talk like a BBC announcer. What did you see?"

"I saw they were in love with each other, if that's anything to do with it."

"There you are!" Maggie's tone was triumphant. "So you've twigged it at last. You've got him!"

"Look here, Maggie, this isn't Monday Night at Eight or Itma or even Twenty Questions. What bee have you got in your bonnet? Get it out and let's have a look at it."

"Well, don't you see? If the master knew what we know, our bright friend Mr Frank Roscoe wouldn't be long at Jasmine Lodge."

Boone's eyes narrowed. "Maggie, I always said you were the goods. That's right! If Mr Efficiency Roscoe pokes his nose in where it's not wanted, we'll have him on toast.

That's the best news I've heard since he came. I think I'll have a word with the master."

"You'll have to be careful, Arthur. It's a bit risky. It'll take some thinking out."

"Trust me. With any luck our friend's stay won't be long. You're a good girl, Maggie. You deserve all you're going to get."

With this somewhat doubtful benediction the conference came to an end.

It was perhaps a pity that both Sir Roland and Boone postponed their prospective interviews, each hoping that in his own case the unpleasant task would become unnecessary.

The date of Juliet's sudden happiness marked for Dulcie the beginning of a period of growing anxiety and fear.

This was not connected with her work at Harley Street. All there was functioning smoothly. The scheme was bringing in money in larger and larger amounts. In one never-to-be-forgotten week she made £94 10s. 0d., exclusive of her salary. Not once had there been the faintest breath of suspicion.

Her worry was due to something quite different. For several weeks after their separation Frank had remained his old self, not all that was to be desired admittedly, but a good helper and friend. Suddenly this had altered. He now seemed always in a hurry and he was frequently prevented from coming to Town. He had grown cooler and seemed to care less whether they met. He was more touchy and readier to go off the deep end on the slightest word of criticism. His temper indeed was now very hard to put up with. He had also become secretive and she could learn little of what was happening at Jasmine Lodge.

Something had gone wrong. But what? It was nothing in the job itself, because of the time which had passed before the change appeared. Then it had developed suddenly, showing that some definite incident had occurred to cause it. And since the results still obtained, the influence of that incident must have continued.

As has been said before, Dulcie was of a jealous temperament and it was not long before suspicion leaped into her mind. What women were there at Jasmine Lodge? Frank had mentioned only Lady and Miss Chatterton, and his references to neither had been flattering. But Frank was tricky. Dulcie now asked had these references a purpose? She loved Frank, but where women were concerned, she had absolutely no faith in him whatever.

Living a rather lonely life, there was little to divert her thoughts, and her suspicions began to fester in her mind. They grew till they became an obsession. More and more she felt that Frank's loyalty was the one thing that mattered. More and more intolerable became her doubts, till at last she realised that at all costs she must know where she stood. Better to face the worst than to continue in this ghastly uncertainty.

But how to learn the truth was not so obvious. To ask Frank the direct question would be futile. He would certainly prevaricate. Besides, she did not want him to know of her doubts. At best he would be most unpleasant, at worst, he might use them as an excuse for breaking with her altogether.

Then like a physical blow she remembered that he had never actually promised to marry her. It had been tacitly understood, at least by her. Fearfully now his omission took on a new significance. She began asking herself had he ever really intended it.

So worried did she grow that at last the idea of employing a private detective to watch Jasmine Lodge occurred to her. She had money for such things now. But this somehow seemed mean. Also she shrank from revealing her private woes to a stranger. Further, if Frank got to know, it would be the end of everything between them.

At last she thought that without confiding in anyone she might herself be able to find out a good deal. She had never attempted detective work, but if other people could do it, why not she? She had read many detective novels and believed she knew how to set about it. With eagerness she began devising plans.

As a result on the next Saturday afternoon she dyed her beautiful auburn hair a dull brown and with a wash darkened her complexion. She put on a pair of plain glass tortoiseshell spectacles, which she bought at a theatrical supplies shop. Being rather under medium height she usually wore high heels: now she decreased her inches by putting on other shoes. Always dressing with extreme neatness, she selected clothes which made her look shapeless and slovenly. When she had finished she was satisfied that except at very close quarters she was unrecognisable.

She went down to Staines by bus to avoid the railway station, as Frank always travelled by train. He had often described the place and she had no difficulty in finding Jasmine Lodge. Opposite the gate was a copse, and she slipped unseen into this, hid behind some shrubs and waited.

For a long time nothing happened. Then about five a limousine appeared coming out of the gate. It was driven by a uniformed chauffeur and beside him sat a young woman. The car turned towards the town and was quickly out of sight. Ten minutes later it reappeared, this time without the lady. It turned into the drive and vanished.

Another five minutes and Dulcie's heart leaped. Frank was coming along the drive.

She crouched down, waiting. He reached the gate and also turned towards the town. Dulcie waited till he was a hundred yards ahead, then followed, walking with a slouching stoop very different to her usual brisk step and upright carriage. Except for the two of them, the road was deserted.

She had scarcely left her retreat when he reached a bend and disappeared. Fearful that she should lose him, she ran quickly forward and peeped round the corner, keeping herself pressed against the hedge bounding the footpath so as to remain invisible.

It was well for her that she did so. Just as she caught sight of Frank, only some sixty yards ahead, he stopped, glanced quickly in both directions, then with a suggestion of furtiveness, he stepped quickly across the road and disappeared through the hedge. Obviously he had not seen her.

She decided to wait thirty seconds before attempting to follow. At the end of the time she glanced once more round the bend. This time the stretch of road was no longer unoccupied. A woman was walking towards her, and as she approached Dulcie saw that she was the lady of the limousine.

Dulcie remained motionless, her heart pounding with excitement. The woman reached the place where Frank had turned aside, then she also looked both ways and with equal furtiveness crossed the road and vanished.

Without hesitation Dulcie followed. Though seething in a white heat she did not lose her caution. The place was a plantation of small trees, and taking all the cover she could, she stealthily followed the other.

Then in a little clearing where a fallen trunk made a convenient seat she saw Frank, evidently waiting. When the woman appeared he hurried to meet her and they became clasped in each other's arms. Dulcie almost choked with fury, but she crouched unseen and watched through the branches. Presently the two seated themselves on the trunk and began an eager conversation. Then they took out some papers and their heads went down as they looked at them.

This was Dulcie's opportunity. With the utmost care she backed away, keeping herself screened by the shrubs. A few moments later she regained the road.

Scarcely knowing what she was doing, she returned to Staines and took a bus back to London.

On the next two Sundays Frank wrote that he was urgently engaged in extra work for Sir Roland and was terribly sorry that he could not get up to Town. Dulcie was relieved and she wrote him sweetly worded notes saying she could well understand that business calls would occasionally prevent their meeting, and not to worry.

But during that fortnight she had become changed from a somewhat weak and clinging, but otherwise ordinary young woman, to an avenging fury in female form. As she brooded over Frank's treatment of her she could scarcely retain the outward appearance of sanity. Her love for him had turned to a bitter hate. What she wanted was to make him suffer: to pay him out for the misery he was causing her. Nothing seemed so desirable as an adequate revenge.

But how to obtain it was the difficulty. The more she thought over the problem, the more impossible it seemed to grow. Fuel was added to the fire when she realised that once again Frank had been too clever for her.

Her first idea had been to go to Juliet Chatterton and tell her all about Frank. Then arguing from her own experience, she realised that Juliet would not believe her. Next she considered approaching Sir Roland, who would certainly believe her without question.

But what would be the result? A word from Frank and the Burt fraud would come out. No doubt he could not give that word openly or he would be asked how he knew. But trust Frank to get round a difficulty of that kind!

Now with almost insane rage Dulcie saw what she had so far overlooked. Frank had pinned the whole fraud on to her and cleared himself! She now worked it without help. Even that last move of handing her over the stamp had, she believed, been conceived with the same idea. She had thought he was being helpful. Now she knew. If the thing came out there would be nothing against him but her accusation, and what would that be worth except to convict herself?

If Dulcie had hated him before, from this point her main object in life was to destroy him. She could not do it openly because of the fraud: after all if she were sent to prison she could not do it at all. She must therefore be circumspect. She must pretend to be friendly. She must contain herself till she found a way in which she could strike.

The more she knew about Juliet Chatterton, the better for her plans. On the next Saturday afternoon she therefore made herself up in her previous disguise and again visited Staines. She had noticed not far from Jasmine Lodge a small teashop, and to this she went early, before it filled up.

When the waitress brought her order she held her in talk. She was, she explained, a stranger to the district and thought it delightful country. And this teashop was just the kind of place she liked, so completely rural and surrounded by this beautiful garden, and yet everything so nice and up to date.

The girl seemed surprised to find a patron who was appreciative rather than critical. She perceptibly thawed, and as for the moment she was disengaged, she stopped as if ready for a chat.

"I like the whole area," went on Dulcie, "except that I've just had a rather horrible experience. I was almost run over a few minutes ago. The nearest thing you can imagine! I was crossing the road when a big car swept in from a crossroad and came straight for me. Just absolutely straight for me and didn't slack up or anything?"

"A shime," said the waitress.

"I should think so," Dulcie agreed. "If I hadn't jumped with all my strength I'd have been down. The nearest thing you ever saw."

"They don't care what they do, these car people," asserted the waitress. "Road 'ogs, that's what they are."

"And that wasn't all," Dulcie went on, warming to her subject. "If you can believe it, she didn't stop. It was a woman driving alone and she never stopped! One would think she might at least have got out and said she was sorry. But not she! Never took the slightest notice of it. Just drove on."

"A shime," repeated the waitress. "You should 'ave told the police."

"I thought of doing it, then I thought they'd ask the number of the car, and I hadn't taken it."

"Just what they would 'ave done. But you couldn't be expected to think of that all on the sudden."

"I should have," Dulcie admitted, "but I didn't. It was a big dark blue car, the sort they call a limousine, I think. Very posh and all that."

The waitress seemed interested. "What was the woman like?" she queried.

"Well," said Dulcie slowly; she had to be careful not to have seen too much in the fraction of a second, "I couldn't distinguish much of her face, but she seemed to be dressed," and she described Juliet's appearance as she had seen her on her previous visit.

The waitress nodded. "That's right," she said. "I can tell you who it was. That was Miss Chatterton, that was. Lives a bit further along the road 'ere. Place they call Jasmine Lodge."

Dulcie nodded casually. "Well, I wish someone would teach her manners, whoever she is. She's a public danger."

"It was a shime right enough. But that wasn't like Miss Chatterton all the same. The cook there's a friend of mine and I've 'eard a lot about the family. She 'as a good word for Miss Juliet."

"Oh well," Dulcie shrugged magnanimously, "we all make mistakes. Perhaps she didn't see me." Then after a pause, "Some money in that house, I imagine from the car?"

"You're telling me. Just rolling, the lot of them. Two maids, cook, personal attendant, chauffeur, gardener, private secretary, two cars, tennis court, two boats and a punt, every blessed thing you can think of."

"Some people have all the luck."

"I'm not so sure of that neither. Sir Roland's a cripple. Rheumatism. Can only 'obble about with two sticks. And he's lost 'is only son. Killed in a motor accident. Money's a lot, but it's not everything."

"That's true, but it isn't everyone who sees it. Then if the son's dead, what happens to the money? Is there a Mrs Chatterton, or I suppose it would be Lady Chatterton?"

"That's right, Lady Chatterton. His second wife. Very nice lady, my friend says. I don't know what'll 'appen to the money, but there are only the two ladies for it."

Dulcie felt that she need ask no more questions. Here was the link she had suspected. Of course the Chattertons' cook was not their lawyer, but Dulcie did not doubt that her information was correct. That Juliet Chatterton would come into money seemed a necessary antecedent of Frank's interest in her.

Just then some other customers came in and the waitress drifted off. Dulcie was not sorry, for she had plenty to occupy her mind. How could she put a spoke in Frank's wheel without getting herself arrested for the fraud?

She pondered over the problem all the way back to town, but when she reached her flat she had not solved it.

– 7 –

TRAGEDY

The passage of some weeks brought the date to the 19th of August. Sylvia Chatterton sat at the writing table in the small private sitting-room which opened off her bedroom. She had been checking the household accounts, but now she laid down her pen and sat back, gazing vacantly through the window in front of her.

The room faced south like her husband's study, but the view was even more attractive owing to its being from the first floor. On this day the country was looking its best. A bright warm sun put a vivid yet mellow light into the atmosphere. The garden, lying immediately below, suggested an archipelago of brilliantly-coloured islands in a sea of emerald green. At its foot the river formed a broad band across the landscape, clear as a mirror and reflecting here the blue of the sky and there the greens and browns of trees. Beyond it the ground sloped gently up to a low range of well-wooded hills.

From the tennis court came the thuds of hard strokes and the cheery voices of the players, but Sylvia could only get glimpses of the white figures through the branches of the three great beeches. Deryk Firmore was back on short leave and he and Juliet were playing Tom and Marjory Allgood, neighbours who lived just across the river. More to the right, in the angle between the two rivers, was the clump of bushes representing Sir Roland's sun trap. A gap in the shrubs in the nearest side formed the entrance, but the path leading in twisted in the depth of the bushes, and Lady Chatterton could not see through. Some distance from the opening ran a herbaceous border, and stooping over it was Weekes, the gardener.

It was a prospect calculated to please, and yet Lady Chatterton's face wore an anxious look. The fact was that she was worried about her husband. For some weeks he had been ailing both mentally and physically. During these weeks he had grown increasingly depressed, a new symptom in a hitherto courageous and well-balanced man. Worse still, he had lost interest in his book and this, Lady Chatterton believed, was the one thing that was keeping him alive. She had wanted to call in the doctor, but he had positively refused. In such matters he was irritating and irrational. She thought he must have something on his mind and wished he would confide in her, but her tentative efforts to offer sympathy had met with little response.

As she stared absently out of the window, she saw Sir Roland. He was walking painfully towards the sun trap, a stick in one hand and leaning with the other on the arm of Boone, who carried a second stick. It cut her to the heart to see how frail and bent he looked, and she wondered un-happily whether this was a mere passing indisposition or the beginning of the inevitable end. She would have given anything to help him, but experience had taught her that there was nothing that she could do.

Presently she noticed Boone returning to the house. He had, she felt sure, settled Sir Roland in his chair under the oak, where he would sit in the sun perhaps till six o'clock. It was now, she saw, a little after eleven. Boone doubtless was going to get him his soup, and as a matter of fact a little later she saw him carrying it out.

With a sigh she busied herself in her work, then happening to glance up, she saw Boone walking smartly down again towards the sun trap. Evidently he had brought back the empty soup bowl to the house and wanted to see her husband about something else.

As he reached the sun trap, Frank emerged from its entrance. He was too far away to see his face clearly, but something in his movements told her he was upset. He started towards the house, then as Boone spoke to him, he stopped.

The two men held a short conversation, then both came on to the house. Wondering vaguely what they were discussing, she again bent over her books.

She was interrupted by a knock at the door. Frank entered. He was looking startled.

"Excuse me for interrupting you, Lady Chatterton, but Mr Boone and I are not very happy about Sir Roland. I went out to him to the sun trap just now with a question about his book. But he wouldn't listen. He looked very strange: I could scarcely describe it, unhappy and excited, almost a little wild."

Sylvia had a dreadful premonition of evil. She put down her pen and leant back as if to wait for a coming blow.

"I didn't like his appearance at all," Frank continued, "and I was coming to tell you about it when I met Mr Boone. He had noticed the same thing and was actually on his way to report to you when he saw me going into the sun trap. He therefore followed me down to see what I thought. We decided you should know."

Sylvia rose. "Thank you. I'll go out at once. Come with me, please, both of you. If he's ill I may need help."

They went downstairs and out into the garden. It was full of the sounds and scents of summer, somnolent, comfortable, reassuring. Then suddenly its peace was broken. There was a sharp report. The sound of a shot. It came from the sun trap.

The three stopped and exchanged dismayed glances. After a moment of rigid listening, they hurried forward. As they reached the entrance Deryk Firmore and Tom Allgood ran up, followed by Juliet. Weekes straightened up from the flower bed and hastily joined the party.

"Don't come in, Cousin Sylvia," cried Firmore. "Let us look first." He disappeared into the enclosure, followed by Allgood, Frank and Boone.

Sylvia felt she could not remain outside. She went after the others. At once she was brought up sharply by what she saw.

Sir Roland lay back in his chair, a huddled shapeless mass. Near his right temple was a small bullet wound, from which a thin stream of blood had run down. Unmistakably he was dead.

With clasped hands, Sylvia stood as if gripped in a vice. So this was the end, the end of her husband, the end of the happy years of her married life! Little loss to him, for he was old and ailing and to himself his life must have been a burden. But for her a bitter sorrow. She had loved the old man dearly, and to look after him and to help him had been her work and her joy. Now that was over.

She stepped forward. The men were talking in low tones, with the girls behind them, for Marjory Allgood had now followed the others. "We mustn't touch anything," Firmore was saying. He turned back. "I'm terribly afraid, Cousin Sylvia, that we'll have to tell the police. You see," and he pointed to the ground at the side of Sir Roland's chair.

The old man's right arm hung down and on the grass just below it lay a small chased pistol, obviously having fallen from the nerveless hand.

So that was it. Suicide! A sharp pang pierced Lady Chatterton's heart. Oh, if only she had known! If she'd realized, she might have helped him. Her sympathy might have prevented the tragedy.

Once again Firmore's voice came to her as from a great distance. "I wish you'd ring them up, Roscoe," he was saying, "first Dr Maunsel and then the police."

"You should go in, Lady Chatterton," Allgood said solicitously as Frank disappeared, "and you girls. You can't do anything here. Take them in, Deryk. Boone and I will watch till the doctor comes."

Sylvia saw that he was right. She could not help, and to remain would be uselessly trying for herself and embarrassing to the men. With another long look at the motionless figure she slowly turned and moved towards the house.

"Come, Juliet and Marjory," she said. "We can do nothing and presently we'd be in the way. Leave the men to arrange everything. Don't trouble to come, Deryk. We'll be all right."

She had realised that at her husband's age and in his state of health she might lose him at any time, and had often considered what life without him would mean for her. Yet now she felt stunned. Perhaps it was the suddenness, perhaps the knowledge that he had died by his own hand, but what had happened had struck her like a physical blow.

Time began passing on leaden wings as first the doctor and then the police arrived and went into the sun trap. The three women sat together, the girls talking in low tones, Sylvia for the most part remaining silent. At length after an eternity Dr Maunsel came in. He looked distressed and made a sign to the two girls, who slipped silently away.

"Dear Lady Chatterton," he began, and his voice sounded strangely troubled, "I can't begin to say how sorry I am about this. But there is just one thing that may be a comfort to you. It was instantaneous. There was no suffering."

Dr Maunsel was an old family friend and Sylvia liked and respected him. She believed implicitly both in his straightforward character and professional skill. She knew he would be kind and sympathetic, but she was not prepared for the depth of feeling he showed. Her heart warmed to him.

"Thank you," she said in a low voice, "it's good of you. I just can't realise it. It was so – so unlike him. But he was ill. You know he was ill?"

"He certainly was not normal," Maunsel returned unhappily. "No one is who takes that way out."

"I knew he wasn't well," she went on, "but I had absolutely no idea he was as bad as that. Oh, *poor* Roland! How he must have suffered!"

Maunsel, besides being a loyal friend and a good doctor, was an accomplished man of the world. There were few delicate situations with which he could not have dealt tactfully. Yet now he seemed at a loss. He moved nervously, cleared his throat, and gave other indications of doubt and discomfort. In spite of her preoccupation Sylvia could not help noticing it.

"What is it?" she asked sharply. "Is there something more that I don't know?"

Little beads of perspiration showed on the doctor's forehead. With a quick movement he wiped them off.

"My dear," he answered in deeply sympathetic tones, "I'm afraid there is. You must be brave, Lady Chatterton, for this will be a shock to you. I shouldn't tell you, but I fear it will come out at the inquest and you ought to know it before that."

Her face slowly paled and she gripped the arm of her chair till her knuckles showed white. "Tell me," she muttered.

"There was a paper in his pocket, a letter dated for yesterday." He paused in evident distress. "It said – I just don't know how to tell you what it said."

"Go on," she whispered.

Again he wiped his brow. "It said – that the writer – had been in prison. It declared that he had been sent there by Sir Roland."

"Well, what if he had?" she returned sharply. "When Sir Roland was Governor on the West Coast such a thing must often have happened."

"It was not in his capacity as Governor. The letter said that it was due to evidence Sir Roland had given."

"Suppose it was," she said more sharply still. "I don't see what you're getting at, Dr Maunsel."

"There's still more to be told. It said – of course I needn't assure you I don't believe it – but it said that Sir Roland's evidence was false, and that it was given to save himself."

She stared. "To save himself?" she repeated blankly. "I don't understand. What do you mean?"

"I can only repeat what the letter said. It suggested that Sir Roland was guilty of some crime and had given false evidence to put the blame on the writer. He – "

Anger flashed from Sylvia's eyes. "How can you bring yourself, Dr Maunsel, to repeat such an odious lie? Why, it's absurd! Surely you knew enough of my husband to know that it couldn't be true?"

"I told you I didn't believe it," he answered miserably. "But it's not what we believe. The trouble is that the coroner is likely to take the matter seriously. That isn't quite all. I'm afraid you must hear the rest."

She looked her question with a heart-rending suggestion of bracing herself to meet a blow.

"The writer said he didn't want Sir Roland's life, but he did want – his disgrace and imprisonment and – "

"Oh!" she covered her eyes with her hands. "Infamous! Who wrote it?"

"We don't know. It was signed Sandy Archer, but bore no address. The writer said he now had proofs to put before the authorities."

"Oh," Sylvia moaned again. "It couldn't be! No one who knew my husband could believe it! It's a malicious lie! Or – or a mistake."

"Of course we who knew him realise that, but we'll have to prove it. Dear Lady Chatterton, you do understand that I had to tell you because the coroner will certainly read the letter, and you had to be prepared for it."

"Oh, Doctor, what does it mean? Was it attempted blackmail?"

"I imagine so. If we can find the writer we shall soon learn. In fact," the doctor suddenly grew more confident, "something has just occurred to me, and I rather think we have him on toast. If he doesn't come forward it will be an admission that the accusation is false. If he does, it will be to meet a charge of blackmail. Yes, I think we'll deal with him all right. Now another matter," he went on quickly as if thankful to be rid of the subject. "I believe I know your wishes, but I must be sure: you would like the funeral from here?"

"Why of course. Where else?"

"The remains might lie in the mortuary and the funeral could be from the church."

"No, no, I'd rather have it from here."

"I was sure of it. Then that will be arranged."

"Deryk is staying in the house: he'll see to things."

"Dear lady, we'll all be glad to help. As far as that's concerned, don't give anything a thought. All will be done as you would like." He looked at her penetratingly. "How brave you are! But you mustn't try yourself too highly, for that will bring a reaction. I'll send you a dose which will give you an untroubled night."

A few more words of kindly sympathy and Sylvia Chatterton was alone. She locked the door and sat down once again at her desk, gazing sightlessly before her as she deliberately nerved herself to meet the ordeal which was coming.

Was this ghastly letter true? Often she had had hints that in his younger days her husband had been far from the almost saint he had latterly become. Was it possible that he had committed some crime for which he had incriminated another? Was it possible that he had lived for years knowing that another was suffering in prison for his fault?

No! she thought with a welling sense of relief. It just wasn't possible! Whatever he might have done, Roland could not have lived so foul a lie! He might have been passionate or bad-tempered, but he was never mean or cowardly or dishonourable.

If so, this letter could only be an attempt at blackmail. But since Roland was dead, the writer would not come forward. That fact alone would disprove its contents. The doctor had been right, the letter would not prove so serious after all.

Then a hideous thought struck her. Why had her husband committed suicide? Was it because of the letter? If so, would it not follow that Roland had known that the charge was true?

Why *had* he taken his life? Sylvia racked her brains. Because he was depressed and ill? That was it, of course. For some weeks he had been growing worse, and this was the natural result. He had not appeared to be worrying over any special trouble: it was just that everything had got too much for him. The letter probably was just the last straw.

At this point Sylvia's meditations were interrupted. There was a knock, and she opened the door to find Deryk Firmore waiting.

"Sorry to intrude and all that, Cousin Sylvia," he said, "but there's a matter I think you ought to consider. To be candid, I didn't think of it myself: it was that fellow Roscoe who suggested it. Said it wasn't his business and that he didn't like to butt in, but that he thought he ought to mention it. Got his head screwed on all right, that chap."

"Yes, Deryk. What is it?"

"Well," even Deryk seemed embarrassed, "it's about that letter. Nasty business that. Not that one believes it of course, but it may make trouble."

"What is your suggestion?"

"Really Roscoe's, you know. He thought you ought to be represented at the inquest. I mean, a lawyer to look after your interests, so he put it. It seemed to me sense and I thought I'd mention it."

Sylvia felt shocked. The proposal brought into its true perspective the seriousness of the letter. She had been thinking of it as a vile and hideous insinuation, but now it became an actual menace, something with power to hurt, something against which they would need protection.

As to the idea itself, she could not make up her mind. She did not know enough about such matters. She wondered if Frank did.

"I wish you'd call Mr Roscoe," she said at length. "As it's his idea, I think we might discuss it with him."

Firmore seemed surprised and for the moment she thought he was going to protest. Instead he nodded and disappeared. In a moment he returned with Frank. She pointed to chairs.

"Captain Firmore has told me of your suggestion, Mr Roscoe," she began, "and I am grateful to you for it. But to be quite candid I'm not satisfied that it would be a good thing. I thought we three might talk it over."

"Thank you, Lady Chatterton," said Frank.

"If there's going to be trouble about this letter," she went on, "I quite see that a lawyer would be desirable. What I'm afraid of is that the mere fact that we were represented would look as if we took it seriously. I'm not sure that we shouldn't treat it as completely negligible."

"That's a point certainly," Deryk remarked.

"What do you think, Mr Roscoe?" Sylvia asked, as Frank did not speak.

"I agree with you and Captain Firmore," he answered, "that the point should be considered. Since you ask my opinion I should suggest that you put it to your solicitor. I mean, tell him the facts and let him decide whether or not representation is desirable."

To Sylvia this appeared horse sense. "I'll do it," she declared, "and thank you for the idea. Deryk, will you ring up Mr Cummings and ask him to come round as soon as possible. You can tell him it's about the inquest without going into details."

When Cummings heard of the letter he was obviously perturbed. He strongly advised representation, and it was agreed that he should be present himself.

For Sylvia Chatterton some dreadful hours followed. The remains were taken to the mortuary, to be brought back later to the house. The grounds and house swarmed with policemen, and Inspector Pardoe of the local constabulary questioned her at length. Nothing could have exceeded his respectful sympathy, but the interview had been trying. Now there was the inquest. That, she foresaw, would be *horrible*. Well, she must just set her teeth and go through with it. Everyone at least was kind. They would not make it worse for her than they could help.

– 8 –

INQUEST

The tragedy had been a profound shock to Juliet Chatterton also. She, too, had loved her father, though perhaps with less intensity than had her stepmother. As a child she had regarded him not only with respect and affection, but also with some awe, and subconsciously the latter feeling had persisted. Now with bitterness she regretted that she had ever contemplated acting against his wishes, should he have failed to see eye to eye with her about Frank.

At first she thought only of her father and with sympathy of the blow his death would be to Sylvia. But she would have been less than human if she had not presently considered the effect it might have on her own fortunes. Here surely was the opening of the way to her marriage. She could not but wish to discuss it with Frank, but he declared it would be unwise for them to meet in private until the household had once more settled down. In this she saw he was right. No time could be less propitious than the present for anything to come out about their love.

Then all these ideas were swept out of her mind as Deryk clumsily blurted out the news of the letter. At first she did not believe him. Such a thing was unthinkable and Deryk should have known better than to repeat it. When in her mind's eye she saw her father sitting in his chair before the fire, she felt that to suspect him of so appalling a crime was merely silly.

Yet there was the letter, and there was the suicide. She *knew* there must be some explanation other than the apparent one, though what it might be she could not imagine.

She was called to the conference with Mr Cummings and was shocked to find how seriously he took the matter. "It's not what we think," he had explained, unconsciously repeating the doctor, "it's what the coroner will do. And without doubt he'll insist on the letter being read. It will then be for us to disprove the statement."

"How do you think we should do that?" Sylvia had asked.

"I'd rather not say till I've considered the affair further," he had replied. "Naturally we should try to trace the writer, and if we fail we might consider any trial in which Sir Roland was concerned. But I don't myself believe that will be necessary. I don't think for a moment the letter will stand."

Deryk had asked what he meant by that, and Mr Cummings had said he was sure it would be discredited without the need of research, perhaps at the inquest. But he had not explained why he thought so.

The hours dragged slowly but relentlessly away without bringing anything further to light. An atmosphere of tragedy hung over Jasmine Lodge like a menacing cloud. Everyone spoke in hushed tones and kept within the grounds. Frank remained out of sight except in the presence of others. Juliet felt terribly depressed and lonely.

Then came the second morning after the tragedy, bringing with it the inquest. With the same distress and apprehension as her stepmother she nerved herself for the ordeal.

The inquest was held in a hall not far from Jasmine Lodge. Juliet drove there with Sylvia, Marjory Allgood and Deryk, the others walking. The place was well filled, for though the area was semi-country, Sir Roland had been well known and the tragedy had aroused keen interest.

The room was long and narrow and running down it was a table surrounded by chairs. At the head was the coroner's seat, with on his left a place for his clerk. The first chair at the side of the table to his right was reserved, so Juliet learned later, for a witness box, and next to it sat Mr Cummings, tall and elderly, with a high forehead and a shrewd eye. Beside him was Sylvia, and further along the table Juliet, Deryk, Marjory, Tom, Frank and Boone took their places. Seven chairs opposite them remained empty, but at the bottom of the table were Dr Maunsel, Inspector Pardoe and two other police representatives, while a couple of reporters were huddled over card tables further back. Sitting alone in a corner was a girl with a pencil and pad, obviously ready to take notes. Behind all these were members of the general public.

To Juliet the whole thing seemed somehow informal and yet sinister. Mr Cummings was speaking gravely to Sylvia, and Deryk and Tom Allgood were talking across Marjory. Dr Maunsel and Inspector Pardoe were deep in some discussion, while from the rest of the room rose a continual hum of conversation. Juliet was struck by the varying expressions around her. Her family and friends who had suffered the loss and were to give evidence looked drawn and anxious, while those who had come out of curiosity appeared happily expectant. Only the doctor and the police seemed normal, men who as a matter of routine were about to carry out their ordinary commonplace duties.

A few moments before ten the coroner arrived with his clerk. Cummings introduced him to Sylvia as Mr Lawson, and Juliet could hear him saying how sorry he was for the cause which had brought them together. Juliet thought his face honest and trustworthy, but his expression suggested that he was not one who would encourage liberties.

He bowed to the company and sat down, and while he was unpacking his briefcase Inspector Pardoe approached and they had a whispered conversation. Then he looked up.

"I have decided to sit with a jury," he announced, and busied himself with a legal-looking document.

Names were called and then seven people, five men and two women, advanced and took the seven vacant chairs. Juliet felt as if she were divided into two persons. Half of her, the essential half, seemed numb, as if she had got past caring what happened. The other half of her mind she could not control. It wandered off into irrelevant speculations. While the numb part waited listlessly for the actual proceedings to begin, the other part watched the assembling of the jurors and speculated as to their personalities. How ordinary they looked and yet how representative! Or was that the same thing? Three of the men were slow, heavy and unemotional, no doubt possessing shrewdness and common sense, but apparently without the slightest approach to intellectuality or imagination. Another was small, agile and had a fussy manner. A busybody who would poke his nose into his neighbours' affairs and find deep-laid plots in the most trivial actions? If so, a dangerous man to have on a jury! The fifth was again different. He was tall and thin with a satirical expression, a man doubtless who would discuss "isms" and strive for dialectic advantage rather than the elucidation of truth. The two women presented an interesting contrast. One was thin, spiky and sour looking. She would see everything through jaundiced eyes and put the worst construction on all actions. The other was placid and comfortable looking with a pleasant expression and a kindly smile: one who would listen to the witnesses with sympathy and understanding and give the benefit of the doubt every time. Interesting to put them all in a play and watch their mutual reactions! As jurors, it was not unlikely that the sum total of their views should approximate to the truth.

But Juliet told herself that this was no time for daydreaming. The proceedings were getting underway. When the jurors had been sworn, the coroner addressed the gathering. He briefly stated for what purpose they were assembled and expressed a formal but not unkindly sympathy with the relatives of the deceased. He then asked the jury if they wished to inspect the remains. A whispered colloquy ensued, then the foreman said they would like to do so and they all trooped out.

When they returned the first witness was called, Captain Deryk Firmore. Juliet wondered how he would comport himself under the ordeal. She expected him to be a little short with the coroner, for she knew he hated to be asked questions. But she soon saw that she had wronged him. He answered everything quietly and politely and seemed as much at ease as if he was chatting over his wine after dinner. Seldom had she admired him more.

He deposed that he was a relative of the deceased and gave details of his life. He was at present staying at Jasmine Lodge and had done so on many occasions in the past. He had known the deceased intimately and identified the remains. They were those of his second cousin, Sir Roland

Chatterton. He then described the layout of the grounds and sun trap.

"You were the first to make the discovery of Sir Roland's death?" went on the coroner.

"I did go first into the sun trap," Deryk returned, "but we were all together, practically everyone who is here," and he indicated the right side of the table.

"Let us have it in detail. What were you doing at the time?"

Deryk told of the tennis, continuing: "I was at the end nearest the sun trap. We had stopped playing for a moment to enable Miss Allgood to adjust her shoe. Just then I heard a shot. It wasn't very loud and seemed to come from the sun trap. I noticed Tom Allgood drop his racquet and begin running towards the sun trap. I did the same, and being nearer, got there first. I went in and saw Sir Roland."

"You were followed in?"

"Yes. When I looked up there was a crowd behind me. Lady Chatterton, Miss Chatterton, Tom Allgood, Frank Roscoe, the attendant, Boone, and the gardener, Weekes. Miss Allgood came in two or three minutes later."

"What did you do?"

"I saw Sir Roland was dead and I asked Mr Roscoe to ring up the doctor and police. Then we got the ladies away. Mr Allgood and Mr Boone and I waited there for Dr Maunsel and the police."

"Was anything touched before the police came?"

"No, I saw to that. Even Dr Maunsel contented himself with a mere inspection."

"Thank you, Captain Firmore."

When Deryk had testified that he saw no one leave the sun trap and that no one was there when he entered, Lawson intimated that he had finished.

"Would any member of the jury like to ask the witness a question?" he inquired, looking at his seven supporters.

All shook their heads and he thanked Deryk again and told him he might stand down. As the young man resumed his place beside her Juliet murmured a word of congratulation on his bearing, which, she told him, had encouraged her to meet her own ordeal. Then her attention was recalled to the proceedings.

Dr Maunsel had moved to the witness chair and was giving details of his life and medical qualifications. Once again Juliet was struck by his kindly dependable manner. She felt instinctively that he was trustworthy and a person to whom one would be glad to go in time of trouble. Now his quiet, matter-of-fact bearing seemed to rob the tragedy of much of its horror, and make it something which could be dealt with normally and by ordinary means. Lawson was particularly polite to him.

"On Tuesday last you were called in to Jasmine Lodge?" he began.

"Yes, I was paying a call and I was rung up from home. I broke off my visit and hurried to Jasmine Lodge. There Mr Roscoe met me and took me to the sun trap."

"Please tell the jury in your own words what you did."

"I found the deceased lying back in a chaise longue under a large oak tree. There was a bullet wound about an inch below his right temple, which had bled slightly. I saw at once that he was dead and therefore did not move him till the police arrived."

"After that what did you do?"

"When the body was moved I extracted the bullet, which had penetrated slightly upwards and backwards and had lodged in the brain. I handed the bullet to Inspector Pardoe."

"Did you do anything else?"

"I made a general external examination to satisfy myself that there was no other injury. There was none. I was not asked to make a post-mortem and therefore did not do so."

"Quite. Can you tell the court how long death had taken place before you saw the deceased?"

"A very short time. A matter of minutes, I should think, but I could not give an accurate figure."

"Might it have occurred when the shot was heard?"

"Certainly. I should think just about then."

"Do you consider the wound could have been self-inflicted?"

"Unquestionably, though of course I can't say definitely that it was."

"Were you the deceased's ordinary medical attendant?"

"Yes, I visited him for several years."

"In what state of health was he?"

"Rather frail. He was seriously crippled by rheumatoid arthritis and could move about only with aid of sticks. Otherwise he was in normal health for a man of his years."

"It has been deposed and will be given in evidence that latterly he had been very depressed. Can you tell the court anything about that?"

The doctor shook his head. "I was not called in to see him about that, and therefore know nothing of it at first hand."

Lawson glanced over his notes. "Thank you, Dr Maunsel, that's all I want." He looked at the jury and repeated his invitation to them to ask questions. No one taking advantage of this, Maunsel returned to his place.

Inspector Pardoe was the next witness. He stepped briskly forward and went through the preliminaries with quiet assurance.

"I am taking the police statement rather earlier than is customary in these inquiries, Inspector," Lawson told him, "because I understand you will give evidence about which I may want to question the others. Now will you please tell the court what you know of this sad affair?"

Pardoe was comparatively young and was very much the policeman on duty. He had a long sallow face with a strong jaw and a particularly sharp eye. To Juliet he seemed competent and very wide awake. He made a sort of little ducking bow to Lawson and began in an official voice, untempered with apparent feeling or interest.

"A telephone call from Jasmine Lodge was received at the police station at eleven fifty-three on Tuesday last, reporting Sir Roland's death and asking for assistance. I proceeded there at once and on arrival was shown by Mr Roscoe to an enclosure in the garden which I was informed is called the sun trap. There I found Dr Maunsel, Captain Deryk Firmore, Mr Tom Allgood and Mr Boone. Dr Maunsel was examining the remains of a man whom I recognised as Sir Roland Chatterton."

"Yes, Inspector?"

"The doctor informed me that Sir Roland was dead and I saw the bullet wound he has described. Two of the other gentlemen stated that they had been playing tennis and had heard a shot and hurried over. I then made an examination of the place. Beside the chair in which the deceased was lying was a table with books and papers, and leaning up against it were two sticks. The chair faced the river and was protected from direct sunlight by the branches of the tree. The deceased's right arm was hanging down, and on the grass below the open hand was a small ornamental pistol, which from the smell of powder I believed had been recently discharged. It bore Sir Roland's fingerprints and his only. I have since found that it was one of a pair belonging to himself which were kept in the safe in his study. The case and the other pistol were in the desk. The shot had been fired from close to the head, for there was powder blackening on the skin."

"Continue, please."

"I could find no other traces which seemed to me material, with one exception. Crumpled in the left side pocket of the deceased's jacket was a letter signed Sandy Archer. It bore no address, but was dated for the previous day. It was typed on a single sheet from a cheap block. This, sir, is it."

Inspector Pardoe handed a paper to the coroner. As the latter read it his face lengthened. "This is an unexpected and distressing letter," he said with obvious concern, "but I'm afraid it's my duty to read it," and this he proceeded to do.

18th August.

You thought you had done cleverly when by your lying evidence you let me rot in jail for the best years of my life for your crime. Since I came out I have done nothing but search for proof to convict you. I have got it now, and I have come back to this country to settle our account. Do not be afraid for your miserable life. I want you to live to have your turn of prison and disgrace.

SANDY ARCHER.

Though Juliet was prepared for something horrible, the wording of the letter struck her like a physical blow. Incredible! Her upright honourable father! She could not have believed such a letter possible.

Absorbed in her thoughts as she was, she could not fail to notice the sudden change which had come over the assembly. The proceedings had been decorous, businesslike and unemotional, indeed, rather inhuman considering that sudden death was under review. Now a breath of life had stirred the dry bones. People sat with staring eyes and bated breath. A very ordinary tragedy unexpectedly promised thrilling revelations.

Lawson resumed his interrogation. "Have you discovered any incident in the deceased's life to which this letter could refer?"

"No, sir," Pardoe answered, "but of course we have not yet had time to go thoroughly into the matter."

"Have you identified the writer?"

"No, sir."

"Have you been able to trace how the deceased received the letter?"

"I have made inquiries about that. The deceased's attendant informed me that four letters came by that morning's post. I found three in the wastepaper basket in the deceased's bedroom. I presume that this was the fourth."

"What led you to make that presumption?"

"The dates, sir. All four letters were dated for the previous day."

"What about envelopes? Did you find them?"

"Yes, sir. Three were in the wastepaper basket with the letters. The fourth was lying on the table beside the deceased's chair. The postmarks on all four were also dated for the previous day."

"And you therefore assumed they came by the morning delivery. Well, that seems reasonable. Would the letter found in the deceased's pocket have fitted the envelope lying on the table?"

"Yes, sir."

"I presume there was nothing in any way remarkable about that fourth envelope?"

"Well, there was, sir. I was just going to tell you. On the back of it at the top left-hand corner were the two capital letters SA They were in ink, small and faint and by no means obvious."

"SA? The writer's initials presumably?"

"I thought so, sir."

"Could they have been clearly seen by anyone who was looking for them?"

"Oh yes, perfectly clearly."

"An interesting point, Inspector. Very well. Now you heard Dr Maunsel say that while he believed the wound could have been self-inflicted, he could not say definitely that it had been. Do you agree with that?"

"Yes, sir. The powder blackening on the skin and the direction of the bullet showed that the shot had been fired from where the deceased could have held the pistol. But these results would of course have followed if anyone else had fired it."

"Quite. The doctor said he handed you the bullet. Can you say if it was fired from the pistol found on the ground?"

"Yes, sir, it had been."

"And you said the pistol belonged to the deceased and was in his safe. Was the safe kept locked?"

"It was locked when I examined it. I don't know if it was kept so."

"Then anyone who had a key could have got the pistol?"

"Certainly."

"Did you look for traces of any unknown person's presence in the sun trap?"

"I made a careful search. I could find no such trace."

"Are you of opinion that some unknown might have been present at the time of the shot?"

"No, sir. I feel sure that no one was there but the deceased."

"Please tell the jury what led you to that conclusion."

"I can only repeat the evidence I received. It was not my personal observation."

"I note the reservation. Please proceed."

"At the time of the shot the whole land exterior of the sun trap was under observation. The north side containing the entrance was in the view of Lady Chatterton, Mr Roscoe and Mr Boone, who were approaching from the house, and of the gardener, Weekes, who was working at some little distance. The east side was overlooked by the four tennis players, one of whom, Miss Allgood, remained for a couple of minutes after the others to put on her shoe, of which the lace had just broken. It is impossible therefore that anyone could have left from either of these sides. The other two sides were bounded by water, the Thames on the south and the Merrow on the west."

"I follow. We shall get that evidence from the witnesses later. Now tell me. Could anyone have committed the crime and then hidden, either in the bushes or along the shore, until the spectators had entered the sun trap, and then slipped away?"

"I believe that to be quite impossible. No one could have hidden in the bushes without leaving traces, and there were none. There was no hiding place along the riverbanks, which slope gradually down to the water. Further, all the witnesses state that no boat was near."

"That sounds conclusive, Inspector." The coroner consulted his notes, intimated that he had finished, and put his customary question. The fussy juror put up his hand.

"Yes, sir?"

"I should like to ask, Mr Coroner, in view of your last questions, whether the Inspector thinks it possible that anyone other than the deceased could have fired the shot?"

"I think the witness has already answered that, but as you have asked the question, I pass it on. What do you say, Inspector?"

"I think only the deceased could have fired, sir."

The fussy juror intimated that he was satisfied and Lawson called, "Lady Chatterton."

Juliet felt more sympathy for her stepmother than ever before. The questions she would be asked in such publicity would be trying enough under any circumstances, but this ghastly business of the letter would make them an absolute nightmare. How dreadful the letter was she had scarcely yet herself realised: her attention had been too much taken up with what was happening. Even now she had little time to think of it as her eyes followed Pardoe to his seat.

Sylvia moved to the witness chair with evident unwillingness and her strained expression and compressed lips showed that she was striving hard for composure. The coroner was gentle with her.

"I'm sorry, Lady Chatterton, to have to call you, but I'm afraid I've no option. I can only assure you I will be as quick as possible."

"Thank you," she answered.

Formal questions followed in which she gave her maiden name, said that she was Sir Roland's second wife, and that she had married him thirteen years earlier. During the last ten of these they had lived at Jasmine Lodge.

"Now you have heard Dr Maunsel telling of the deceased's rheumatoid arthritis and general health," went on Lawson, "so I don't wish to go over that again, but apart from that was there any recent change of health?"

"Yes," she answered in a hard dead voice. "For some time he had been specially poorly and depressed."

"That's what I want. When did this depression set in?"

"It began very gradually and slowly got worse. I could not give an exact date."

"A rough estimate, please?"

"I should say it began six or eight weeks ago."

Lawson nodded. "What form did the depression take?"

"My husband was always cheerful in spite of his rheumatism. He lost that cheerfulness and became gloomy. He had been mentally alert and fully alive to all that was going on, but he no longer wished to hear the news. His great interest had been a book he was writing. Even this failed to rouse him from a sort of despondent reverie."

"Did you think he had something on his mind?"

"No, I thought he was physically less well and that it reacted on his spirits."

"But you did not obtain medical advice?"

"No. I should have liked to and suggested it, but he was very much opposed to it. I felt that to insist would worry him unnecessarily."

"I follow. Now here is a rather difficult question. Do you think that this depression and what you have called a despondent reverie might have been caused by the receipt of unpleasant tidings, such as an earlier letter on the subject of that which was read?"

Sylvia thought this over before replying. "I had not considered the point," she said at last, "but speaking on the spur of the moment, I should think not. If such a letter had been received, I should have expected a sudden marked change. That did not take place. The depression began too gradually to fix any actual point of commencement."

"Thank you, that's very clear. Now here, I'm afraid, is a painful question. Can you think of any circumstances to which the letter could refer?"

Sylvia's deep resentment came out in her manner. "Absolutely none! I can't believe that there were such circumstances. Whatever faults my husband had, cowardice was not one. Nor was falsehood."

Lawson bowed as if he accepted this. "The deceased was a Government official in a West African colony, was he not?"

"Yes, he held various offices and was Governor for five years."

"Quite; his distinguished career is well known. Now coming to last Tuesday. Did you see the deceased on that day?"

"Oh yes." Her voice again became dead. "When I heard he was not getting up for breakfast I went into his room and talked to him in bed. Then again after breakfast I went in and sat with him for ten or fifteen minutes."

"Were those the last occasions on which you saw him alive?"

"The last on which I spoke to him. Later about a quarter past eleven I saw from my window Boone helping him to the sun trap."

"When you saw the deceased after breakfast had the letters come?"

"Oh yes, they generally came before breakfast."

"Do you know if the deceased had read his when you saw him?"

"I don't actually know, but normally he would have done so."

"Did you notice any additional depression or mental upset, such as might have been expected from the receipt of the letter I have just read?"

"No, nothing of the kind. He was depressed, but not more so than during the previous week."

"Thank you, Lady Chatterton. You said you saw the deceased going to the sun trap. Did you notice anyone else going there or coming away?"

Sylvia described the movements of Frank and Boone, their subsequent report to her and her decision to visit the sun trap. She told of hearing the shot while on the way and what she had seen on entering the sun trap.

This concluded Lawson's examination. No one else wished to ask any questions, and with obvious relief, which was shared by Juliet, the witness returned to her place.

– 9 –

VERDICT

At intervals Juliet had watched the girl who was taking notes in the corner. She wondered who she was. She had asked Deryk his opinion, but he had dismissed the subject with a careless glance and the words, "Press, I expect." Juliet did not think the girl was connected with the press. She believed there was a strong freemasonry among reporters and the two men at the card tables obviously belonged to the fraternity. But the girl had not spoken to them. Moreover, she wrote a great deal more than the questions and answers, which were all the others noted. Juliet would have liked to talk to her, but of course this was impossible.

The next witness was Arthur Boone, Sir Roland's attendant. He deposed that he was forty-six years of age and held certain nursing qualifications, which he detailed. He had spent several years as a nurse in a mental institute, but disliking the work, he had tried for private employment and been engaged by Sir Roland. He had been with him for nine years. Sir Roland had on more than one occasion indicated that he had given satisfaction.

"What did your duties consist of?" went on the coroner.

"I had to do almost everything for the deceased," Boone replied, "dress him, cut up his food, help him about, get

143

him what he wanted. He was unable to do much for himself."

"Had you noticed this depression which has been mentioned?"

Boone had noticed it and described it very much as had Sylvia. He was unable to account for it, but for the same reasons as she, considered it was due to ill health rather than to the receipt of unpleasant news.

"On Tuesday last the deceased did not get up at his usual time?"

"No, sir, he was not feeling very well. He normally got up for breakfast, but not always. He would perhaps stay in bed for one or two days in the week."

"What time did he rise on this day?"

"About half past ten."

"I should like to get a picture of how the deceased spent his morning. Please tell the jury in your own words what happened up till half past ten."

"At eight I took Sir Roland a cup of tea and drew back the curtains in his room. As usual, he was awake when I went in. Then he said he felt tired and would not rise for breakfast. At nine-thirty I took him his breakfast and letters. I was in and out of the room on various occasions until he got up, but I don't think he spoke to me. He was lying still, awake, not reading."

"Tell me about the letters. Where did you find them?"

"I took them from the box on the hall door. When I was going up with the breakfast I put the tray down on the hall table for a moment while I went for the letters. I looked through them and put Sir Roland's on his tray. I left the others on the hall table where the rest of the family could get them."

"How many had the deceased?"

"Four, sir."

"Did you see the envelopes of the three found in the bedroom wastepaper basket?"

"Inspector Pardoe showed them to me, sir."

"Could you identify them as having come that morning?"

"One of them certainly, it was a deep blue with large handwriting. The other two were not in any way remarkable."

"Can you tell the jury what the fourth envelope was like?"

"All three other than the blue one were of business shape and with typewritten addresses."

"Did you notice the letters SA on the back of one of them?"

"No, sir, but I didn't look at their backs."

Lawson nodded. "Now you helped the deceased to dress?"

"Yes, sir."

"It's common knowledge that the deceased was always well dressed. Was he, in your opinion, particular about his clothes?"

"That's correct, sir, he was most particular. He would consider carefully what suit to wear and what socks and tie should go with it. The trousers had always to be perfectly creased, and he would never allow any bulky or heavy object in any pocket, in case it dragged the cloth."

"And on last Tuesday morning? Did he make any remark?"

"No, sir, except that he would wear his light grey. But there was nothing for him to remark about. If all had not been in order I should pretty soon have heard of it."

"Very well, when he was dressed, what happened?"

"He went out to the sun trap. I gave him an arm and carried his books and his second stick and settled him with his rug in his lounge chair."

"Now have I got that right? He got up about half past ten, dressed, and went straight out. About what time did he reach the sun trap?"

"I should say about a quarter past eleven."

"And then?"

"Then I came in and heated his soup and took it out to him."

"How long was it between the time you left him and when you returned with the soup?"

"About fifteen minutes."

"Bringing it to about half past eleven. Now when you returned did you notice any difference in his appearance?"

"Yes, sir. He was lying back in his chair staring up into the air as if he was lost in thought. He was very pale and looked ill and haggard. His expression frightened me. It's hard to describe, but it was strained, almost desperate, if you understand me."

"Do you mean that he looked as if he was facing some calamity?"

"That describes it exactly, sir."

"Yes?"

"His hand was lying on his knees and it held a paper. It looked like a letter. When he saw me he pushed it into his pocket, as if to hide it."

"Which pocket?"

"The left outside pocket of his jacket."

"Was the envelope lying on the table when you took out the soup?"

"Yes, sir, I saw it when I put the soup down."

"What happened next?"

"I asked him if he was not feeling well. He looked at me dully and did not answer. Then I said the soup would do him good. He said, 'Put it on the table. I'll take it presently.' I was beginning to say that it would get cold quickly when he said sharply. 'Leave it there. That's all I want now.' "

"What did you do?"

"When Sir Roland gave me a direction like that he expected it to be carried out. I left the soup and went back towards the house. I decided I ought to report to Lady Chatterton."

"How long were you in the sun trap?"

Boone considered. "A very short time, sir: I wouldn't be sure how long. Four or five minutes, I should say."

"You said you went back towards the house. Did you not actually reach it?"

"No, sir, not then. When I was on my way to the back I saw Mr Roscoe leave the front door at the other end of the house, and go towards the sun trap. I waited to see if he was going in, and when I saw he was I went back so as to compare notes about Sir Roland. Just as I reached the entrance he came out."

"Yes?"

"He also thought there was something wrong and that we should tell Lady Chatterton. We decided to do so together and went back to the house."

Lawson leant back in his chair. "Now, Mr Boone, here's a more difficult question. From your training and the nature of your work you're probably as good a judge of this as anyone. Did the deceased at any time make any remark or show any sign that might have suggested that he was contemplating suicide?"

Boone shook his head with decision. "Absolutely nothing of the kind, sir."

Lawson busied himself for some moments with his notes. Then he leant back. "Any questions?" He looked round. "Then that will do in the meantime, Mr Boone. But please don't go away, in case we want your evidence on some other point."

He had not said this to any of the other witnesses, and Juliet wondered what it could signify. However she had no time to ponder it, for he went on: "Call Frank Roscoe!"

At this Juliet's heart leaped as if hers had been the name mentioned. She felt intensely for Frank as he walked to the witness chair. Yet, she told herself, she need not be nervous. He would not be. He would give his evidence as he did everything else: supremely well.

As with the previous witnesses, the interrogation at first was formal and Frank told briefly of his previous life and qualifications, how he had answered Sir Roland's advertisement, and about the work he did in connection with the deceased's correspondence and book.

"Coming then to last Tuesday," went on the coroner, "will you tell the jury what you did up till the occurrence of the tragedy?"

"After breakfast I met Mr Boone, who told me that Sir Roland was not getting up. I therefore went to his room to see if he had any special instructions for me. He had none, but told me to carry on with some research I was engaged on. I did so."

"What was the nature of the research?"

"It was checking the relationships between persons he had mentioned in the book. I had a *Debrett* and a *Who's Who* and other reference books."

"I follow. Please continue."

"During the morning a point arose upon which I wanted Sir Roland's opinion. He had referred to Sir Herbert

Whitaker and I believed it should have been Sir Charles. I could not get on till I knew, so I went to his room to ask him. He wasn't there, so I felt sure he was either in the study or had gone out."

"What time was that?"

"About half past eleven, I should say."

"Yes?"

"I looked into the study, but he wasn't there, so I went to the sun trap. He was sitting under the oak."

"Please describe what you saw in detail."

Frank's story was practically the same as Boone's. He also had asked Sir Roland if he was not feeling well.

"What did the deceased say?"

"He glanced at me as if he hardly knew me and muttered in a sort of testy way, 'Yes, yes, all right.' I then began to put my question, but he cut me short. 'Later on,' he said almost in a whisper. 'Don't worry me now. I'm tired.' "

"What did you do?"

"I didn't know what to do. I felt sure he wasn't well and I didn't like to leave him. But he obviously wanted to be alone. I did wait perhaps for a minute and then he pointedly closed his eyes, so I came away."

"How long were you in the sun trap?"

"Oh, just a few moments: not more than one or two minutes."

Frank then described his meeting with Boone, their discussion, their report to Sylvia, their hearing the shot and what followed, confirming the previous witnesses on all points.

Lawson turned over his notes. "Now tell me about the book the deceased was writing. What was its subject?"

"It was an autobiography. He had done about half of it."

"Did that cover his life in West Africa?"

"Partly. It gave his parentage, youth, education and Foreign Office work in London, India and West Africa. I understand he was afterwards Governor of his colony, but the book had not reached that stage."

"I don't think we want to go through it in detail, but I presume you have done so?"

"Yes, it was necessary for me to make up the early chapters in order to understand what we were working at."

"Quite so. Now you have heard this letter read. Was there anything mentioned in the book, or any notes or other information to which in your opinion the letter could apply?"

"Nothing whatever."

"Did the deceased ever mention anything to which you think it might have applied?"

"Never."

Lawson nodded and again consulted his notes. "Now Inspector Pardoe has told us that the pistols were kept in the safe. I presume that was locked?"

"Yes, always."

"Who had the key? Or perhaps I should first ask if there was more than one?"

"There was only one key and that was kept by Sir Roland."

"Then he was able to open the safe?"

"Oh yes. He could get to it with the help of his sticks, and support himself while he unlocked it. He could not do it easily, but he could do it."

"Did you ever open the safe for him?"

"No, never."

"Have you seen into it?"

"Once. I went into the room when it was open. He swung it shut, but he was slow and I glanced in. I didn't mean to look – it was nothing to me – but I couldn't help seeing."

"What was inside?"

"Papers mostly. There were some drawers in the lower part and open shelving above. I really only caught a glimpse."

"Did you see the pistols?"

"No, sir."

"Did you know of their existence?"

"No, he never mentioned them and I never saw them."

"Was the manuscript of the book kept in the safe?"

"No, there was a large cupboard where it and the notes and the books of reference were kept."

"Who kept the key of the cupboard?"

"There were two. Sir Roland kept one and I the other."

"Very well. And there is nothing else that you can tell us that might have a bearing on this sad event?"

"Nothing whatever, sir."

"Thank you."

Juliet was feeling a warm satisfaction. It had been as she expected. Frank *had* been a model witness. He had given his evidence coolly, clearly and concisely, and his manner to the coroner had been just right. Never was there such a person as Frank!

Then Juliet's heart gave another leap, for the next name to be called was her own. But she soon found that she had no cause for nervousness. The coroner was sympathetic and his questions were easily answered. Indeed, before she had grown accustomed to her prominent position, she found herself back in her place, her ordeal over.

Three other witnesses followed her, whose statements, like her own, merely corroborated the facts already known.

Tom Allgood practically repeated Deryk's evidence about hearing the shot and finding the body. Weekes, on his part, stated that no one could have entered or left the sun trap by the north side unseen by him, and that no one other than those mentioned had done so.

Marjory Allgood told how her shoelace had broken and how she had stopped the set and taken her shoe off to adjust the lace. It was then that they had heard the shot. The other three had hurried away, but she could not follow till she had put on her shoe. This occupied perhaps one or two minutes. During that time no one had left the sun trap on the east side, either through the bushes or along the river bank.

Marjory was the last witness and when she stood down a little buzz of movement and whispered conversation ran through the assembly. Mr Lawson did nothing to check it, but busied himself setting his notes in order. Juliet had been immensely impressed by the proceedings so far. Never could she have imagined so detailed an inquiry. She felt that the jury could have known no more, had they seen the entire affair taking place before their eyes. What everyone had done was crystal clear. All their actions were natural and reasonable and all their stories dovetailed together. She could not see what more could be said about it.

But the coroner had other ideas. He now began to address the jury.

"Members of the jury, as you doubtless know, your duty is now to decide on three matters: first, you will state, if you can, the identity of the deceased. Second, you will declare, with the same proviso, the cause of death, not only the actual physical cause, but also how this came to be suffered. Here I need scarcely remind you that in such cases the three possibilities of accident, suicide and murder must always be taken into consideration. Lastly you must say, again if you can, whether any person or persons are to blame for the death, and if so, whom.

"Now let me very briefly review the facts which have come out in evidence.

"First, it has been deposed that the deceased was Sir Roland Chatterton, and as this has not been questioned, you will naturally find a verdict accordingly. Then you have heard some account of the deceased's distinguished career, of his marrying his second wife the present Lady Chatterton, of his taking up residence at Jasmine Lodge, and of his becoming crippled from rheumatoid arthritis. This affliction required the employment of two helpers, Mr Boone, his personal attendant and male nurse, and Mr Roscoe, his secretary, both of whom you have seen.

"But though the deceased was thus crippled, he was until from six to eight weeks ago a happy and otherwise a healthy man. Then he became less well, growing mentally depressed and physically feebler. This deterioration began gradually and gradually grew worse. The witnesses agree that it seemed a loss of health rather than the result of a shock.

"Let us come now to the events of last Tuesday," and Lawson recapitulated Sir Roland's feeling ill and remaining in bed till about half past ten, his getting up, dressing, and going to the sun trap about a quarter past eleven, and his then taking his soup. "Now Mr Boone tells us," he continued, "that so far as he could judge, the deceased was at this time in a normal condition of mind, no worse than for at least a week previously. But when he visited the sun trap a short time later, he found him very much agitated. Mr Roscoe then saw him, and both men were so much impressed by his appearance and manner that they went immediately to report to Lady Chatterton.

"Now you have to ask yourselves what produced this sudden change. Here we have the evidence of the threatening letter, and you must decide whether this was or was not the cause.

"Just consider once more this matter of the letter. You have heard that four letters came that morning," and Mr Lawson summarised the evidence, continuing: "If you assume that the envelope on the table beside the deceased contained the threatening letter, you may or may not regard its presence there as indicating that he did not open the letter until he reached the sun trap. In this case you may or may not consider that the information it conveyed was the cause of the change in his condition. That is a matter for you alone.

"A possible reason why the deceased should not have opened this fourth letter with the other three may suggest itself to you, namely that he recognised the envelope, and foreseeing a possibly painful message, decided to wait to open it till he was alone. That he could have recognised it is obvious owing to the letters SA on its back. While you may weigh this suggestion, you must remember that it has not been proved. You may also consider whether SA might or might not have stood for Sandy Archer.

"I must remind you that with the contents of the letter you are not concerned. It is no part of your duty to weigh the deceased's conduct or to pass judgment on anything he may or may not have done in the past. You are entitled to, and indeed you must, reach a conclusion in your own mind as to whether the letter was genuine or spurious. But beyond that you must not go.

"Now with regard to the point I mentioned, whether the death was due to accident, suicide or murder, you will have to form your own judgment. No evidence suggesting that it could have been accident has been put before you and I do not think therefore that you will have much difficulty in rejecting this theory.

"So far as murder is concerned there is a considerable amount of evidence, but you may consider it negative. Firstly, no suggestion of murder has been made at any point in the evidence. Secondly, no motive for murder has been indicated against anyone. Thirdly, no person was found in the sun trap when the witnesses ran in. Fourthly, no person could have left the sun trap after the others entered. Lastly, the powder blackening proves that the shot could not have been fired from a distance. In the light of all this evidence, I do not doubt that you will dismiss the idea of murder.

"We are then left with the possibility of suicide. Here also there is some suggestive evidence. Firstly, as I have said, if the death was neither accident nor murder, it could only have been suicide. Secondly, if you believe the letter to be genuine, the deceased had what he might have considered a sufficient reason for the act. Thirdly, the deceased was in an abnormal and very depressed condition of mind. You will consider whether this might or might not have rendered him less liable to stand up to the shock of disagreeable news. Fourthly, the pistol was his own, and on it were his fingerprints and his alone. Fifthly, as we have seen, the deceased was alone when the shot was fired, and it was fired from close to his head.

"These are the main points in the case as I see it. If there is any question any member of the jury would like to ask me, I shall try to answer it. If not, I will ask you please to retire and consider your verdict."

There was movement and whispering among the jurors and then the foreman announced that they did not require to leave their places. They were agreed that the deceased was Sir Roland Chatterton, that death was due to a pistol shot wound, self-inflicted while the balance of his mind was disturbed.

NOTE

The reader has now been given all the information which enabled Inspector French to prove what really occurred in connection with Sir Roland Chatterton's death.

– 10 –

DOUBTS

We must here go back one day in our narrative and follow Dulcie as she went upon her lawful occasions on the day after the tragedy.

As one of the minor signs of increasing affluence, she now bought a *Telegraph* each morning on her way to Harley Street. Having glanced over the headlines on arrival at her office, she put it aside till lunch time. Then in a secluded corner of the small restaurant she patronised she read what she had time for, finishing during supper at her flat.

This programme she carried out on the Wednesday in question. But it was not until she turned a page near the end of her lunch that her eye fell on a short paragraph.

DEATH OF SIR ROLAND CHATTERTON
Yesterday morning Sir Roland Chatterton, KCB, KBE, was found shot at his residence, Jasmine Lodge, near Staines, Middlesex. He had been in poor health and very depressed for some weeks and was alone when the shot was fired. An inquest will be held tomorrow. Sir Roland had a distinguished career...

Dulcie sat staring at the paragraph as if held in a vice. This was startling news. It might affect her, and closely. What about Frank? Would he lose his job, and if so, where would he seek another? Apparently he had been very comfortable at Jasmine Lodge, and it was unlikely that he would be so lucky twice running. At all events he need not come to her looking for sympathy and help in new questionable schemes.

Then she thought with still another surge of hatred that if he did come with some horrible proposition, she would have to listen. More than listen, she would have to agree. She was in his power. He could prove her complicity in the fraud, but she could not incriminate him. With complete safety to himself he could arrange that the affair should come out, but against him she had only her unsupported word.

She wondered why he had not written. If he had posted a letter in the early evening she would have received it before leaving the flat. It looked as if he did not care whether or not she knew.

That was it! He did not care because his interest was centred in another woman! No doubt he wanted to marry Miss Chatterton, believing that one day she would be rich. And of course there would be the enhanced social position.

Suddenly it occurred to her that this death might affect him in a very different way from that she had at first supposed. What if the Chatterton woman were now rich in her own right? If so, the marriage would be much more advantageous. Dulcie wondered with an intense curiosity whether Frank had achieved an engagement before the tragedy.

Certainly luck pursued Frank! Assuming the engagement had materialised, what could be more timely than this death? Whatever position the old man had taken up, from Frank's point of view, he was better out of the way.

Yes, Frank was just about the luckiest person she had ever known.

Then it was that the seed of doubt first entered her mind. Luck? Was Frank's persistent good fortune always due to luck? Had he not himself usually done something to bring it about? And if so...Once again Dulcie grew rigid as the full implications of her doubt smote on her mind.

No! She was wrong. Frank was dishonest and deserved her hate, but he was not – he could not be – a murderer!

A moment later she almost smiled with relief. Sir Roland had been alone when the shot was fired. What did that mean? Obviously that no one else was near enough to have shot him: in other words, that he had committed suicide.

Dulcie tried to banish from her mind her horrible suspicion. But she could not. As the afternoon wore away it loomed larger and larger in her consciousness. Gradually she saw that its truth or falsehood might very materially affect herself.

It was a dreadful thought, but it was true that if Frank were arrested and convicted, she would be safe! At least safe from him, for of course there was always a small amount of danger in the fraud itself. As the shrinking rabbit is fascinated by the snake, so the idea drew her. If Frank were guilty and his guilt were proved, she would be free.

But what if he were guilty, yet were not suspected? This might easily happen, he was so diabolically clever. Then she would still be at his mercy...

She continued her ruminations until a further point occurred to her. Suppose she were in a position to insinuate her suspicion? At once their positions would be reversed. She would have him in her power. Of course she did not mean actually to take such an action. It would be sufficient if he knew she could do so. With this knowledge he would not dare to mention the fraud, fearing what else might come out. Dulcie held her breath as she considered the possibilities.

But *was* he guilty? And could she find out? She did not know and she felt anxious and baffled. She did not even know what had taken place, still less what the police were doing.

It was as she was sipping her cup of afternoon tea that it suddenly occurred to her that there was a way in which she could secretly find out the facts. She went in to Burt and told him that she had a wild toothache and was afraid that if she carried on she might make a mistake in her work. If he could spare her for an hour she would run down to her dentist and have something done.

As she had foreseen, Burt was sympathetic and told her not to come back that evening. She went immediately to a large secretarial establishment and asked for the principal.

"I want a stenographer for the whole of tomorrow," she explained, having given the name of Miss Edwards. "It's for a rather unusual piece of work. I am trying to write a detective story, and in my book there comes the suicide of an old gentleman who has moved in good society. I do not know in sufficient detail how inquests are conducted, and I have for some time been looking out for such a suicide, so as to attend the inquest. I have just seen this," and she showed the *Telegraph* paragraph, "and it seems the sort of inquiry I want. But unhappily an unavoidable engagement prevents my going myself. Can you send a girl?"

The principal thought she could.

"I'm afraid I shall want rather a lot," Dulcie went on, "not only a verbal record of everything that is said, but also as much descriptive matter as can be squeezed in."

The principal thought that this also might be managed. She had a very good girl, who, she was sure, could do it, but for such skilled work her charges would be high. Dulcie was not interested in the terms, but she thought it unwise to say so and discussed them in detail.

On reaching her flat she found a note from Frank. In it he said very briefly that no doubt she had seen an account of Sir Roland's suicide in the papers, that this would make changes and that he expected shortly to be out of a job, but that he would write again as soon as anything was settled.

For a moment Dulcie felt that such a letter could only have been written by an innocent man. Then she remembered Frank's duplicity and decided she would let her stenographer carry on. Besides, Frank would never know what she had done.

Next day, though her toothache was miraculously cured, the hours dragged interminably. It took all the resolution she possessed to carry on her work, and she found herself sitting for long periods brooding over what might be happening at Staines. A short paragraph in the *Standard* told her that the jury had returned a verdict of suicide. But that did not resolve her doubts. If Frank had had a hand in it, such a verdict would naturally be reached. She would have given a year's pay to go again to the secretarial establishment and demand the report, but she felt that too great an interest would be suspicious.

It was not indeed till she returned from work at lunchtime on Saturday that she found awaiting Miss Edwards a bulky envelope containing what looked like the manuscript of a small book. She deliberately laid it aside, had a slow and comfortable lunch, and then instead of her usual long Saturday afternoon tramp, she settled down in her easiest chair to read the document.

The stenographer had made a job of it. There was first a description of the scene before the proceedings opened, with a plan of the room showing where the principal actors sat. Then the arrival of the coroner was recounted with the preliminaries of calling and swearing the jury, their going to view the body, and the interest which was obviously taken in a strange stenographer apparently unconnected with the press. There were even shrewd interpolations giving the witnesses' apparent reactions to the questions. Dulcie felt that the high fee had been more than earned.

But the further she read, the less need there seemed to have been to obtain the record. Sir Roland had unquestionably committed suicide, and her suspicions were unfounded. For once she had misjudged Frank. The jury had returned the obvious verdict, indeed if she had been on it herself, she would have voted with them.

She was surprised to find how sure she had been of Frank's guilt. Now she saw that this had been due to wishful thinking, partly due to the bitterness of her resentment, and partly to the hope that he had done something by which she could get him into her power. But she had been wrong.

And if she had been wrong about the tragedy, might she not also have been wrong about Juliet Chatterton? Might she not have read into their interview more than was really there? Then a further reaction set in. No, she had made no mistake! Their furtive glances! Their passionate embrace! The girl was in love with Frank. Whether he loved her for herself or only for her money Dulcie could not know, but she was certain beyond possibility of doubt that he was working for the marriage. Then she saw that there was even further proof of her theories. If the two had considered that Sir Roland were likely to consent to such a match, would there be any need for a furtive meeting? Of course not! Their association was undoubtedly clandestine.

But from that there followed her original doubt. If Frank were making love to Juliet Chatterton and believed that Sir Roland would not give his consent to the marriage and might therefore cut Juliet out of his will, would not the suicide be too good to be true? Having in her thoughts made a complete circle, Dulcie was now back where she had started.

Once more she read the evidence, finally concentrating on the coroner's summing up. He had, she thought, done it well. He had given the salient points fairly, omitting none. But as she pondered further she saw that there were only two which really mattered. The first was that no one except Sir Roland was in the sun trap when the shot was fired, the second, that no one could have left it after that moment.

Frank then definitely was innocent. So bitter were her feelings that it was with profound disappointment that she reached the conclusion. The first chance she had had of regaining her freedom had petered out. For hours she considered the position, then she concluded that nothing more could be done. She would just have to carry on as things were.

That night, having lain brooding for some hours, a further idea flashed into her mind. She would not give way so tamely, admitting defeat before the battle had been joined. Admittedly the coroner had not been able to visualise Frank's guilt, nor had she. But for that there was a reason in both cases. The coroner had not suspected murder, so he naturally had not considered methods. On the other hand she who did suspect murder knew little of its possibilities. Suppose an expert shared her suspicions, might he not find a method?

For her freedom there was still something that she could do! In a way that would not injure Frank she would put her suspicions before an expert. Though scarcely hopeful as to the result, it would at least be worth trying.

She knew the expert to consult. He was a Mr Anthony Liddell, a rising young barrister. She had heard him spoken of as brilliant and painstaking and certain to reach the head of his profession. That Sunday she posted a note to him asking if she might call on him one evening to consult him on a rather unusual point of law.

The Liddells had been patients of her father, and though she herself had never met them, through him she had heard of the son, Anthony. She remembered Dr Heath telling of an interview he had had with the young man and how impressed he had been with his ability. It seemed that Mr Liddell, who was a solicitor, had wished his son to enter his office and succeed him, but Anthony was more interested in medicine. It was Dr Heath who had suggested the compromise which to his delight had eventually been adopted. Anthony would read for the bar and would then specialise in forensic medicine with a view to concentrating on criminal cases.

He had done so with success, though so far he had appeared for the defence only. But he had already made something of a reputation and he was everywhere looked on as a coming man. Dulcie thought that no one could be better qualified to advise her.

By return of post there came a note saying that Liddell would be at Dulcie's service in his rooms in Lincoln's Inn at eight-thirty on the following evening.

Nervousness was not one of Dulcie's weaknesses, yet she could not overcome a feeling of anxiety as she ascended the young barrister's staircase. In what she was doing there was a danger that things might go further than she had intended. If Liddell was as wide awake as he was supposed to be, he might conceivably see through her little subterfuge. Whether Frank were innocent or guilty, it was a serious step to take. However by calling she was burning her boats and she could only now go through with it.

The tall, rather good-looking young man who opened the door seemed far from formidable, and with his pleasant manners and friendly smile he put her at her ease as far as this was possible.

"Miss Heath?" he exclaimed, holding out his hand. "Come in. I had your note and I shall be glad to do anything I can to help you." He drew up a second armchair to the open window. "Won't you sit down? Cigarette?"

Dulcie thanked him as he held out first a silver case and then a lighter. He seemed in no hurry to come to business, chatting lightly on a variety of topics. But eventually he asked in what way he could be of service.

"I've come to you, Mr Liddell," Dulcie answered, "after much hesitation. I have an uneasy feeling that I should not presume to trouble a man of your standing with what can only be a trifle, or even something which you can scarcely take seriously."

"If your idea is to arouse my interest," he smiled, "you're certainly going the right way about it. I shall now not be satisfied till I hear your problem."

"Then I must plunge, or I may not have courage to go on," Dulcie smiled also. "It's about a book."

"A book? Yes?"

"The fact is, I'm trying to write a detective story and I'm ignorant of certain technical matters which you could certainly advise me on, if you would. Of course I needn't say it would be a business matter between us and I should expect to pay the same fees as if the case were a real one."

"Well, no one could say fairer than that. I like detective stories and I should probably be very much interested in yours. What's the difficulty? Some point of law? Or is it police procedure?"

"No," she declared. "It's much worse than either. It's really something that, as the author, I should do myself, something that I've no right to ask of anyone else. As a matter of fact it's a little help with the plot."

"Oh," he said, "that's certainly unusual. Now suppose you begin at the beginning and tell me all about it."

"Thank you," she answered gratefully, "you're very kind. My book is about the murder of an elderly country gentleman, but murder is not suspected at first. It's only afterwards that doubts arise and the affair gradually comes out. I'm afraid so far it's not very original."

"It's a situation which can bear repeating," Liddell suggested. "In my view it all depends on the details."

"Yes, I agree of course. Well, I was not too sure of how an inquest was carried on, so I watched the papers for the sudden death of someone in somewhat the same position as my old country gentleman, with a view to attending the inquest and seeing for myself."

"The way to succeed," Liddell approved. "I congratulate you."

"I hope you're not doing it too soon. After weeks of waiting I saw this," and she handed him the cutting about Sir Roland's death. "It seemed to me the very thing and I decided to attend it."

"And did you?"

"No. As it happened I had an unavoidable engagement. But I had waited so long for the kind of case I wanted that

166

I felt I could not miss it. So I did what I thought was the next best thing," and she told about engaging the stenographer. "Here," she handed over the bulky type-script, "is her report."

He laughed. "As I said, the way to succeed. I do admire thoroughness. Continue, please."

"The verdict was suicide, and so far as I can see, could only have been suicide. It seemed quite obvious from the evidence, as no doubt you will agree if you are good enough to look through it. Now when I read it it struck me what a perfectly magnificent story it would make if I could put in similar evidence in my book. I mean, evidence which appeared to point equally obviously to suicide, and yet the affair would turn out to be murder in the end."

He looked at her whimsically. "No doubt," he declared. "A natural, but if I may say so, not a very original desire. Every detective novelist would like to do just that. And the reason they don't is surely obvious?" He paused to let this sink in, then continued: "What I mean is, if the evidence points to suicide, it's presumably because it *was* suicide. If it was murder, would the evidence not necessarily be different?"

Dulcie leant forward eagerly. "That's the point, Mr Liddell. I want to see whether with this evidence a scheme of murder could be devised. It would make such a splendid book. I have to confess I don't myself see exactly how it could be done. But I wondered whether you perhaps might."

Liddell smoked for a moment in silence. "My dear young lady," he then said in mild protest, "that's surely a rather tall order. What you seem to want is for me to devise your plot, and that's a job not for a barrister but for a novelist. But perhaps I have misunderstood you?"

Dulcie's heart began to sink, but she rallied her courage and tried to answer easily.

"I think I haven't made myself quite clear. I don't for one moment suggest that you should devise a possible crime. Obviously, as you say, that would be a novelist's job, not a barrister's. What I meant was that with your great knowledge of crime you might see at a glance how murder could have been committed in this case. All I would ask would be a hint of a possible method. It would then of course be for me to work out the details."

"Oh," he smiled, "your idea's clear enough, and from your point of view it's certainly a good one. I mean, it would be good if you could carry it out. But to be quite candid," he grew serious, "I fear you're asking an impossibility."

"Perhaps I am, Mr Liddell. I realise that at best it would be only a chance. But will you not give me that chance? All I ask is that you should read the notes of the inquest and see whether any helpful idea occurs to you. If it does, my first book becomes a bestseller. If it doesn't I'm no worse off than before."

"I'm not so sure of that. You'd have lost the fee I should charge you, because I'd have to charge for the time I spent reading the notes, even if nothing came of it."

Dulcie smiled happily, feeling that she had won her case. "If that's all," she returned, "I should thankfully take the risk. To succeed would be an immense thing not only for this book, but for my whole future as a writer. For a chance of success the fee would be a legitimate expenditure. Please don't think of that. If you would be so terribly good as to try, I should be more than grateful."

"I confess I'd be interested," he returned. "But to charge you a fee without having done what you want would go against the grain. And yet it would be earned."

Dulcie got up. "Of course it would," she said finally. "Then that's settled and I can't say how grateful I am to you."

He laughed, then moved to the door. "I'll tell you what I think would be a help," he said, pausing as if a sudden idea had struck him: "to read the draft of your story as far as it has gone. I could then see better how this new idea might be worked into it."

Dulcie felt slightly embarrassed. She had not foreseen such a request. "I'm afraid I've not actually written the draft yet," she answered. "I've been concentrating on the plot, and of that I have only a series of disconnected notes, unintelligible to anyone but myself."

He nodded. "Ah well, it doesn't matter. Then I'll read your report of the inquest and if by some unlikely chance I'm able to suggest anything which might help you, I'll let you know."

While Dulcie was thus commencing her operations against Frank, events at Jasmine Lodge had pursued their predestined course.

After two restless and unhappy days during which no one could settle down to their usual tasks, there came the funeral. It was private, and melancholy as are all such. Except to Sylvia and to a lesser extent Juliet, it was an unpleasant formality and all felt relief when it was over. The others were more interested in what was to follow: the reading of the will. This indeed filled their minds to the exclusion of almost all else.

"We may have a bit of luck," Boone said to Maggie Green, by no means for the first time. "The old boy was open-handed enough, I will say that for him. I've been with him for nine years: he may have remembered me."

"Oh, Arthur, if we get enough for the pub!"

Boone thought it unlucky to anticipate good fortune. "Talk sense, woman," he grunted severely. "If we get a quarter of it I'll be more than pleased."

"It's usual, isn't it? I mean for the staff to be mentioned in the will?"

"Well, I wouldn't go so far as to say that," Boone returned cautiously. "But plenty of employers do it. I don't think I've too bad a chance. After all, I did a lot for him."

"After all, you were paid for doing it," Maggie pointed out.

This Boone considered an improper remark and the conversation showed signs of coming to a standstill. But before it did so she broke the deadlock. "Why not have a word with Roscoe?" she suggested. "He was well in with the master and may have seen his papers."

"He said he hadn't at the inquest. I'm not too fond of Mr Inquisitive Roscoe. I don't feel like discussing things with him."

But Boone was apparently too much on edge to keep the matter entirely to himself. He mentioned it to Weekes, as the oldest member of the Jasmine Lodge staff. Weekes of course knew no more than anyone else, but it was evident that he also harboured similar hopes.

Excitement rose among the staff when instructions were received that they were to be present at the reading of the will. This presaged a feast of good things. Seldom has an order been more enthusiastically obeyed.

At length the great moment arrived. The household assembled in the dining-room, where at the head of the table Mr Cummings had already taken his place. He was commendably brief. As soon as all had taken their places, he made a few pertinent remarks and went straight on to the reading of the document, which he said he had not drawn up, but which he had found in the deceased's safe.

It was simple enough as wills go. Jasmine Lodge and an ample sum to maintain it were left to Sylvia during her life, and practically all that remained, together with the reversion of Sylvia's legacy, went to Juliet. "It has not been possible," Mr Cummings broke off to explain, "to ascertain just what this means, but roughly speaking and subject to future correction, I believe it will not be far short of £130,000."

"Those," he went on, "are the two main items, but there are several smaller ones," and he reverted to his reading. A number of charities benefited, then came the eagerly expected clause. No member of the staff had been forgotten. The secretary and personal attendant were to get the sum of £50 for every year or part of a year they had spent in Sir Roland's service, and all other members were left £25 on similar terms.

There was carefully suppressed jubilation in Jasmine Lodge that night. Boone in particular seemed unable to disguise his surprise and delight. His nine years of service would bring him in £450, and when the £25 a year for Maggie Green's four years was added, there would be enough to buy the licensed house with a little over.

Changes were doubtless imminent at Jasmine Lodge, but with the one great exception, matters temporarily resumed their accustomed course.

When Dulcie had gone, Liddell remained gazing absently out of the open window, while he turned her strange commission over in his mind. He had to admit that his interest had been keenly aroused. It was not so much in Dulcie's idea for her book, though that might be entertaining enough. What had excited his curiosity was the

171

lady herself. He wondered if her statement was the undiluted truth. He wondered if the plot for the book was the real object of her call. In fact he wondered if it even featured in her motive.

It was with this in his mind that he had asked to read the draft of the book. His request had obviously embarrassed her. If the story of the book were gospel, why should it have done so? She had in fact admitted that the draft in question did not exist. Strongly he suspected that it had never been contemplated. Indeed the more he pondered the matter, the more convinced he became that the book was a myth. Almost certainly her interest lay in some other direction.

But where? As to this he could of course form no opinion till he had read the typescript. He weighed it in his hand. This extraordinarily voluminous account must have cost her something, and she was evidently prepared to pay him a good fee. Something about the death of Sir Roland Chatterton was clearly vital to her.

With a growing interest he read the script, which he soon realised was a verbatim report. He found it convincing. The verdict returned was certainly the correct one. What could Miss Heath's idea be?

Then like a flash a theory shot into his mind. She suspected murder! She knew something which had not come out at the inquest and which she had not told him.

The more he thought this over, the more likely it seemed. Yet it by no means explained her action. Suppose she did suspect murder, what was she employing him to do?

Was it that she feared some innocent friend of her own might be accused? Liddell doubted it. With such a fear she would certainly have taken no action. The inquest had passed off safely and her obvious policy would be to let sleeping dogs lie. To consult a lawyer might bring into the open the very evidence she wished kept secret.

The same reasoning would apply if she thought her hypothetical friend guilty. She would wish the circumstances to be forgotten.

Then he wondered if she were a friend either of the deceased baronet or of his family. If so, she would naturally want the murderer to be brought to justice. While these were the only theories Liddell could evolve, he was by no means satisfied with them.

Next evening he reread the typescript, and then settled down to consider it as he would had it formed the basis of one of his briefs.

Firstly, what was the evidence for suicide?

The chief point, he thought, was the deceased's state of health, which all concerned had agreed had produced a deep mental depression. This in itself was enough to account for suicide, but if to it were added the receipt of the threatening letter, the act would be accounted for fully. Under the circumstances suicide was not only possible, it was likely.

Then as to murder. When the shot was fired, the deceased was alone. The police were not likely to be mistaken on such a point and the Inspector's evidence was definite. Moreover, it could not have been fired from a distance. This was shown not only by the powder blackening, but also by the fact that the bullet which had caused death had come from the pistol found on the ground beneath the deceased's hand.

This proof was corroborated, firstly, by the fact that the position of every member of the household had been established at the time of the tragedy, and secondly, that no unknown could have hidden in or about the sun trap.

Lastly, no motive for murder had been suggested against anyone.

Liddell felt that it would be foolish of him to give the matter any further thought. No verdict other than that of the coroner's jury could have been returned. It was therefore impossible that he could do what Miss Heath pretended to want.

On the other hand the lady was obviously no fool, and what was so clear to the jury and to him must be clear to her also. Why, if so, had she come along with her story?

His interest was now so keenly aroused that he could not banish the affair from his mind. If Miss Heath suspected murder, she must have good reason for doing so. Was there any action that he could take to clear the matter up?

First he thought of bluffing Dulcie: of putting it to her that he was aware of her suspicions, and that in the interests of justice she must divulge them. But on further thought he believed this would fail. She would almost certainly express astonishment that he could have so far misunderstood her, and would stick to her story about the book.

Was there then no way in which he could test the matter? For a long time he puzzled over it and then at last he thought he saw light. If Miss Heath really only wanted information for a book, it followed that she had no personal knowledge of Jasmine Lodge or its occupants. If on the other hand she suspected murder, it would undoubtedly mean that she was acquainted with someone there.

Could he find out? He thought so, but it would cost money. Was it worth it? His reason said no, his curiosity, yes.

His curiosity eventually won. Next day he called at the office of Messrs Miller & Mackintosh, private inquiry agents, and asked for Mr Mackintosh.

- 11 -

SAPPING AND MINING

Stewart Mackintosh sat hunched over the desk in his small office in the microscopic flat his firm occupied in Arundel Street, Strand. He was working on a report covering the activities of a lady and gentleman whose respective husband and wife were curious as to how the two passed their spare time. As a result of the report divorce proceedings would probably be initiated and fees would swell the coffers of Messrs Miller & Mackintosh.

Though divorce and its preliminaries was a profitable line for the firm, it was by no means its only interest. The partners undertook all kinds of inquiries except those appertaining to actual crime. Where the law was known to have been broken they would indeed make subsidiary investigations on behalf of a client, but only after acquainting the police of the district concerned. In this way they kept on the right side of authority, sometimes being lucky enough to help the official forces and sometimes getting a useful hint in return.

The business had been started by Miller, an ex-Scotland Yard detective-sergeant, who had retired as soon as the rules of his service permitted. Mackintosh was his brother-in-law, a former solicitor's clerk, whose hobby, and indeed mania, was detection. The two were hard-working and

175

painstaking, and had done a good deal better for themselves than if they had remained in their original jobs. Miller, who was a big beefy man, interviewed new clients, carefully impressing them with his strength and driving force. Also he dealt with the more timorous witnesses, who might be bounced and badgered into saying more than they intended. Mackintosh on the other hand was undersized and insignificant looking, and when dressed in nondescript and rather shabby clothes, as he usually was, could pass almost anywhere unnoticed. Though helped by an assistant, it was he who did the most of the shadowing and the watching of residences.

Mackintosh had just returned from lunch and was settling down to another chapter in the Adventures of the Lady and Gentleman, when the indoor staff, a stout young woman with a Semitic cast of features, ushered in Anthony Liddell. Mackintosh rose to his feet.

"This is an honour, Mr Liddell," he declared. "Will you please take a seat?"

Liddell, who had frequently come across the little man in court and thought highly of him, wished him good afternoon. "Busy at present?" he went on.

"Can't complain, sir; can't complain," Mackintosh answered with a faint suggestion of a Scottish accent. "Enough to keep us alive, if not so much more. Was there anything you wanted done?"

"A little job for myself in person. Very private, you understand."

Some reproach showed in Mackintosh's features. "All our work, sir, as you know, is strictly private."

"I know of course. But in this case I don't want it even to be known that inquiries are being made."

"You've come to the right place for that, sir. Our strong suit, as you might say."

"I know that too, but there was no harm in mentioning it. It's an unusual piece of work and I dare say it won't be easy, but I expect you'll manage it all right."

"Well, sir, as you know again, we'll do our best, and we can't say more than that."

"Good enough." Liddell laid a slip of paper on the desk. "That's the name and address of a lady, Miss Dulcie Heath. I can't tell you anything about her, because I don't know it myself, having only met her once. Now you'll see there's another address, Jasmine Lodge."

"Where the owner committed suicide a few days ago? Let's see, I can't just mind the name. I read about it, but I didn't take any special heed to it. It wasna my affair."

"Sir Roland Chatterton. That's the place."

"Yes, sir? I've got you so far."

"What I want to know is whether the lady, Miss Heath, has or has had any association with Jasmine Lodge, or with anyone who is connected with it. I'm afraid it will mean looking into Miss Heath's life, and as I said, I don't want her to know you're at work."

"I follow. I think with any ordinary luck we can find that out for you. You don't know if the lady has a job, and if so, what?"

"I'm afraid I don't."

"Could you describe her?"

Liddell did so and Mackintosh went on: "Well, the work will probably take a bit of time. What about costs, sir? Is there a limit we're not to overstep?"

"Not exactly, but you might report at intervals and you can then give me a hint of how the money's mounting. If it gets too high I'll just have to ask you to stop."

"I'd be sorry if we stopped before you'd got all you wanted."

"Perhaps you won't."

When the detective had again assured his visitor of his unstinted efforts on his behalf, Liddell took his leave. Mackintosh picked up a new folder, marked it "Miss Dulcie Heath", and having dropped the paper with the addresses into it, he put it away in his file. Then he returned to the errant lady and gentleman, scarcely lifting his head till his report was complete. Lastly he went in to see his partner. They discussed the new inquiry and arranged the work so that next day the junior partner should be free.

That evening after supper Mackintosh went out to prospect. Shuffling along with his hat pulled down over his eyes, he passed through Dulcie's street, observed her house, and noted places which offered suitable cover to an observer.

Early next morning he began strolling up and down the main street opposite where hers debouched. In due course a lady left the house and from Liddell's description he saw that it was Dulcie. He turned into an entry from which he watched her pass, then followed. When she queued for a bus he took up a position some places behind her in the line. He avoided her in the bus, and when in Wigmore Street he saw her preparing to alight, he stepped out before her and walked off without a backward glance. Then halting at a shop window, he allowed himself a peep after her. He was just in time to see her turning into Harley Street. Sprinting to the corner, he followed slowly up the other side. When he observed her let herself in with a key to No. 779 he felt that his immediate task was completed and turned back the way he had come. A telephone call to his office, where reference books were available, told him that No. 779 was occupied by Mr Bartholomew Burt and gave a précis of Mr Burt's qualifications and career.

So far Mackintosh's action had been purely routine and easy at that, but his next step was not so clear. Owing to the use of the door key, as well as the time of her arrival, it was obvious that Miss Heath was not a patient. She was probably a nurse or receptionist or secretary, or a combination of all three. How was he to find out? He thought of making some excuse to call or telephone, but rejected both because he did not want the lady to see him or hear his voice.

Finally he decided that nothing more could be done till evening, and delighted his partner by turning up at the office and doing a lot of clerical work. By five o'clock he was back in Harley Street, this time in his small ten-horse car. He parked near No. 779, choosing his position so that if Dulcie walked to Wigmore Street, she would face the car and pass it closely. One of his most cherished possessions was a miniature camera of superlative quality, and this he now drew from its case and fixed by a clamp to the side window, focussing for the footpath and the level of the face of a passer-by. Then he pulled out a newspaper, and while reading with absorption, awaited developments.

Presently a man appeared, and stepping into a Rolls-Royce which had just glided up to the door, was driven magnificently away. Obviously Burt. Some half-hour later Dulcie left, walking past the car as he had hoped. While ostensibly still buried in his paper, with the corner of his eye he watched her progress, and an exposure was made at the psychological moment.

He was about to turn the car and follow her when the door of No. 779 again opened and a man emerged.

His appearance and walk seemed unprofessional and Mackintosh put him down as an attendant. Instantly it flashed into his mind that here might be his most promising informant. He slipped in his clutch and followed him.

Fortunately the quarry took a bus: if he had gone by Tube the agent would have been sunk. The chase continued to the Euston Road, where the man dismounted, and after walking a block or two, turned into a narrow street. Mackintosh parked near the corner and followed on foot. Presently the man stopped, took a key from his pocket, and let himself into a house. Having noted that it was No. 22 Green Street, Mackintosh returned to his car.

The use of the key indicated that the house was where the man lived and it seemed likely that he would now have his evening meal. Everything depended on what he did after that. Mackintosh drove to a nearby restaurant, had a hasty supper, parked his car in a side street, and inside thirty minutes was back in sight of No. 22.

For nearly an hour he watched, lounging about as far as possible from the house. Then his persistence was rewarded. The man appeared, walking off in a leisurely way. When he turned a corner his pursuer was close behind him, being just in time to see him entering a large public house. The agent waited for five minutes, then followed him in.

The place was fairly full, most of the tables being occupied in addition to the line of people at the bar. Mackintosh felt his luck was in as he saw his quarry seated alone at a small table in a corner. He bought a pint, then moved away from the bar, obviously looking for a seat. He was careful to look only where none was vacant, as he edged closer to his man. Finally he stopped beside him.

"This place taken, mate?" he asked.

"No," said the man. "Sit down."

"Nice house this," went on Mackintosh. "I've never been here before. Just on my way to the station and I thought I could do with a pint."

A desultory conversation ensued, but as it was leading nowhere, Mackintosh thought he should bring matters to a head. He leant forward and spoke more confidentially.

"I'm looking for a bit of advice," he said, "maybe you could help me?" Then glancing at the other's glass, he went on: "But first, have another pint with me."

The man didn't mind if he did.

"It's this way," Mackintosh explained when their wants had been supplied, "I'm out of a job: chauffeur, gardener, handyman about a place. You wouldn't know by chance of anything in that line?"

" 'Fraid not," said the man. "I'm not in the way of knowing about vacancies. There's a chauffeur where I work, but he's not leaving. Been out long?"

"No, only last week. Sort of tragic, it was. The old man got ill and the local doctor said there should be an immediate operation. But the family waited to get one of these big pots down from Town, chap called Burt, I believe. But he came too late. Before they could do anything the old man had popped off."

The other looked interested for the first time. "Burt, did you say?" he asked. "Not Bartholomew Burt of Harley Street?"

"That's the man, yes. I remember the two Bs in his name."

"Well, that's a bit of a coincidence, that is. It's Bartholomew Burt of Harley Street that I work for. General attendant at the consulting-rooms."

181

"Bless my soul! I'll say it's a coincidence! If you read that in a book you wouldn't believe it. Well, I wasn't saying anything against him. This trouble wasn't his fault."

"Oh, Burt's all right. Good at his job, at least they say so. And good to work for too."

Mackintosh thought he could now get down to it. "What's your job like?" he queried. "Did you have to have any special sort of training?"

"No, not me. I worked in a railway cloakroom here in London: seven years of it I put in. It was all right, but I was tired of it and thought I'd like a change. I saw Burt's ad, and applied and got the job."

"You like it?"

"So far, only I get tired of places. But I'll stick to this for a while. I've scarcely been there six months yet."

"It sounds the sort of thing that would suit me. What have you to do, if I'm not asking too much?"

The man was ready enough to talk about himself and his activities, but Mackintosh wanted something more. When he had again declared that such a job would be ideal for himself, he turned to another point. Speaking with less interest, as if he were only prolonging the conversation from politeness, he asked if Burt had a large staff.

"Only two, not counting the chauffeur," the man answered, "myself and Miss Heath. She's receptionist and secretary. She's all right. I get on well enough with her."

Mackintosh looked at his watch. "I must be going," he said. "I've to call at Euston for a suitcase and take it to my sister's. But let's have another pint first." He gave the order. "Look here, mate. If I leave my address will you drop me a card if you hear of a vacancy with the other doctors? My name's Duncan, James Duncan."

"Mine's Rider, John Rider. Yes, I don't mind, but I warn you it's not likely I'll hear of anything."

Mackintosh took a stamped postcard from his pocket, wrote on it "James Duncan" and an imaginary address, handed it across, and with thanks and a hearty good night took his leave.

He was not very satisfied with his day's work, but at least he had obtained this man's name and address and forged a connecting link with Dulcie.

Having arranged for the assistant to shadow Dulcie when she was not at Harley Street, Mackintosh next morning took an early train to Staines. He asked his way to Jasmine Lodge and saw what he could of the place without actually going into the grounds. Wishing to observe those who entered and left, he followed Dulcie's plan of some weeks before: screened himself in the wood and settled down to watch the gate.

It proved an unproductive vigil. After an hour's wait a blue limousine left, driven by a chauffeur with a young lady at the back. Another hour passed and the car and its occupants returned. A few minutes later a tallish, dark, athletic-looking man walked smartly out and turned towards the town. Another hour and he reappeared and went up the drive.

Mackintosh felt that this was getting him nowhere. He had grown hungry, and as he noticed a small restaurant not far away along the road, he went there and ordered lunch. He was early, and when the waitress brought his soup, he held her in conversation.

He had little idea that his actions were not original. As luck would have it, he sat in the same seat as had Dulcie on her detective expedition, though unhappily for him he did not talk to the same girl. At the moment she had no other customers and appeared glad of a chat. Mackintosh led the talk to Jasmine Lodge and then proved an appreciative listener.

"You're right when you say there'll be changes," she remarked. "Sir Roland's attendant, Mr Boone will surely be going, and it's not likely they'll keep Mr Roscoe, his secretary. But beyond that I can't say. Mr Weekes, the gardener is a fairly old man and he might take the opportunity to retire, but again I can't say."

"That's interesting to me," Mackintosh told her. "I'm out of a job and a gardener's would suit me fine. I'll call and ask if there's an opening, and thanks a lot for your help."

Mackintosh had now obtained a list of the members of the establishment with a more or less vague thumbnail sketch of each. Three of them he had undoubtedly seen: Miss Chatterton and the chauffeur in the car, and Roscoe walking. As he returned to his hiding place in the wood he felt his next step must be to contact some of these persons. The most promising were undoubtedly the two who would probably be leaving: the secretary or the personal attendant.

Shortly after three the young lady he had seen in the car left with an older woman, both walking. Obviously the two Chattertons. They turned towards the country. Ten minutes later a middle-aged rather pessimistic-looking man came down the drive and walked off towards the Town.

This, Mackintosh realised, could only be Boone, the attendant. Here was an opportunity which should not be missed, and when the man had disappeared round the bend in the road, he slipped out of the wood and followed. He let him go on far ahead, closing up only as they approached the town. Boone called in one or two shops and then did what Mackintosh was hoping he would, pushed through the swing doors of the Jolly Fisherman. Five minutes later Mackintosh did the same.

There followed an almost exact repetition of the events of the previous evening. Boone was standing alone at the bar and Mackintosh moved near him as he gave his order. He began to chat to Boone, then when the ice was at least cracked, he bent towards him and spoke more confidentially.

"Excuse me, but aren't you Mr Boone of Jasmine Lodge?"

The man glanced at him suspiciously. "That's right," he admitted, "but I don't know you."

"Of course you don't," said Mackintosh. "I only know you because I was making inquiries about Jasmine Lodge and you were pointed out to me as being there. I wonder if you could give me a bit of information? Will you have another pint with me?"

Like Rider the night before, Boone didn't mind if he did, Mackintosh carried the two pints to a table and they sat down.

"My trouble's not what you'd call an uncommon one," he began. "I'm out of work. I read about Sir Roland's death and I wondered if there might be changes and if I'd have a chance?"

"What is your line?" Boone asked.

"Chauffeur, gardener, general handyman."

"Well, I wouldn't know. I'll be leaving because my job's finished, and I expect Mr Roscoe, the secretary, will be too, though of course I can't say about that. But they've already got a chauffeur and a gardener and I don't suppose either'll be leaving."

"It doesn't seem hopeful, I'm afraid," Mackintosh said despondently. "All the same, thanks for what you've told

185

me. Matter of fact it's a bit of a coincidence about you and me, for we both seem to have lost our jobs for the same reason. My boss has just died too. But he was a bachelor and the house is being closed."

"Been with him long?"

"Four years," Mackintosh answered, memorising the period.

"Oh well, that's not too bad. Myself, I'm not sorry to be leaving. I was there too long: nine years. You tend to get into a groove if you stay too long in the same place."

"That's a fact. I was sorry to leave because the place suited me better than I'll likely get again. But I agree it's bad to be too long anywhere."

"Too long's bad, but too short's worse," Boone declared. "If you don't stay long enough in a place it's hard to get another. They think there's something wrong with you. Now this trouble at Jasmine Lodge won't do me any harm, but it's a bit hard on Frank Roscoe, the secretary. He's not been there very long. I don't know where he was before, but if he only had a short engagement it'll begin to count against him."

"I see what you mean. But surely Sir Roland's death would be a good enough reason for the last move?"

"I suppose it would. All the same, a longer stay would have been better."

So far, though Mackintosh had been gaining inform-ation, he had learnt nothing of any apparent value. When he got up to leave, his new friend did so too. They stood for a moment chatting on the doorstep, Mackintosh having decided that his business would lie in the opposite direction to Boone's.

It was then that Mackintosh had his first stroke of luck. They were just about to part when Boone pointed across the road. "Why there's Miss Green, our house parlourmaid. Which reminds me I have some commissions to do."

Mackintosh bade him good afternoon and turning, kept the woman in sight. He thought that as the means had been offered to him, he might as well get another angle on the household. When Boone was out of sight, he stepped up to her.

"I beg your pardon," he began, raising his hat politely, "but I think you're Miss Green of Jasmine Lodge?"

"Why yes," she said, waiting for him to explain himself.

"My employer sent me down to see if I could pick up a bit of information, and he told me to offer a pound or two for it. It occurred to me that you might be able to give it to me, if you would."

"What do you want to know?"

"Well, I can tell you here if you'd rather. But not to keep you standing, might I suggest a cup of tea?" He pointed to a teashop which conveniently revealed itself across the road.

She hesitated, then agreed.

"The fact is," he went on when the order had been given, "my employer is dissatisfied with his house and he has heard of Jasmine Lodge and thinks it would be the very place for him. When he read of Sir Roland's death he wondered whether the house would be for sale. I suppose you couldn't give me a hint?"

"I certainly could not," Miss Green answered shortly. "Why don't you go to Lady Chatterton or the agents?"

He smiled ruefully. "Well, I have a certain amount of nerve, but it wouldn't run to asking such a question of Lady Chatterton and I don't know the agents. Could you give me their name?"

"I'm afraid I don't know it."

She was not encouraging, but as Mackintosh could scarcely put the question he wished to ask without some previous conversation to lead up to it, he struggled on manfully.

"It's a bit awkward," he said apologetically. "Unless you're right on the spot, so fine a property is liable to be snapped up before you've a chance to bid for it. My boss naturally didn't want to butt in if nothing was doing, but if it was for sale he didn't want someone else to get there first. I'm sorry if I've bothered you, but I thought you might know."

She seemed mollified. She hadn't heard the idea suggested, but if she were to give her own opinion, she thought it very unlikely that Lady Chatterton would move.

They chatted on during tea and then Mackintosh thought he might prepare for his question. "Well," he said, "I'm grateful to you. From what you've told me I think I've been on a wild goose chase. I need scarcely trouble to find the agents. Now I was given this to pass on to whoever gave me my information, so I hope you will accept it," and he put a pound note on the table beside her.

She shook her head and declared she had done nothing to earn it, but he insisted, and protesting, she allowed herself to be persuaded. "I'll have something to say to Miss Heath when I get back," he went on. "It was she who started the idea?"

"Miss Heath?"

"Well, you know her, don't you? She knows Jasmine Lodge, for she described it in pretty complete detail. That's her photograph."

Miss Green looked at the little picture and shook her head. "I've never seen the lady before," she declared, "and if she'd been at Jasmine Lodge I would have, for I open the door."

Mackintosh expressed a not too interested surprise. "That's strange, for she seemed to know it well. Perhaps she visited it on your day out?"

"Must have done. She wasn't there at any other time."

The agent put the photograph back in his pocket. "Oh well, it doesn't matter; she's heard of it somehow," he said carelessly, and changed the subject. But presently he skilfully brought it back to the occupants of Jasmine Lodge. He felt he could ask no more direct questions, but from suggestions he learnt that Miss Green liked and trusted them all, with the single exception of the secretary. He, she explained, was a comparative newcomer, and she had somehow taken a dislike to him. She could not say why, for he was always civil enough, but there it was.

"You say Mr Roscoe was a newcomer?" he went on. "What does that mean? A few weeks?"

"Oh more than that," she answered. "I remember the date of his arrival for," she smiled, "it happened to be my birthday. It was on Monday the 10th March last."

"If that was a newcomer," Mackintosh smiled back, "it means that all the rest of you have been there for several years," to which she agreed.

On his way back to Town Mackintosh thought over his day. He had learnt a lot about Jasmine Lodge and its occupants, but nothing that helped him to answer Liddell's question. So far as he had gone, it looked as if Dulcie Heath had had no connection with the place, but he was not sure enough of this to report accordingly. Then he told himself he ought not to mind his lack of results. He was doing honest work and it was bringing in good money, and what more could he want?

189

Just as they were approaching Paddington an idea struck him. It was just under six months since the 10th March when Roscoe had gone to Jasmine Lodge. Curiously enough the only other date he had heard in the affair was also just under six months: when Rider had gone as attendant to Burt. Strange how these coincidences occurred!

There could be no connection of course. Mackintosh put the idea out of his mind. But that evening when he was resting idly after supper it returned. Could Miss Heath's post coupled with Liddell's question constitute a connection? He didn't think so. And yet, the similarity of dates was interesting.

Learning on Monday morning that nothing had been discovered by Dulcie's shadower, the agent found himself bankrupt of ideas as to his next step. It was this, rather than any belief in what it might bring forth, that prompted him to look a little further into the matter of the dates. A few hours would cover the inquiry and then he might dismiss the matter with an easy mind.

John Rider had said that he had been employed in the cloakroom of a London station before going to Burt. Mackintosh now began visiting the principal stations. His procedure at each was the same. Going to the cloakroom, he asked if Rider was there. Then he explained that he had just arrived from Australia and that he wanted to find his old pal.

He tried King's Cross, St Pancras and some other stations without result, but at Charing Cross he struck oil. The man on duty remembered Rider, though he could not give the date he had left. Mackintosh explained that he particularly wanted to know this, as he was in doubt as to whether Rider had received a letter he had sent him from

Australia. The man suggested a call at the offices, and there after a good deal of delay the date was turned up. It was Wednesday, 6th March. The clerk recalled the affair with irritation, because Rider had not given proper notice.

Mackintosh thought this last fact suggestive. It looked as if the Harley Street position had become vacant on the following Monday. But that Monday, 10th March, Roscoe began work at Jasmine Lodge. Mackintosh drew a deep breath as he asked himself: Where was Roscoe during the previous week!

He went back to the office and saw his partner. "See, Bob," he told him, "it's time you did a spot of work on this Liddell case. Go and doll yourself up as a country squire or something and call on Burt: Mr Bartholomew Burt, 779 Harley Street. Say you've had an application from a man named Frank Roscoe for a job as private secretary, and that Roscoe had given his name as a reference. See what happens."

"Hang it all, Stewart, I must know more than that," Miller retorted irritably. "I'm not a ruddy thought-reader. Who is this Roscoe and what's the connection?"

Mackintosh told him and Miller rang up Burt for a non-professional interview. A woman's voice answered, but as this was probably Dulcie Heath, Miller's business was naturally with Burt himself. He presently received an appointment for five-twenty that afternoon, on his own condition that he would not take up more than five minutes of Burt's time.

Miller was apologetic to the surgeon. He explained that he would not occupy as much as the allotted five minutes, but that he had asked to see him because he considered a personal interview worth a dozen letters. In brief what he wanted was, and he put his question.

191

Burt's answer was equally to the point. Roscoe had been with him, not as secretary, but as attendant, though Burt believed he was capable of much more important work. While with him he had given every satisfaction. Burt obviously could not recommend him as a secretary, but if he did clerical work as well as that for which Burt had employed him, Mr Miller would be lucky to get him.

The news delighted Mackintosh. His long shot had got a bull's eye! Not only would his good work be profitable in itself, but it would raise the firm's stock in a valuable quarter. With satisfaction he settled down to draft a report for Liddell.

– 12 –

FRIENDLY EXAMINATION

During dinner that evening Anthony Liddell received a telephone message saying that Stewart Mackintosh would like a word with him. Liddell suggested his chambers in an hour's time.

Since giving his commission to the detective agency Liddell had been occupied with a murder case which was shortly coming on at the Old Bailey, and in which he was leading for the defence. He had therefore given little thought to Dulcie, and he now almost regretted having allowed himself to become mixed up in her business. That there was nothing in his suspicions he now felt certain, and he was going to pay away good money for the indulgence of a not very intelligent whim. On the other hand he would be glad of anything which might divert his mind from the murder case.

When Mackintosh arrived, Liddell waved him to an armchair and put cigarettes beside him. "I didn't expect to hear from you so soon," he declared. "If you've got something to report, you certainly haven't been idle."

"I had a bit of luck, sir, and that's a fact," Mackintosh answered. He was pleased by his reception. Indeed Liddell's good manners and genuine kindliness were one of the principal causes of his popularity. He always tried to put himself in the place of the other fellow and to act accordingly.

"Luck's quite a help sometimes," he agreed. "Well, I'll be interested to hear your results."

Mackintosh unfolded his report. "You were right, sir, in your surmise," he said, laying it on his knees. "There is a connection between Miss Heath and Jasmine Lodge, but it seems to be a rather unusual one."

Liddell felt a sudden thrill. All his suspicions surged back into his mind. "Tell me," he said, and he could not keep the interest from his tones.

"First," Mackintosh continued, still further pleased by these manifestations, "I shadowed Miss Heath and found out where she worked. She is receptionist and secretary to Mr Bartholomew Burt, the surgeon, of 779 Harley Street." He paused, but as Liddell only nodded, he continued: "I then went down to Staines and made inquiries about the Jasmine Lodge household. It consists of," and he enumerated the members. "All of these have been there for several years with one exception, Mr Frank Roscoe, who started work there just under six months ago, on Monday 10th March, to be exact."

"How did you manage to find all that out in the time?" Liddell queried, not only because he was interested to know, but because he thought a little judicious appreciation might be useful.

Mackintosh was too wise to claim any special credit. "Easily enough," he explained. "I saw one of the staff go into the local – it was Mr Boone, the late Sir Roland's personal attendant. I followed him in, and on the excuse of looking for a job, got a lot of information about the household."

"It sounds good to me. Go ahead."

"On the previous night I had done the same with a man who left the Harley Street house just after Miss Heath. I followed him to a licensed house and we got into conversation. He told me he had gone to Mr Burt just under six months earlier."

Liddell glanced at the other sharply. From his manner Mackintosh had evidently expected him to be impressed. "I don't follow," he said.

"Well, sir, there was a bit of a coincidence about the dates. Mr Roscoe had gone to Jasmine Lodge about the same time that Rider, that's Mr Burt's attendant, had gone to Harley Street."

"I still don't follow."

"I'm not surprised either. It wasn't much of a hope, but out of curiosity I thought I'd find out the exact date Rider started work. He left his former position suddenly on Wednesday, 5th March."

"Five days earlier!"

"Exactly. Then I wondered if that could mean anything interesting and I got my partner to go with a tale to Mr Burt, that Roscoe had applied to him for a job and had given his name as a reference. It was a long shot, but it got home."

Liddell stared. "You don't mean that Roscoe had been there?"

"Just what I do mean. He had been with Mr Burt for about a year and had left to take up the Jasmine Lodge appointment. So there, sir, is the connection with Miss Heath that you wanted."

Liddell was really startled, but Mackintosh must not see that. "I congratulate you, Mr Mackintosh," he said warmly. "A fine piece of work! That was all I asked you to find out. Was it, as a matter of fact, all you learned?"

Mackintosh hesitated. "Well, there's just one other item, but I scarcely like to mention it. I can't state it as a fact: it's only a bit suggestive."

"Let's have it all the same."

"Miss Heath wasn't known at Jasmine Lodge. So far as I could learn, and I asked the parlourmaid who opened the door to visitors, she'd never been there. Now of course that may mean nothing, but on the other hand it may mean that she and Roscoe wished to keep their acquaintanceship secret."

Liddell considered this. "I don't think we can build much on that," he said at length. "Unless they were very close friends, and I gather there's no evidence of that, there would be no reason why Miss Heath should visit there."

"That's correct, sir, but I thought I ought to mention it. Well, that's all I have to say except that you'll find what I've told you in my report," and he handed it over.

For a moment Liddell was tempted to confide wholly in this wise and capable man, then he thought that for the moment at least it would be better to keep his suspicions to himself. He therefore congratulated his visitor again and let him go.

To say that Liddell was impressed by what he had learnt would be to understate his reactions. He now felt no doubt that Dulcie suspected murder, and as he was satisfied that she was anything but a fool, he believed also she must have adequate reasons.

In the light of Mackintosh's information he was able to go a step further. If Dulcie's connection with the household were through Roscoe and Roscoe alone, her motive could not be regret for Sir Roland's death and desire to bring his murderer to justice. On the contrary, if she suspected Roscoe, her object could scarcely be other than to protect him from discovery. But her recent action was a curious way to set about it. If she wanted to help him, would she not have kept quiet? In other words, if the dogs were sleeping so satisfactorily, why not let them lie?

Liddell kept on telling himself that Sir Roland's death was no business of his. All he had to do was to see this girl and tell her he could not devise the plot she desired, and so far as he was concerned, the affair would be over. But he found he could not do so. The thing had gripped his imagination and he could not forget it.

For two days he hesitated, then his curiosity again overrode his judgment. He wrote to Dulcie asking her to call on the following evening.

For Dulcie also the last few days had been filled with curiosity and not a little anxiety. She was frightened by the step she had taken. To wonder in her own mind whether Frank could be guilty was one thing, to pass on her doubts quite another. This Mr Liddell was reputed to be extraordinarily shrewd, indeed that was why she had gone to him. Might that very shrewdness not lead him to see through her subterfuge and learn more about her than she wished?

All the same, when she received his note asking her to call, she did not hesitate. She must hear what he had to say. Almost certainly it would be that he was unable to help with her plot. If so, as far as he was concerned, the matter would come to an end. What should she then do? Well, that could wait till after the interview.

Liddell was quite as courteous as on her first visit, in fact, he welcomed her as an old friend. He then declared he had not yet had coffee and asked her to join him. It was not till this was over and cigarettes were alight that he turned to business.

"I've read your report," he told her, "and very interesting I've found it. I certainly agree with you that if you could retain these incidents and yet prove the case one of murder, you'd have a fine book."

"But you don't see how it could be done?" she asked smiling.

"I'm sorry to have to admit it, but you're correct. I have really tried quite hard, but I do not see how under such circumstances the affair could be other than suicide."

"I was afraid so," she returned. "At least," she realised what she had said from his amused smile, "I – I don't mean – That is – " she broke off in confusion.

"I know very well what you mean," he grinned. "Naturally you're disappointed over your plot. You thought I could help and I've failed you. Well, I'm disappointed too. But you see, the evidence is very strong."

"I realise that of course. I did say I was afraid I was asking you an impossibility."

"It's strong because there are two separate lines of testimony and I really think that either alone would be accepted as proof. First, take the deceased's frame of mind and that extraordinary business about the letter. There's the motive all right: amply sufficient. Second, consider the actual circumstances of the death; the fact that the deceased was alone at the time of the shot and that no one afterwards left the sun trap, that the bullet came from the gun lying at his hand, and that there was powder blackening on the wound showing that the pistol was within a few inches of the head when it was fired. No, I'm afraid no one could make murder out of that, though I grant you it's a great pity." He grinned again.

Though Dulcie had expected some such reply, she listened to it with bitter disappointment. Frank had won again! There was nothing that she could hold over him and she remained in his power. His usual luck! And hers! Whatever happened, she lost!

She was recalled by Liddell's voice. "You've asked me several questions, Miss Heath, and though I can't claim a right to do so, I'd like to ask you one. May I?"

"Why of course, Mr Liddell," she answered, mildly surprised. "Anything I can tell you."

"Why do you think Frank Roscoe guilty?"

Dulcie's heart shot into her throat. She simply could not believe her ears. *What* was it that this man had said? It could not be – no, it simply *could* not be that – he suspected. If he had learnt that she knew Frank, what else did he know? For a moment she could not reply.

"I don't think I understand – " she managed to stammer at length, but he broke in with a friendly smile.

"My dear young lady, of course you do. If I had any doubt before, which I hadn't, you've dispelled it now, absolutely and for ever. But why should you mind my knowing? It's no disgrace to suspect someone of murder, and you have been so correct and discreet in your attempted search for truth, that no one could criticise you."

Dulcie's mouth was dry. She felt absolute panic. If this smiling man knew so much, had he discovered the fraud? She strove to pull herself together and answer carelessly, but for the life of her she could not. In fact before she was able to reply Liddell spoke again.

"You'd make a very bad conspirator, Miss Heath, so I feel I can rely on everything you say. It's quite obvious that you think Roscoe guilty, and you haven't denied it, so let's start with that. I'm correct, am I not, in believing that you're not really writing a book, but that you didn't see how Roscoe could have done it, and wanted me to solve your problem? If so, again I congratulate you on your discretion."

Still she could not reply and he went on more seriously. "There are one or two things that I'm sure you know, but which at the moment may have slipped your memory. The first is that you have employed me to act on your behalf. My duty therefore is to you, it being understood of course that this involves no breach of trust to the State or morality in general. I mean that in acting for a client I can't become party to a crime, but otherwise what my client confides to me is secret. You follow that?"

At last Dulcie forced herself to speak. "Oh yes, I understand that all right."

Relief was surging back into her heart. If this man knew about the fraud he surely would not speak in so friendly a way. And if he did not, perhaps she had scored! Now that his interest had been aroused he might concentrate further, and yet give her her hold over Frank. But he was speaking again.

"Very well, unless you're party to the crime of murdering Sir Roland, which," he smiled, "is on the face of it, unlikely, you can tell me your doubts about Mr Roscoe with perfect security. But there's something else you must consider. *If* Sir Roland was murdered, and *if* you know anything which might throw light on the tragedy, it is your duty to come forward with your information. It's really rather serious: I expect you're not aware of how serious it is. Do you know that if it can be proved that anyone has vital information with regard to a murder, and if he fails to advise the authorities, he can be charged as an accessory after the fact and sent to penal servitude? Therefore you must consider your course of action very carefully."

Dulcie listened with renewed uneasiness. The affair was going much further than she had anticipated. "Why do you suppose I think Mr Roscoe guilty?" she asked in a low voice.

"It's pretty clear from your statement, isn't it?" he returned, which irritated her because she could not see how. "But that really is not the important question. What matters is your answer to mine: *why* do you think him guilty?"

She hesitated. "I don't really," she began, but he stopped her.

"Now," he said, "we've settled that. You'd just admitted it. Better answer the question."

"Well," she replied, still speaking hesitatingly, "what I mean is that I've no proof. You're right to a certain extent, but I don't suspect Mr Roscoe: all I wondered was whether he could be guilty. The evidence seemed conclusive, but I wasn't sure."

"Exactly. And why were you not sure?"

"Perhaps I should say that Mr Roscoe is not a stranger to me."

"I know. Mr Burt, 779 Harley Street."

Once again Dulcie's heart missed a beat. Once again, what *did* this man know? In spite of herself she shivered.

She saw that Liddell was watching her closely. Then he smiled encouragement. "Now you've gone so far, better tell me all," he advised. She thought his manner showed interest, but not criticism and slowly she took courage.

"I can't imagine how you know about Harley Street," she said rather unsteadily, "but you're correct. Mr Roscoe was out of work and he took a temporary job with Mr Burt."

Liddell nodded.

"It was not a suitable position for Mr Roscoe and he only took it until he could find something better. He was a qualified secretary, you understand."

"Quite."

"Then he saw Sir Roland's advertisement. He applied and got the job and moved to Jasmine Lodge."

"Yes, that I had gathered also."

Dulcie's courage was returning. As before, she felt that Liddell could not be so friendly if he knew of the fraud. Further, she did not see how what she had said could really injure Frank.

"Mr Roscoe has very good manners and he can be very agreeable to women." Dulcie did not realise the bitterness of her tone, though once again she noticed Liddell looking at her shrewdly. "There is Miss Chatterton at Jasmine Lodge."

"Do you mean that Roscoe was making advances to her?"

"I thought so."

"I'm afraid you'll have to tell me just why you thought so."

This wasn't quite so easy as Dulcie had expected. "Frankly, Mr Roscoe always had an eye to the main chance, if you understand me. Miss Chatterton was not engaged, Sir Roland was rich, Lady Chatterton was his second wife and his son was dead. It seemed clear that Miss Chatterton would come in for something worthwhile."

Liddell openly stared. "Are you trying to tell me that Roscoe wanted to marry Miss Chatterton for her money?"

"I told you I had no proof. That's why I made no accusation."

"But you suspected it?"

"No, not really. I only wondered about it."

Liddell grew more serious. "Now Miss Heath, you needn't tell me you suspected such a thing without any evidence, for of course you did suspect it. What made you think it?"

Another difficult question. Dulcie did not want her own relations to Frank to come out. That would be humiliating, besides getting too near the fraud. "He was that kind," she said shortly, and again unconscious bitterness sounded in her voice.

"No doubt," Liddell persisted, "but even that could scarcely account for your belief. I want the definite evidence that you obviously have."

Dulcie thought she could safely tell of her journey to Staines. "If you must know, it was something I saw. I was down one day at Staines," and she described what had taken place.

Liddell nodded. "That's certainly suggestive enough. Did either of them see you?"

"No."

"If Roscoe did not see you at that time, he did not see you when he came out of the drive. Where were you?"

She hesitated, slightly confused, and again becoming anxious as to where these questions might lead. "I happened to be in a wood opposite the gate."

"Happened?" he queried. "Do you mean that you had hidden in the wood so as to watch the drive unobserved?"

"I don't think you've any right to make such an insinuation," she declared. "I was in the wood and I saw the drive."

"You knew Mr Roscoe at Harley Street, and you saw him coming out of the Jasmine Lodge gate from a hidden position in a wood, and you didn't call to him or run out to speak to him. Miss Heath, do be sensible. Obviously you were watching the place to learn what you could. Don't be annoyed with me. If I am to help you, I must know the facts."

This she thought reassuring. Once again, he would not speak in this way if he knew of the fraud. "Well," she said with simulated unwillingness, "I suppose I must confess. I *was* watching the place."

"Of course you were. That's a lot better. And it follows that you suspected a courtship *before* you saw Roscoe and Miss Chatterton turn up the path." He looked at her sharply. "Excuse a personal question, Miss Heath, but with the serious suggestion of murder in the background this must be cleared up. Had Mr Roscoe ever made love to you? Or perhaps I might put it, was there any understanding between you?"

Dulcie began to feel helpless in his hands. Whatever happened she *must not* be forced into damaging admissions. All the same, to agree that they had been friendly would do no harm.

"We had been friends," she answered.

"Was there an actual engagement?"

She hesitated and he went on quickly: "I see there was. You were engaged, and you were afraid that he would break off the engagement and take up with Miss Chatterton because of her wealth? That was it, wasn't it?"

She hung her head. "I suppose so," she admitted gloomily.

"Well, don't be depressed about it. If he's that kind, you're well rid of him. Now all that's reasonable enough. Also it makes your observation of them quite natural. I suppose what aroused your suspicions was a cooling in Roscoe's manner to you?"

"Yes, that was it."

"Exactly. I think it's all quite clear now, and I can also understand and sympathise with your hesitation in admitting it." A thought seemed to strike him. "Tell me, were you acquainted with Roscoe before you met him in Harley Street?"

Dulcie didn't see why she should deny it.

"Which of you was there first?" he went on.

"I was."

"Then I presume you were instrumental in his going there?"

"Yes," and Dulcie told of Frank's return from Italy and his desire for a temporary post.

"I see. Now we must consider this carefully, Miss Heath. You suspected that Roscoe might have murdered Sir Roland for the following reasons: just stop me if I go wrong. First, he had an eye for the main chance, and though you didn't say it, you obviously think him unscrupulous. Second, you were engaged, but after he went to Jasmine Lodge, you found him growing cool towards yourself. Third, at Jasmine Lodge there was a Miss Chatterton, not engaged, and certain to inherit a good sum. Fourth, Roscoe is a man who can make himself very attractive to women, and you thought it possible that Miss Chatterton might have fallen in love with him. Fifth, you saw them in each others' arms. Sixth, I don't think you put this into words, but you implied it: Sir Roland died at an extraordinarily convenient time for Roscoe. He would certainly have objected to such a match, and if his daughter persisted, he might cut her out of his will. Seventh, Roscoe was the last person to see the old man alive; in fact he was with him five minutes before his death. Is all that correct?"

Not appreciating his training, she was amazed at how completely he had read her mind and how strongly he had put the case. "It's quite correct," she muttered unwillingly.

"And against the theory of his guilt there is only one thing: that neither of us can see how he could have done it. On the other hand, since you suspect him, you must believe him very able."

"He's certainly that."

Liddell remained silent, obviously in thought. "Well, I congratulate you. You've made a strong case and you've acted discreetly. It all really does go back to the problem you put up to me at our first interview: could murder have been committed under the circumstances of the case? I'll have to think over that again."

Dulcie left the chambers still uneasy as to how much Liddell actually knew and how her action might affect Frank. Yet as she thought over what had taken place, she believed that no harm had been done. The evidence showed that Frank was innocent, so they could not hurt him, and it was obvious that Liddell had no suspicion of the fraud. All would yet be well!

SUPERINTENDENT FRENCH

Liddell on his part was wholly pleased with the interview. Dulcie had been more malleable than he had anticipated and he thought that she knew little of which she had not told him. Her story moreover was consistent and he unquestioningly believed it. Of course some slight modifications of it were required, but these he could supply for himself. She had not, for example, told him that jealousy of Juliet Chatterton and hatred of Roscoe for his treatment of her were the spurs which had driven her to action. But these motives leaped out of every word that she had said, and it was they which made her conduct credible.

All the same Liddell was also uneasy. The affair had left him with a very pretty problem. Did the warning he had given to Dulcie now apply to himself? Had he information regarding a murder which he could not keep to himself without incurring the guilt of an accessory after the fact?

Of course in a sense he had no information at all. Nothing that he had heard proved either Roscoe or anyone else guilty. But Liddell was too honest a man to be satisfied with this plea. If he had justification for a reasonable suspicion of the crime, was it not his duty to declare it? To answer that he must first decide whether he *had* such suspicion. He took a pad and jotted down the items, considering each as he did so.

All seven points which he had made to Dulcie were suspicious, but not one was conclusive. Even the entire seven taken together were not conclusive. They made a case for investigation, but that only.

The ruling factor seemed to be the actual occurrences at the death. Could Roscoe have committed the murder or could he not? For the second time Liddell reached this conclusion, just as Dulcie had done earlier.

Till late that night he pondered the problem. The only way in which he could imagine Roscoe guilty was if the man had used some delayed action appliance, something he could have set while with Sir Roland and which would have fired the pistol after he had left. But to Liddell this seemed out of the question. The police were quite as alive to delayed action appliances as he was, and had the use of such been possible, it would certainly have been commented on at the inquest. If all this were correct, Roscoe's innocence seemed unquestionable.

When Liddell reached this conclusion he felt he might banish the whole affair from his mind. But he could not. The doubt instilled by Dulcie remained and kept gnawing away in his consciousness. He found he could not wholly concentrate on his other business. Was there a murderer at large in Jasmine Lodge? If so, he alone was in a position to take action about it. What was he going to do?

In the end it was consideration for Juliet Chatterton which brought him to a decision. If Roscoe had killed Sir Roland, it might be because he wanted Juliet to marry him. And he might persuade her to do so. This would indeed be a tragedy, perhaps greater than that of the death itself.

Liddell would not be justified in keeping silence unless he were sure that such a thing could not take place.

But what steps should he take? Being in doubt, Liddell did nothing for a couple of days, then, his conscience giving him no peace, he came to a decision.

Among the many Scotland Yard officers with whom he had come in contact in the course of his profession was one whom he respected and trusted, not only as a skilful investigator and a shrewd man of the world, but also as kindly and honourable. His name was French. He had been a Chief Inspector when Liddell had first met him, but recently he had been promoted to the rank of Superintendent. Admittedly it would be unfair to bother him with a case outside his own work, but he was a man who never thought it a trouble to do anyone a good turn, and if Miss Chatterton's possible situation were put to him, he would certainly give the matter consideration. Liddell rang him up, explained that he wanted advice, and asked him to dinner on the following evening.

It was not until they had finished the meal and were seated in easy chairs with tobacco and coffee that Liddell broached the subject of their meeting. "I feel a complete idiot about this," he began with a somewhat twisted smile, "bothering you with an affair which I ought to be able to settle off my own bat. But the fact is that I've got some information which is worrying me, and it occurred to me that your experience might enable you to throw light on a doubtful point."

French, evidently surprised, murmured that he would be glad to do anything he could.

"First, I should say that it's an unofficial application. I'm consulting you as a private individual, not as an officer of the Yard. I hope that's all right?"

French looked at him with a twinkle in his eye. "If it was anyone but you, Mr Liddell, I'd ask a question or two at this point. But with you it doesn't matter."

"You mean that you don't want to be let in on a crime and then asked to keep it dark?" Liddell grinned. "Well, you needn't worry. I don't know whether the thing is criminal or not, but naturally if it is, the proper authorities must be told."

French looked somewhat pained. "I was joking, sir. You don't need to give me an assurance like that."

"I know that of course. But let me tell you what happened. A fortnight ago I had a note from a Miss Dulcie Heath," and he went on to tell of her call, the reading of the typescript, Mackintosh's report and his second interview with Dulcie. French listened with obvious interest.

"An unusual story," he commented when Liddell paused. "The lady certainly has put up a case, but then you've suggested her motive. If she was jealous and resentful, she'd tend to see Roscoe guilty of a crime. She'd want to see it. Our old friend wishful thinking again."

"You think there's nothing in it?"

"I don't say that; I'd have to study the evidence in detail first. All I mean is that if the lady felt herself badly treated she might wish this man to be guilty, and the wish might be father to the thought."

"I appreciate that, but I don't think it accounts for everything. Those seven points must be either true or false, and if they're true they'll want some explaining. Suppose we go over them again? First, that Roscoe had an eye for the main chance and was unscrupulous."

"Nothing in that; I mean, it may be just Miss Heath's bias. If necessary of course we could test it by tracing his career."

"Very well; that Roscoe and Miss Heath were engaged, but after he went to Jasmine Lodge he cooled off towards her, that at Jasmine Lodge there was an heiress, that she was not engaged, that Roscoe could make himself very attractive to women, and that Miss Chatterton had in point of fact fallen in love with him."

French carefully knocked out the ashes of his pipe. "Well, we know there's a Miss Chatterton at Jasmine Lodge, who has inherited a lot of money from her father. We don't know that she's not engaged, though if she had been, it would probably have come out at the inquest. In any case it's easy to find out. But to all the other points my criticism applies. That Roscoe was engaged to Miss Heath and cooled off we have on her testimony only. Since she fell for him she'd naturally think him attractive to women. That Miss Chatterton had fallen for him is Miss Heath's story. So far, to be candid, I don't think there's much to go on."

"The clandestine meeting?"

"Was there one?"

"Well, at least it was a convenient time for Roscoe for the old gentleman to pop off."

"Only if Miss Heath's unsupported statement is true."

"Then you think I should drop it?"

"I think if Miss Heath has allowed her judgment to become warped, there's nothing in it. But she may not have. If her statement is true the thing certainly wants looking into."

"I came pretty much to that conclusion myself. What I wanted to know was whether under the circumstances established at the inquest Roscoe could have murdered Sir Roland. Because if not, the question's automatically settled."

French made a gesture of agreement. "Now you're talking, Mr Liddell. I agree that's the first point to establish. But I don't know that we can do it now. We should want more exact particulars from the officers who examined the body."

"You can't see any way in which it might have been done?"

"No, sir, I have to admit I cannot. Just think of it. If Roscoe was guilty he'd have had to rig some apparatus to fire the shot after he had left. Well, under normal circumstances that would be easy enough. But speaking on our present information, there are two things about this case which make it practically impossible."

"Those are?"

"First, the gun was close to the deceased's head when the shot was fired. Now no one could have rigged an apparatus to hold the gun in such a position without the deceased's knowledge. And if he knew about it he wouldn't sit still and wait until it shot him. That is, unless he was incapacitated from some other cause."

"You mean drugged? There was no suggestion of that in the medical evidence."

"Exactly, though it might be worthwhile having a word with the doctor. But there's a further point which alone would seem to rule out any kind of delayed action apparatus. If such had been used, some trace of it would remain. Well, obviously there was nothing or it would have been mentioned at the inquest. But here again an interview with the local inspector might be useful."

"It scarcely seems worth considering further."

"There are two other points to be thought of," French went on. "It seems to have been admitted that the deceased's state of health would fully account for the suicide. If Roscoe was guilty, is it assumed that he brought that illness about? That doesn't seem very likely."

"Could he have done it?"

"I doubt it. I suppose a doctor could, but I doubt if a layman would have the knowledge or could have got the drugs. Could you believe further, that if the deceased had been drugged over a period of weeks, the police doctor wouldn't have had something to say about it? I don't think I could."

"I suppose your other point was the letter? If Roscoe were guilty, he must have written that."

"Yes, but again that's not very likely. On the evidence the letter was genuine. If not, what had so seriously upset the deceased between the time he went out to the sun trap and when the attendant brought him his soup?"

"Was he upset?" Liddell smiled.

"Oh, come now, sir! Both Roscoe and Boone said so. If it was a lie, those two must have conspired together to tell it. You're hardly going to argue that they carried out the murder jointly? You know as well as I do that people don't do that except in the rarest circumstances."

"I expect you're right. Altogether it seems a false alarm."

"If you ask me, Mr Liddell, it's just another jealous and spiteful woman trying to get her own back on the man who has hurt her self-conceit."

"You may be right. By the way, there was one thing which interested me: a trifle of course and having nothing to do with this other affair. Every time I spoke of Harley Street, and particularly about Roscoe being there, Miss Heath seemed scared. I suppose I'm becoming fanciful, but I imagined there might be more in that connection than met the eye."

French smiled. "I see that at all costs you're going to have an inquiry. Well, a word or two to Mr Burt should clear that up."

Though Liddell could not but agree with all that French had said, he was by no means satisfied with the interview as far as it had gone. He believed that Dulcie was jealous and vindictive, but he could not believe that she was so wholly evil as to desire the death of an innocent man to gratify her spleen. He thought, rightly or wrongly, that she was honest to the extent of herself really believing the secretary guilty. He was inclined to accept her story of Roscoe's unscrupulous eye to the main chance, also that he was contemplating a marriage with Juliet Chatterton. He turned again to French.

"I confess, Superintendent, that while everything you have said seems unanswerable, a little doubt keeps gnawing in my mind. I suppose you could scarcely look a little further into the matter? See the doctor and the local superintendent as you suggested?"

French moved uneasily. "Well, Mr Liddell, I think you know as much about that as I do. I should be very willing to do what you suggest, but, you know, I couldn't start in on a case without orders. If you want the matter gone into further, I'm afraid you'll have to apply to Major Lethbridge, the Chief Constable."

"What sort is he, do you know?"

"Very nice man. He'll do anything he can for you."

"May I mention that I've discussed the affair with you?"

"Of course, if you wish to."

They had some drinks and further chat, and when the barrister had expressed his thanks, French took his leave.

Liddell did not thereupon dismiss the subject from his thoughts. Quite definitely he was not satisfied, and until he was, his conscience would give him little peace. If Roscoe were a murderer Miss Chatterton must be protected from a disastrous marriage.

Next morning with determination he picked up his telephone receiver and dialled Lethbridge's number.

Major Lethbridge was elderly and in poor health, and in view of his retirement, which was impending, he was not anxious to take on more work than was absolutely necessary. But when Liddell rang him up to ask if he might call to obtain his advice on a certain matter which was giving him some anxiety, the Chief Constable was interested. It was not often that a barrister of assured position couched such a request in such terms. They discussed a meeting, and finding that both were engaged during the day, Lethbridge unwittingly copied Liddell's procedure with French, and asked the young man to dine on the following evening.

Lethbridge was a bachelor and he welcomed so interesting a companion to his otherwise solitary meal. Their respective callings gave them plenty to talk about, and as is usual in such circumstances, it turned out that they had many mutual friends. It was not until dinner was over and coffee had been disposed of that the Chief Constable turned to the matter in hand.

Liddell repeated his story of Dulcie's call and the subsequent incidents down to his interview with French "Though French did not himself seem impressed," he concluded, "he admitted that a case for inquiry had been made, so my next obvious move was to put these facts before you. If you're satisfied, of course the matter is at an end. On the other hand if you consider Miss Heath's actions constitute fresh evidence, you may feel that some further investigation is called for. I'm sorry to trouble you with all this, but to be quite candid, I feel a certain responsibility which I should like to share."

For some moments Major Lethbridge sat silently smoking. "Your story," he said at last, "has certainly made me think. I may as well admit to you that I was never entirely happy about the case, though for quite a different reason from that which you put forward. I happened to know Sir Roland, not exactly intimately, but fairly well. He and I met when he was Governor of one of the West African colonies. I thought then that he was a very fine man, and when his rheumatism developed and he retired and settled down at Jasmine Lodge, I naturally called. We visited each other at intervals, and among other things he discussed his book with me. I was therefore able to form some opinion of his personality, and I have to admit that when I first heard of the suicide I simply couldn't believe it. It seemed the last thing that such a man would do."

"That's certainly interesting, Major. No doubt you therefore ordered a specially careful investigation?"

"Naturally. I saw that one of our best fellows was put on to it, Inspector Pardoe, and told him to take nothing for granted, but to go into it as if it was a murder case. He did so very thoroughly. For instance, a specialist checked that the fatal bullet actually was fired from the pistol found. I'm bound to say that Pardoe produced an unanswerable report."

"Does this matter of Miss Heath tend to shake your opinion?"

Again the Chief Constable paused. "Yes and no," he returned at length. "As I saw the affair, or rather as I see it now, there are three points against the suicide and one in favour of it."

"Three to one on murder!" Liddell exclaimed. "Why, that's a decision for Miss Heath!"

"You may not think so," Lethbridge answered dryly, "when you hear them. Against the suicide theory was first the deceased's personality, as I have said. But this was offset by the fact that he had been for some weeks suffering from an increasing depression. Now I did not see him since his illness began, therefore I can form no personal opinion of its effects on him. But his wife and the others who knew him well agreed that he was greatly changed. The argument from his personality therefore seemed washed out."

"Yes, I see that."

"The second item which made me doubtful was the threatening letter. That Sir Roland, at *any* time in his career, could have committed a serious crime and lied someone else into prison for it, appeared to me absurd. No one who met him could have doubted his fine sense of honour. At first, again, I just could not believe the tale."

"You changed your mind?"

"The circumstances which Pardoe unearthed forced me to do so. Sir Roland evidently knew whom the letter was from before he opened it, presumably because it bore the letters, SA, and he evidently knew it would contain bad news, because he waited to open it till he was alone. I puzzled over it and evolved a theory: I need scarcely say I can't prove it. For what it's worth, it's this. That Sir Roland did give evidence which led to the conviction of some man for a crime which he had not committed. That Sir Roland gave this evidence in good faith, believing it to be true. Perhaps it was true, but incomplete, and it therefore led to a miscarriage of justice. At all events Sir Roland's conscience was clear of evil intention. Then I supposed that some weeks ago he had learnt what had happened, perhaps from a letter of similar appearance to that we're discussing. This would horrify him, but he might only partially understand the case and therefore would try to find out more detail. But the very thought of such a possibility would bring about the depression."

Liddell was impressed. "That's very ingenious," he declared.

"Well, it was my idea. Now you come along with further evidence which constitutes my third item. And you will notice it's substantially of the same kind as the other two."

"I'm afraid I don't follow that, Major."

"Well, like them at first hearing it seems conclusive, and again like them, further thought shows that there may be nothing in it. The seven points which you put up are very strong till French comes along and knocks them into a cocked hat with his jealous woman theory."

"I see that now. You said there were three points against suicide and one for. What is the one?"

"Simply that murder could not have been committed."

Liddell laughed. "Somewhat uncompromising! Does it mean you are satisfied, and think nothing more need be done?"

This time Major Lethbridge made a longer pause than ever. "No," he said presently, "I confess that I'm still worried. My intellect tells me it was suicide, my feelings that Sir Roland was never guilty of such an act. Call this intuition if you will. Now reason," he smiled, "is convincing and intuition misleading: hence my conclusion."

Liddell nodded. "What you say, Major, is absolutely unanswerable, and yet I share your dissatisfaction." He paused. "I suppose murder *is* absolutely ruled out by the conditions? What about delayed action appliances?"

"Well, what about them? Can you think of any such which could have been used?"

"No, but I'm not an authority."

"We went into it, I may tell you, very carefully, and we couldn't either. There simply was no possibility that any apparatus could be designed to fulfil the two conditions which obtained: first, that the gun should be fired from close to the deceased's head and second, that the apparatus should automatically dissolve itself into nothing. No, if it was murder, it was done by some human being who was present at the time the shot was fired."

"And there wasn't anyone?"

"And there wasn't anyone."

Liddell moved as if to bring the conference to an end. "I think, Major, you've dispelled my doubts. I hadn't seen it just as you put it, but I can't imagine your being anything but right."

Though Liddell spoke with assurance, Lethbridge could see he was not convinced. Nor was Lethbridge himself. That intuition which he had labelled as misleading still warned him to be careful. As both men stood up he shook his head.

"I'm still dissatisfied," he declared. Then coming to a sudden decision, he continued: "I'll tell you what I'll do. I'll have another talk with my superintendent and Pardoe and perhaps with French. If we can see any justification for reopening the case, I shall not hesitate to do so. But I think it's unlikely that we shall."

Lethbridge felt exasperated by the turn events had taken. Acting on the advice of his subordinates, he had stifled his gnawing doubt that all was not well with the case. Now he dared do so no longer. He knew that his decision would mean unpleasantness all round. His men would naturally oppose the overriding of their opinions and the stultifying of their reports, and the coroner would be annoyed that his jury's finding was called in question. Particularly Lethbridge believed that the appeal to the Yard, which he intended to propose, would be very ill-received. Then he told himself he must not mind. Since he was taking a salary he supposed he ought to do something to earn it.

Next morning he repeated Liddell's story to Superintendent Clements and Inspector Pardoe. To his surprise both men seemed impressed.

"All that about Roscoe might well be true, sir," Clements remarked after thought. "We didn't find out anything of his history, and Miss Chatterton is the sort of girl who might be dazzled by good manners and big talk. But even if it was true, it wouldn't prove murder. And we're still up against our original conclusion: that murder couldn't have been done under the circumstances. What do you say, Pardoe?"

The Inspector hesitated. "I don't deny, sir, I've felt the same dissatisfaction about the case that Major Lethbridge has expressed," he declared, though whether his views were merely diplomatic the CC was not sure. "But I've been brought up by the fact you mention: that under the conditions which existed, murder just couldn't have been committed. If we could suggest any way it could have been done, then I'd be all for reopening the case."

"I know," said Lethbridge, "I admit your point is just. And yet I'm not satisfied. The more I think of the deceased's character, as I knew it myself, the less I can believe in suicide. I grant you that Mr Liddell's story has no bearing on that matter and therefore I shouldn't bring it up, but his story has given new life to the doubt that was already there."

"If we did reopen the case," asked Clements after a pause, "what steps do you suggest we should take?"

"That's not an easy question either," answered Lethbridge, anxious if possible to carry them with him. "There's no use in going over Pardoe's investigation again; I'm satisfied he's given us everything that's to be had. What was in my mind is a different inquiry. I'm inclined to think some knowledge of Roscoe's earlier life might be useful. If we knew that he had always gone straight, I think we could dismiss the affair with an easy mind. If we found previous criminal tendencies we could reconsider the details of the death. Though so far we haven't been able to see it, a clever man might have thought up some trick."

"Tracing his life before he came to this area would be a job for the Yard, don't you think, sir?"

Lethbridge was so taken aback that he almost gave away his satisfaction.

"You think so?" he said doubtfully. "Probably you're right. Well, suppose I have a chat with the Yard, and without asking them to take anything to do with the death, say we'd like a report on Roscoe's history and character. How would that do?"

Lethbridge believed he had been reasonably diplomatic. Clements and Pardoe would think that he had a bee in his bonnet and wouldn't be happy till something was done, but that something would give them no extra work nor would it injure their prestige. They would say to themselves, 'Oh, well, it won't hurt us. Let him get on with it,' and when Clements replied he saw that he had judged them correctly.

"Knowledge of the man's life would certainly be an indication of whether he would contemplate murder to get the money," the super agreed cautiously. "As you say, if this

221

tended to increase our suspicions, we could then consider the next step."

The CC got up. "I'm glad you agree," he declared. "I'll ring up Sir Mortimer and have a word with him."

He did ring up, but only to arrange an appointment. For the detailed conversation he looked forward to, the telephone would be inadequate. Next morning he went up to see the Assistant Commissioner.

– 14 –

THE MACHINERY BEGINS TO CREAK

Superintendent Joseph French was passing through what was for him a slack time. He had been visiting Bath in connection with the distressing murder of an elderly recluse, and since he had returned to the Yard no major cases had come his way. This had given him the opportunity he had been wishing for: to acquaint himself more fully with his new duties as superintendent. He had been clearing out his predecessor's files, which in any case had become overweighted with material. Now in accordance with the usual contrariness of things, it was when his desk was stacked with still unsorted papers that his telephone rang. The fact that the Assistant Commissioner, Sir Mortimer Ellison, wanted to see him immediately did nothing to ease the situation, and some surprisingly lurid language hovered on his lips.

But by the time he reached the AC's room he was the normal French, quiet, unassuming, helpful and competent, or as his brother officers put it, smug. Seated with Sir Mortimer was Major Lethbridge, whom he had previously met on more than one occasion.

"This is Superintendent French," Sir Mortimer was beginning, but Lethbridge got up and shook hands.

"Mr French and I are old friends," he explained. "Congratulations on the 'super'. I was very glad to hear of it."

"Thank you very much, sir," smiled French. "Very kind of you."

Lethbridge turned to the AC. "French and I met in connection with the Arbuthnot case. You remember, French?"

"Yes, indeed, sir," French answered. "Pardoe did some pretty good work over that."

"The Arbuthnot case?" Sir Mortimer put in thoughtfully. "Ah yes, I'd forgotten it for the moment. The butler was murdered by his employer because he had unearthed some dangerous secrets."

"Very nasty case," Lethbridge commented. "Local scandal and all that. Arbuthnot was in everything that was going. It made a lot of unpleasantness."

"I can believe it." Sir Mortimer turned to French. "Major Lethbridge wants to discuss a case with you, French. He says you know something about it through Mr Liddell."

"The Chatterton affair, sir? Yes, Mr Liddell discussed it with me."

"Right. Then will you take the Major to your room. He may want you to undertake some inquiries. If so, do all you can to help him."

"I may have come on a wild goose chase," Lethbridge began when they were settled in French's room, "but I confess that I was never wholly satisfied about Chatterton's death and Mr Liddell's tale has reawakened my dormant suspicions," and he went on to summarise his doubts. "But," he continued, "what I do not see, and neither Clements nor Pardoe can see, is how in the set-up that obtained, murder could have been committed."

"That was my difficulty also, sir. Obviously no one was present at the time of the shot, and therefore if Sir Roland did not fire it himself, it could only have been done by some mechanical means. Nothing of the kind was found, and without human presence it could not have been removed."

Lethbridge laughed. "I realise all that and as you put it, it seems silly to consider the affair further. But in the light of Miss Heath's statement and as one last test I should greatly like to know more of Roscoe's life and character. I mean, suppose he turns out to be an adventurer? Suppose we find him both ingenious and criminal? Should we not then look once more into the possibilities of murder?"

French was not enthusiastic. He agreed – he could not do otherwise – that knowledge of Roscoe's character would undoubtedly be relevant information. Duty made him add that if the Major would like some inquiries to be made, he would be glad to undertake them.

It appeared that this was precisely what the Major had in view. In fact, the point having been established, he got up to prevent further discussion, saying that unless he ran, he would miss his train. French saw him to the door and then went back and looked sadly at his stacks of papers. "The end of that for goodness knows how long!" he told himself. "I know Lethbridge and he'll want one thing after another until the thing develops into a life's work."

With the new case as a case he was by no means pleased. There was nothing to be got out of it and it would mean a lot of useless and boring work. Of course in one sense he might as well spend his time on it as anything else: he could only do a certain amount altogether, and whatever it was, he'd be paid for it just the same. However it was more satisfactory to work on something in which one believed.

His thoughts went back to that tragic event in the sun trap and he began racking his brains to visualise some way in which murder could have been committed. But the more he considered it, the more overwhelming the arguments for suicide appeared. Then he remembered that for him this was not the point. He had expressed this opinion and in spite of it the CC had decided that further inquiries should be made. He therefore must do what he had been asked: look into Roscoe's previous life, and presumably the relations between him and Dulcie Heath. How could that best be done?

He began by rereading the report on the inquest as well as the notes he had taken after his interview with Liddell. Each item he weighed with deliberation. When he had finished there was only one thing which looked promising – in the sense that every other point had already been investigated to the nth power. That was Liddell's statement that any reference to Harley Street seemed to embarrass Dulcie. If everything were in order, why should it? He wondered if he could learn anything about the couple from Burt?

As any approach to the surgeon at the Harley Street house would necessarily become known to Dulcie, he rang him up at his home and begged for an evening interview. Burt fixed that night.

French was impressed by the surgeon. He was pleasant and friendly, and for a man of his eminence, unassuming. He received French in his library, offered him a drink and a cigarette, chatted for a few moments and then asked what he could do for him.

"I've come on rather delicate business, sir," French said and explained that a suspected but unproven crime had led to his inquiry. "You had in your employment some time ago a man named Frank Roscoe, and you have at present a lady, Miss Dulcie Heath. We should like to know anything you can tell us about both these people."

Burt stared. "Good Lord!" he exclaimed, "you don't mean to say you suspect either of crime?"

"We don't *suspect* either, no," French answered, "but some circumstances with which Mr Roscoe is connected require explanation. Miss Heath is not personally involved. It's only in her relations with Roscoe that we're interested."

Burt continued to stare. "I see," he returned, "or rather, I don't. However, curiosity on my part would doubtless be untactful. Carry on, Superintendent. Ask what you will and I'll try to answer it."

"Thank you. Then what can you tell me about Roscoe?"

"Very little, I'm afraid. He came to me on Miss Heath's recommendation; I understood he had just been demobilised. I saw him, liked what I saw, and engaged him."

"Did he give you satisfaction while with you, sir?"

"Complete. He was careful and painstaking and efficient. I could not wish for anyone better."

"Well, that's certainly high praise. You say he was efficient. Does that mean merely that he did his job well, or that he had high qualities of, let us say, resource and ingenuity?"

Burt considered this. "In his work there was little opportunity for resource and ingenuity, but he certainly did cope adequately with any situations which arose."

"I follow. Can you give me the dates when he went to you and when he left?"

For the first time Burt hesitated. "I don't think so. They're in my Harley Street records, not here. But he came about eighteen months ago and stayed for about a year."

"I'm much obliged, sir. If you could let me have his references, if he gave any, that would cover Roscoe."

"He gave me the rector of the parish in which he was brought up and his Army commander. I'm ashamed to say I didn't take either of them up. In fact I built more than I should have done on Miss Heath's recommendation. Roscoe was hard up and I advanced him some of his wages to buy proper clothes."

"Very good of you, sir, if I may say so. Now I'd be grateful for the same particulars about Miss Heath."

"Miss Heath had some training as a nurse, though she is not technically qualified. She also had considerable business experience in a shipping office. By nature she has good manners, in character she is hard-working and efficient. These assets made her just the woman I wanted. She saw my advertisement, applied, and I appointed her."

"And she also has been satisfactory?"

"Very. I consider myself lucky to have her."

"Perhaps you'd kindly let me have her references? Could you ring up in the morning?"

"Certainly."

When next day French received the addresses, he stood for a moment contemplating the heap of papers on his desk. Then he smiled darkly and stretched out his hand for his house telephone. As a result, four of his subordinates received instructions, two to trace Frank's career as a young man and in the Army, the other two, Dulcie's adventures in her training hospital and shipping office respectively. Then, his conscience somewhat eased, he sat down and drew over the first file.

Inspector David Horne was used to getting commissions from French and as a rule he was pleased when this occurred. He found French sympathetic and helpful, ready to make allowances for difficulties and to give credit where it was due. As a result he never spared himself in trying to obtain in the shortest possible time the results French required.

He soon found that the rector Frank had given as reference had retired, but from inquiries in the parish he learnt that Frank had entered the Medical School of London University. He therefore went on to see what the college authorities could tell him. Sending in his card in a sealed envelope to the registrar, he was presently admitted. Dr Nuttall received him with easy, old-fashioned courtesy.

When Horne had explained his requirements Dr Nuttall turned to an index and withdrew a card. "Roscoe, Frank Seymour," he read. "Entered the medical school on the 16th of September, 1931, and left in August, 1935 without taking his degree. That's your man, I presume?"

"Yes, sir. Can you tell me from what school he came to the University?"

"Redwood House, Leicester."

"Had Roscoe a good record there?"

"Yes. Nothing remarkable one way or another."

"And while there? Was he a good worker?"

"Oh yes, no complaint whatever of that."

"His abilities, sir? Would you say he was specially able?"

"Yes and no. The record says that if he was interested he could do splendid work: he was exceptionally ingenious and resourceful and had plenty of initiative. But with routine work he was apt to get slack."

"Many gifted people are like that, are they not? You say he left without taking his degree. How was that?"

As he read further down the card, Dr Nuttall's manner changed slightly. He glanced questioningly at Horne and seemed to grow wary. Horne's interest waxed correspondingly.

"It appears his father died and did not leave the money that was expected. Fees, I presume, were the difficulty."

"I thought, sir, there was some system of grants to meet such cases?"

Dr Nuttall hesitated, then appeared to make up his mind. "Well, I suppose I had better tell you the whole affair. Grants are obtainable in certain cases, but these are at the discretion of the governing body. In this case they did not see their way to offer one."

"Oh," said Horne. "How was that?"

The registrar shrugged. "You said these inquiries were confidential. Very good. During Roscoe's last year several sums of money disappeared: I needn't go into details except to say that as no locks were broken, the thief must have had keys. There was no proof as to who was guilty, but Roscoe was suspected. He was not sent down: as I say there was no proof. But when for other reasons he had to leave, nothing was done to retain him."

"I see. Did the disappearances stop when he left?"

"They did," the registrar answered dryly.

"Apart from these suspected thefts, was his character good?"

"Oh yes. There were no other complaints."

"I suppose you don't know what happened to him after he left?"

"No, I'm afraid not."

This seemed all the information available, and when Horne had expressed his thanks, he took his leave. An hour later the typed fruits of the interview were on French's desk.

French was immediately interested. So far all reports of Roscoe had made him out a paragon, but here was an indication of the cloven hoof. Sadly French saw that further investigation was unavoidable.

The first step would be to find out what Roscoe had done after leaving college. As to this, Miss Heath would probably be his best source of information. French was anxious to see her in any case because of Liddell's statement about her embarrassment on the mention of Harley Street. He felt that a few discreet questions on both subjects might not be out of order.

At this point reports from two other of his men were handed in. From these it appeared that Dulcie Heath had displayed at both hospital and shipping office the same excellent qualities as she was now showing with Burt. In character she certainly seemed efficient, hard-working and trustworthy. Why, more than ever, the embarrassment?

French considered for a few moments, then once again he sent for Inspector Horne.

It was now several days since Dulcie's second interview with Anthony Liddell, and so far she had heard nothing as to the subsequent course of events. When she left his rooms she had felt some anxiety, and as day slowly succeeded day it grew ever keener. Why had Liddell not told her what was happening? She would have given a large proportion of her illicit takings to have known.

She had seen nothing of Frank during these days, for which indeed she was profoundly thankful. He had written that he had been asked to stay on for a week or two in connection with the clearing up of Sir Roland's papers, as Lady Chatterton considered getting someone else to finish the book. This work was heavy and prevented him from coming to Town. Dulcie replied tactfully that she under-stood he must be swamped with details, and would look forward to seeing him when things became easier. In the meantime everything with her was going on normally, and there was nothing except their own longing to necessitate a meeting.

Then at last one evening after supper she had a caller, a young athletic-looking man with good features and excellent manners. He seemed friendly as he announced his name, Detective Inspector Horne of Scotland Yard.

Instantly sheer panic descended on Dulcie. Frank? Harley Street! The fraud? For a dreadful moment she could not even move. Then with determination she pulled herself together.

"Oh yes, Mr Horne?" she answered unsteadily. "What can I do for you?"

"I'm sorry to be a nuisance, Miss Heath," he apologised, "but I've come about a statement you made recently to Mr Liddell." She breathed once more. "He consulted Super-intendent French of our service and Mr French would like to discuss some points with you. He cannot very well leave the Yard, so he sent me to ask if you would be so good as to come and see him instead?"

Her relief was intense. "Oh yes," she answered, "of course I will. When would he like to see me?"

"Well," he smiled, "no time like the present, is there? I have a car here, and if you can come now, I should be glad to drive you there and back."

Feeling that it would be wise, she thanked him and said she would be ready in a moment.

Under normal circumstances a visit to Scotland Yard would have been to Dulcie a prospect full of interest. She had read about the "grim building on the banks of the

Thames" in detective stories, and felt that in one sense she was familiar with its austere rooms and echoing corridors and all that went on therein. Unhappily this occasion was not normal. That gnawing knowledge of what her interference might have done together with the thought of the fraud spoilt everything. She could not overcome the fear it inspired.

But there was nothing terrifying in Horne's manner. He drove quickly and skilfully and for the most part in silence. When occasionally he did speak it was to make some shrewd and humorous comment on the people or things they passed. If it had not been for her laden conscience she would have found him entertaining: as it was, she wondered if he was merely trying to put her off her guard.

Superintendent French, when after traversing the echoing corridors she reached his austere room, was equally pleasant. "This is very kind of you, Miss Heath," he told her. "Won't you sit down? Cigarette?" He handed a box over and produced his lighter. "Too bad dragging you out at this hour of the evening, but we understood you were engaged during the daytime."

"I am," she answered. "As you probably know, I'm receptionist and secretary to Mr Burt of Harley Street."

He nodded. "Yes, of course. It's about your statement to Mr Liddell, as I suppose Horne told you. I'm investigating the points you raised and I hope we'll soon get to the bottom of the affair and have easy minds."

"I hope so indeed, Mr French."

"Perhaps you can help me further. I asked you to call because there were one or two questions which you may be able to answer."

She was regaining confidence. This opening did not suggest trouble: or was it just the police way? "Of course I shall be glad to help," she declared.

"As a matter of fact," French admitted confidentially, "I thought you'd feel like that, so I had the less compunction in asking you to come. Now first about Mr Roscoe. I understand that he left London University in August, 1935, and started work with Mr Burt on the 11th of March last year. I want to know what he did between those dates. Can you tell me?"

"Partly. I'm afraid he had rather a bad time. Probably you know that he believed his father well off, and it was a great shock when he found he had left practically nothing."

"I can imagine it."

"For a while Mr Roscoe tried for the sort of position he could do well, a secretaryship or something of that kind. But he couldn't get anything to suit and at last he took a job as clerk to a builder. Not what he wanted, but the best he could find."

"Where was that?"

"I really don't remember the address: in South London somewhere."

"Did he stay there till he went to Mr Burt?"

"Oh no, he didn't like it and after some time he got another post, clerk to a bookmaker. He didn't stay there long either."

"Do you know the address?"

"I'm afraid I don't. It's a long time ago, you understand."

"What did he do after that?"

"He took a labourer's job. It was dreadful for him, but he couldn't get anything else. I don't know exactly what it was except that it was in a garage."

"What garage was that?"

"Goodwin's in Hammersmith Broadway."

"I see. Was he there long?"

"I can't say how long. He left it about the beginning of the War."

"Do you know why he left?"

"Some dispute with the manager about overtime, he said. The manager seems to have been a brute. In any case Mr Roscoe was well out of it. It wasn't the place for a man of his ability."

"Then he was called up, I suppose?"

"Yes, he was six years with the Army."

"And after he was demobbed he went to Mr Burt?"

"Some time after. He had spent his gratuity."

"And you got him the post?"

"I mentioned his name to Mr Burt, yes. Mr Burt interviewed him and gave him a start."

"I see. How do you like your work with Mr Burt?"

Was she mistaken or was he looking at her with particular keenness? Once again panic surged up in her mind. She strove with all her strength to reply naturally, though she was not sure that she entirely succeeded. But he answered quite pleasantly and she felt sure he suspected nothing.

"By the way," he went on, "I was forgetting to ask you, have you ever seen this man?" He picked up a photograph from his desk and handed it over. "Take it to the window."

Hopelessly puzzled, Dulcie gazed at the frowning visage of a complete stranger. She shook her head.

"No?" said French, taking back the card. "Oh well, it doesn't matter. I think that's all I want to know and I'm much obliged for what you've told me. We'll go carefully into the possibilities at Jasmine Lodge, and if we learn anything, you'll hear about it. Now if you like, Inspector Horne will drive you home."

Again relief filled Dulcie's mind. All had gone well. She had told her tale and quite obviously there was no suspicion. She got up.

"Mr Horne needn't trouble to do that," she answered. "I should like a breath of air and I'll walk part of the way home."

French rang and Horne entered. "Will you show Miss Heath out, Horne," he said. "She says she'll walk home." He smiled at Dulcie. "I have to send him to the door with you, otherwise they wouldn't let you leave."

She thought it a grim reminder, but French was very pleasant as he shook hands.

One small incident took place during her walk with Horne along the corridors. As they turned a corner they came to a section brilliantly illuminated. Horne grumbled when he saw it and turned the extra light off at a switch.

"Careless devils," he complained. "They make photographic enlargements here and they leave the lights on. Other people are very remiss, aren't they, Miss Heath?" and he grinned disarmingly.

When she reached her flat she felt almost contented. She did not think she had said anything to injure Frank and quite obviously not the slightest suspicion as to the fraud had entered the minds of any of them.

HIGH FINANCE

French also was not dissatisfied with the interview. He had obtained what might prove valuable information. The address of the garage in which Roscoe had worked might lead to the revelation of the man's activities between the time he left the University and his joining the Army. This, together with a report from the War Office, might indicate his predisposition or otherwise to murder.

But French's suspicions of Dulcie herself had also been strengthened. Liddell had been right. A reference to Harley Street undoubtedly caused her embarrassment, indeed he thought, even fear. For this reason he had rung for Horne in code, which had the effect of not only summoning the Inspector, but of arranging for a photograph of Dulcie to be taken while she was on her way out. By a hoary trick French had also obtained her fingerprints. This was on general principles, for he did not at the moment require either.

Having a little time at his disposal, he decided that he would himself visit the garage at Hammersmith. It proved a large establishment and a lot of work seemed to be in hand. He asked for the manager.

"My call has nothing to do with your garage, Mr Hudson," he explained. "I want some confidential information about one of your former employees, if you will be kind enough to give it to me. The man's name is Frank Roscoe and he is believed to have left your service about the beginning of the War."

"Roscoe?" repeated the manager somewhat grimly. "Yes, I remember the man. Is he in trouble?"

"No, but he's the victim of some suspicious circumstances and we want to be sure that nothing's wrong."

The manager nodded understandingly. "I can believe it," he declared. Then crossing the room, he looked through a file and withdrew a card. "Here's his record. He came to us in October, 1937 and left in January, 1940. He started as a mechanic's labourer, but we found him an extraordinarily clever natural mechanic though untrained, if I may put it that way. Owing to trade union difficulties I could not promote him directly to a mechanic's position, so I made him a sort of handyman, one who would do any kind of unusual job not covered by union rules. He was willing to tackle anything, and was so successful in his results that he created a good deal of ill will among the others. In fact I had to pay him some money privately, so that the rest should not know what he was getting."

"I know that sort of jealousy is pretty widespread," French agreed. "You found he had ingenuity and resource and initiative?"

"To a marked degree. He could have risen to any position if he had applied himself."

"He did not do so?"

"No. He had to be interested in a thing before he'd put work into it. About routine he was slack and careless."

"Why did he leave you, Mr Hudson?"

The manager looked doubtful. "As a matter of fact, Chief Inspector, I got rid of him because of an unproved suspicion. I don't want to prejudice you against him."

Horne's report from the London University recurred to French. "I appreciate your scruples, but you can at least tell me this: was his dismissal connected with money?"

"Yes," admitted Hudson, "it was."

"Some money was missing and you suspected Roscoe, but could not prove he took it."

Hudson seemed astonished. "How did you know that, Mr French? You're perfectly correct."

"I didn't know it," French admitted. "I was guessing from a similar previous episode."

"Well, whatever you guessed from, you're right enough. Money disappeared from the cash drawer. The thief must have had keys for both office and drawer, for nothing was broken. The thing went on at intervals for a considerable time. We kept a watch but we never caught anyone. Roscoe was always about the premises when it happened, you understand: legitimately of course, his duties brought him there."

"Did you report the matter to the police?"

"Yes, but they were no more successful than we had been." Hudson's voice was dry, but there was a twinkle in his eye.

"Poor lot, aren't they?" said French. "After Roscoe left did the losses cease?"

The manager nodded emphatically. "Yes, and that made me feel that the dismissal was justified."

The parallel with what had taken place at the University was so striking that French felt no doubt of Roscoe's guilt was possible. It might now be taken that the man was ingenious and resourceful, untroubled by moral scruples, and would go to considerable lengths for money. And were not these the very qualities required in a murderer of Sir Roland Chatterton? There was certainly enough in it to justify Lethbridge and Liddell in their desire for investigation. French determined that he would not give the case up until he had satisfied himself beyond yea or nay as to the truth.

Reaching his room, he found a report on Frank's Army career. It was an ordinary enough recital. Frank had been with the Eighth Army from El Alamein to Florence. He had been well conducted without specially distinguishing himself, and had been promoted sergeant in the normal passage of time. A table of his dates was appended.

For some time French considered these facts in his slow methodical way without seeing that they contained anything relative to his inquiry. Then suddenly a point struck him.

Frank had reached Liverpool and been demobbed only ten days before he started work with Burt. Yet according to Miss Heath, he was so hard up when he came to Town that he had to take the first job he could find, even though he was qualified for a much better one. This was confirmed by Burt, who had advanced money to buy a new suit. Why was he hard up? He should have had a comfortable gratuity. What had happened to it?

French recalled Dulcie's words. He had asked if Frank had gone to Burt after being demobbed and she had answered, "Some time after. He had spent his gratuity."

It now appeared that "Some time after" was only ten days. Was this, French wondered, quite straight on Dulcie's part? Of course the statement was literally true, but was it not intended to suggest a longer period during which the gratuity could reasonably disappear? How could a man in Frank's position spend all that money in ten days? French did not believe it normally possible.

Then another point flashed into his mind and he sat up, really excited.

From Burt's, Frank had become private secretary to Sir Roland Chatterton, a wealthy man maintaining an expensive household and living in a luxurious manner. Frank moreover was there as one of the family. Now he could not possibly have obtained or carried on such a job unless he was not only well dressed, but had the necessary possessions to play the part, from a dress suit and good toilet fittings down to incidentals such as a cigarette case and lighter. But these would have cost far more money than the man could have saved. Where had that money come from?

It looked extremely like as if Frank had stolen money both at the University and the garage. French sat drumming his fingers on his desk and gazing unseeingly before him...There was also Dulcie Heath's embarrassment...

That evening he rang up Burt.

"Sorry to trouble you again, Mr Burt, but there's a matter which I feel I must discuss with you, and at your home rather than at Harley Street. Will you please say when you can see me?"

"What about this evening?"

"Nothing could be better, sir."

"Then say nine-ish."

Burt was waiting for him in his study. "Coffee or whisky or beer? They're all here," he invited.

"Nothing I'd like better than a cup of coffee," French answered. "Your hospitality suggests that I must have more frequent business with you in the evenings."

"There's a reason for everything, isn't there? You wanted to talk to me?"

"Yes, and on a rather delicate subject: that of your finances. Tell me in confidence, sir, have you missed any money lately?"

Burt stared, then shook his head. "That's an unexpected question, Superintendent. The answer is no, I haven't. Why do you ask?"

"Just a suspicion, I hope unfounded. As a matter of fact there's reason to suppose that Roscoe is a clever thief and that while with you he obtained a considerable sum of money above his salary."

"Good Lord! That's a most disquieting suggestion. I sincerely hope you're wrong."

"I may be. As I say, it's only a suspicion. But it's rather worse than I've told you. The real fear is that he and Miss Heath have been robbing you."

"Miss Heath also? Oh no! Impossible." Burt shook his head. "I don't believe it for a moment. I've missed nothing."

"I'm afraid we shall have to go into it and make sure."

Burt hesitated, then shrugged. "If there's a doubt I must of course agree to that. How should we set about it?"

"I don't know the details of your financial operations," French pointed out. "I regret to have to ask you to describe them. Then we'll have to go through your papers."

Burt did not seem anxious for this. "I suppose you're right," he admitted gloomily. "Not easy to find the time."

"This is Wednesday evening. What about making a night of it at Harley Street tomorrow?"

"Yes, I could manage that. Say eight-thirty tomorrow evening?"

"Excellent, sir. I'll be there. I'd like to bring one of my men who understands figures. You agree? Right. And just one other thing. If you see Miss Heath, you mustn't let her suspect. Your manner must be quite normal."

"Easier said than done."

"Begin by telling her you have a headache."

As French turned homewards he felt his case was progressing better than he could have hoped.

Promptly at eight-thirty on the Thursday evening French presented himself at 779 Harley Street. He was accompanied by a young Inspector, who though not a chartered accountant, had taken part of the course and could find his way through a complicated mass of figures as well as anyone. Burt had already arrived and he led them to his consulting-room.

"This is Inspector Gould," French explained, "and as he knows more about finance than I do, I propose to turn the proceedings over to him."

Burt shook hands and Gould took up his tale, asking Burt to explain his financial system in so far as it touched his secretary and attendant.

"The attendant," Burt answered, "has nothing whatever to do with finance, and unless Roscoe was working in some special way with Miss Heath, he is necessarily out of this."

"I understood the suggestion was that he might be doing so. Perhaps you would explain Miss Heath's duties?"

"She has a good deal of control, but is surrounded by safeguards which I believe made fraud impossible. First," and Burt went on to describe his methods. As Gould listened his face lengthened.

"It's a pretty good system, sir, if I may say so," he commented. "It's not easy at first sight to find a flaw. The only point which suggests itself is that you don't see your patients' cheques: only Miss Heath handles them. But that seems to be adequately covered by the bank receipts."

Burt made a gesture of agreement. "Exactly. If Miss Heath were to cash a cheque and keep back part of the money for herself, which I suppose is what you had in mind," he looked at French, "she could not get the bank receipts which she provides."

"I follow all that," French returned, "but I'm still not satisfied. If my suspicions are justified, we're up against a very able adversary."

"The system certainly seems all right," Gould remarked, "but we've yet to learn how it's been carried out. If you agree, Mr Burt, I'd suggest a look at your books."

At this second hint Burt nodded. "Most of them are in Miss Heath's room. I have here only her bi-weekly statements and my own private ledger, which she does not handle." He crossed the room to a safe and withdrew a bundle of slips and a small book. "These are Miss Heath's statements of my fees. I know those are right, as I've already told her what to charge. As I've explained, when she leaves these she also leaves the paying-in book with the bank's receipt for the same amounts. I invariably compare statements and counterfoils and never once have I found an error. The totals of the statements I copy into my ledger, as you can see if you look."

"You say Miss Heath keeps the paying-in book. What about a look through her desk?"

"Have you a key, Mr Burt?" French asked.

"I have one," the surgeon answered, "but I don't believe I could find it at the moment."

"Never mind," said French. "We'll manage without. Let us go and investigate."

Burt led the way and French sat down on Dulcie's chair. Taking a tool from his pocket, he began to work. Presently there was a click and the lid was free.

"I always think Mr French could make more by visiting people's houses during their absence than by working at the Yard," Gould remarked to Burt. "What do you say, sir?"

Burt agreed that French's skill might be useful, but French thought that insufficient valuables were kept in desks to make it worth his while. "Now, Gould, here you are," he went on. "Have a run through this little lot."

For some time the two officers worked in silence, removing papers, examining them and replacing them in precisely their former position. Then at last French sat back in his chair.

"Everything there seems OK," he announced in a puzzled tone. "What's your view, Gould?"

The young man agreed. There was no slightest sign of anything amiss.

"It looks as if we'd been barking up the wrong tree," went on French. He turned to Burt. "If so, I'm terribly sorry for giving you all this trouble. But our reasons for suspicion were so good that I daren't give up."

"What more do you propose?"

French shrugged. "The only thing I can suggest is that we consult your bank people tomorrow."

As French spoke he got up from the desk. Then suddenly he stopped, staring at the ground. He pointed.

"What are those wires for, Mr Burt? There, leading up the leg of the desk?"

Burt shook his head helplessly. "I haven't the faintest idea," he declared. "I never saw them before."

"Probably there was a desk lamp at one time. Just follow those up, will you, Gould."

The Inspector was already doing so. "They lead to a flat box under the desk," he exclaimed. "And here's a switch, almost concealed, but arranged so that anyone seated at the desk could operate it."

"Switch on," French directed.

Gould did so. "I'm not sure what the contraption is," he went on, "but it looks uncommonly like a loud speaker."

"A speaker!" Burt sounded incredulous. "Nonsense! How could a speaker be there?"

"Follow the wires in the other direction," French counselled.

"They come from this bell," Gould presently announced. "What bell is this, Mr Burt?"

"It's from the consulting-room. One ring is for Miss Heath and two for the attendant."

"This is a new one on me, sir," Gould declared. "I cannot see what it's for."

"Well," said French, "someone has put it in, and since Mr Burt knows nothing about it, the purpose was probably not too good. Will you ring your bell, sir? Perhaps that may help us?"

Burt left the room. His footsteps died away along the corridor. There was a momentary silence and then very faintly they again became audible. Still more softly came the sound of shuffling papers, then the bell rang stridently.

The two Scotland Yard men looked at each other. "Find out if he moved papers before he pressed the button," directed French, a little breathlessly.

Gould hurried to the consulting-room to put the question. Then the function of the installation became clear as crystal. French did not hear the question, but distinctly he heard Burt's answer, and the sound came from the box under the desk.

He joined the others. "It's a speaker all right," he told them, "and it's arranged so that anything you say at your desk, Mr Burt, can be heard by Miss Heath. The mike must be here somewhere. Find it, Gould."

The discovery was not long delayed. The fact that only the push was connected to the wires led them directly to their goal.

"She wanted to hear what you said to your patients," French went on. "Now why? What advantage could that have been to her?"

Burt shook his head helplessly. He seemed overwhelmed. "I can't imagine," he said with a baffled expression, "and I shouldn't have believed it if I hadn't seen it with my own eyes."

"Well," French declared, "there's our clue. If we find out what the installation was for, we'll be on to everything."

"It's more than the actual installation," Burt continued as if bemused. "It's just incredible that this girl who seemed so competent and so anxious to help me should be working against me, for what else could she have been doing?"

"Money," said French; "somehow I feel sure they were robbing you. Now tomorrow I should like without Miss Heath's knowledge to take her various books to the bank. Could you arrange to send her somewhere so as to leave the coast clear?"

"Oh yes, I'll send her with a case of special apparatus to one of my colleagues. I'll ring him up now."

Burt did so. "That was the principal of the Sanatorium at Petworth," he said. "He'll ring me up tomorrow morning and ask urgently for a special substance. I'll send it off with her at once and it'll take her most of the day."

"That will be fine, sir. Then till tomorrow."

It was after ten next morning when Burt telephoned to say that Dulcie had just left for Petworth. In fifteen minutes French and Gould reached Harley Street.

"I've managed to put off a patient," Burt explained, "so I'll have time to go round with you to the bank. Then I'm afraid I must leave you to do your own researches."

"We'll see to that, sir," French answered. "I suggest that you should come in our car. No point in your chauffeur learning of your visit."

"If it wasn't such an abominably serious matter," Burt declared, "I'd feel like a child playing some silly game. I find it hard to believe, Superintendent, that you're right about a theft. I've been through my ledger and my fees are normal. If I've been robbed, it can only have been to an infinitesimal degree."

"That mike was put in for a purpose, Mr Burt," French answered stubbornly. "We've got to know what it was."

This being unanswerable, Burt attempted no reply and a few minutes later they were shown into the bank manager's room. Mr Harcourt looked shocked when Burt introduced the detectives and explained the purpose of their visit. He instantly pledged all the resources of the bank to aid in learning the truth. Burt then excused himself, and the manager having sent for certain books, they got down to business. Gould read out the counterfoils in Dulcie's paying-in book, and Harcourt found and compared the entries made from the corresponding slips. Nine were checked and found accurate, but at the tenth Harcourt called a halt.

"Half a moment," he interrupted. "What amount did you say?"

" 'Fortescue, cheque for £157 10,' " read Gould. "All paid to current account."

"In other words," put in French, "Fortescue, 150 guineas."

"But I've got a cheque for £189," said Harcourt.

"It makes it easier to put it into guineas," French insisted. "One hundred and eighty guineas."

The manager ignored this. "What's the date of your item?" He looked at Gould.

"Sixth of August."

"But this one's the 6th of August too. I don't understand it. Show me your counterfoil. Yes, that looks all right. I'll have a search made. There may by chance have been two cheques from Fortescue that day."

"Only one is shown in Miss Heath's book."

Harcourt nodded as he rang for his chief clerk. He asked him to turn up the original paying-in slip for the transaction. This showed the amount paid in as £189 and therefore differed from Dulcie's counterfoil. Further search confirmed also that only one cheque from Fortescue had been paid in.

The three men stared at one another. Then French asked for the use of the telephone. The manager pushed it nearer. French made a call.

"Mr Burt?" he said. "Can you recollect a recent patient named Fortescue?"

"Sir Ridley? Yes of course. I operated on him a few weeks ago."

"Do you remember the amount of your fee?"

"Well at this date I couldn't be absolutely sure, but I believe it was 150 guineas."

"It couldn't have been 180?"

"A hundred and eighty? I don't think so. That would have been unusually high for the operation. Why do you ask?"

"A doubtful figure here, sir," French said easily. "What you say has helped us."

He replaced the receiver. "It looks," he said slowly, "as if that was that."

For a moment no one spoke, Gould seemingly pleased and happy, French non-committal, and Harcourt obviously divided between amazement and vexation.

"Don't let us leap to conclusions," French advised. "Suppose we carry on with a few more items?"

Further research put the matter beyond doubt. Five days later a cheque for 160 guineas had been entered as 120 and a cheque for forty had been cashed. Every four or five days after that similar transactions had occurred. With every inward cheque larger than that shown on Dulcie's paying-in counterfoil there was a cheque withdrawing the excess, and when they found that Burt had not received these monies, they felt they had reached finality. With thanks they took leave of the perturbed Mr Harcourt.

With accuracy they replaced Dulcie's books in her desk, and feeling that the scheme involved duplicates, searched till they found them. Then having made an appointment with Burt for that evening, they returned to the Yard.

Burt's horror when he learned what had taken place seemed to French wholly exaggerated. "My patients?" he groaned. "I've defrauded them! I've overcharged them and I've met them afterwards and talked to them as if nothing were wrong!"

French tried to comfort him. "You're not responsible, sir. They've been swindled by a clever thief, for we may feel sure the scheme was Roscoe's and not Miss Heath's. But since it was without your knowledge or consent you can't be blamed."

"I feel I am to blame and I must pay every penny back."

"If you pay half back you'll be dealing generously with them," declared French. "But there, I'm interfering in what's not my business. Sorry."

French had real difficulty in persuading Burt not to move in the matter without permission from the Yard. At first the surgeon would not hear of delay, and it was not until French grew absolutely threatening that he came to heel.

"You force me, sir, to speak bluntly. If you do anything to defeat justice you may have murder on your conscience. The matter which brought us here is not the theft of a few guineas from your patients. It's murder. We think this Roscoe has murdered for money, though as yet we can't prove it. If you let Miss Heath know what we have learnt she will give Roscoe the tip and he may destroy vital evidence. In such a case you will be responsible for his escape and will risk a charge of accessory after the fact."

It was this last phrase that did it. Burt reluctantly promised full co-operation.

For some time further they discussed the affair and gradually all its details became clear in their minds. They saw what the mike and loud speaker were for, noted the part played by the duplicate books, and realised that whoever produced the rubber stamp must have had at least Roscoe's skill.

"It took a pretty ingenious mind to devise the scheme," French said finally, "and what's more, it has taken courage and a lot of ability to work it. Miss Heath must be something of a psychologist. She had not only to make sure that no mention of the amount of the fee was made, but also to determine from the patient's conversation whether he was of the type that would not refer to it afterwards if he thought it excessive."

"A few think it beneath their dignity to speak of money," answered Burt. "They want to show they are above such mundane considerations and can meet any calls no matter how great."

"Roscoe doubtless built his fraud on a knowledge of that weakness. All the same it was a dangerous game and must sooner or later have been discovered."

"Probably by then Roscoe would have fixed it so that there'd only be proof against the girl," suggested Gould.

French nodded. "More than likely, but we'll get him all the same. Well, Mr Burt, we must go back to the Yard, and you'll take no action till you hear further."

Before turning in French reported by telephone to Sir Mortimer Ellison, and having obtained his approval, rang up Major Lethbridge and arranged a meeting for the following morning.

– 16 –

A GLEAM OF LIGHT

When French reached police headquarters at Staines he found that Lethbridge had called Superintendent Clements and Inspector Pardoe into conference to receive his report. French made his statement in detail and all three seemed much impressed by his revelations.

"There!" Lethbridge said triumphantly, "that's just what I expected! Not the details of the fraud of course, but that Roscoe was that type of man. From what Mr French has told us, he undoubtedly has the qualifications and character to commit a baffling murder. And he had the motive. Various witnesses have confirmed the statement about his relations with Miss Chatterton. And of course she comes in for a packet."

"We seem back to our original snag," French declared, "how he could have done it."

"That's it, Mr French," put in Clements heavily. "That's what held us from taking further action. I think we're all agreed, sir," he looked at the CC, "that as long as we can't see how the murder could have been committed, our hands are tied. If once we saw that, I for one would be in favour of reopening the case."

"The Super's put my view also, sir," Pardoe added. "We've discussed it several times."

"Yes, of course that's right," Lethbridge agreed. "But with this fresh information I don't feel that we can drop the matter. What do you say, Super?"

Clements moved his great bulk uneasily. "I'm bound to admit I agree with you and Mr French. I didn't think there was anything in it at first, but this information about the fraud alters the situation. All the same there are serious difficulties in any murder theory. Apart altogether from the method, there's the question of the attendant. Could Roscoe be guilty without Boone knowing? Or were they both in it? That would seem to me hard to believe."

The CC sighed. "What do you say to that, Mr French?"

"I see the Super's difficulty of course, sir: we all must. And that leads on to what we should do. I've thought a good deal about it and I can see only one possible line."

"And what's that?"

"A detailed investigation into Roscoe's life since he went to Jasmine Lodge. I looked at it this way. If he committed the murder, he must have taken a number of steps to bring it about. An investigation would certainly reveal some of them. If we find one action that can't be explained normally, I think we've got him."

"I'm sure we should have."

"And that," went on French, "brings us to our immediate problem: should we arrest Roscoe at once?"

"On what charge?" asked Clements.

"Conspiring with Dulcie Heath to defraud certain of Mr Burt's patients."

"But have you actual proof that he did so?"

"No," answered French, "though I believe that if we searched their rooms we'd get it. But I don't think proof matters. It would simply mean that we'd hold him while we went into the murder."

"It's rather a nice point," Lethbridge said doubtfully. "On the one hand an arrest would make the murder inquiry easier. On the other it would certainly be more satisfactory to find the method first."

With this all the others were in agreement and the conference then went into committee of ways and means. That Clements and Pardoe thought the inquiry should be made, but did not want to make it themselves, soon became clear to Lethbridge, and the more he thought over the problem, the less he blamed them. He believed it highly undesirable that Roscoe should become aware of the inquiry, yet he could not himself see how the information could be secretly obtained. However as far as he was concerned there was one obvious step to be taken and he took it. He turned to French.

"I think, Mr French, we are going to have to ask you if you'll undertake the inquiry: both Clements and Pardoe are full up with other work. Sir Mortimer gave me to understand he would agree?"

"Oh, yes, sir, I've had instructions to do whatever you want."

"Good. Then I'll apply officially for your continued help. As to the question of the arrest, it seems to me that this is entirely outside our jurisdiction. Therefore do what you think best about it."

French, who had no illusions as to the difficulty of the task, smiled inwardly at the CC's neat solution and the satisfaction with which it was received. He could not but agree, and when Lethbridge had promised him every help that the local force could supply, the conference came to an end.

When the CC had gone Clements turned to French. "Anything you'd like to see while you're here?" he asked. "Pardoe, what can we show the Superintendent?"

"What about going over the file with him, sir?" Pardoe asked.

French agreed that this might be useful and Pardoe gave him copies of the photographs which had been taken of the body, the sun trap, and the various residents of Jasmine Lodge, together with enlarged photographs of the typescript of the threatening letter and its envelope, and the expert's report declaring that the bullet lodged in the wound had been fired from the pistol found on the grass. He explained that Roscoe was an excellent amateur mechanic and alone used Sir Roland's finely-equipped workshop. Pardoe then took him out to Jasmine Lodge and they inspected the sun trap, grounds and workshop, even penetrating into the house on the excuse of wanting to see Lady Chatterton, whom they had previously noticed driving out in the car. Indeed when French left Staines he felt he knew as much of the case as did Pardoe.

The question of the arrest of Roscoe was considered again later in the day when French went to report to Sir Mortimer. French repeated the arguments which had already been advanced. The AC thought for some moments without speaking.

"You know the implications of such a situation as well as I do, French," he said at length. "Obviously we don't want to make an arrest until the essentials of the case are complete. Details may properly be filled in after it, but not fundamentals. Now here you cannot see how murder could have been committed. That would appear to me not a detail, but very much a fundamental. The general rule therefore would be: don't arrest until you clear up this point. On the other hand we have to make exceptions in exceptional cases. Are there such exceptions here?"

"It would be convenient to have Roscoe out of the way of course," French answered, "but it's not necessary."

"That's what I think too. Well, suppose you concentrate on method. When you've worked at it a bit we'll consider the arrests again."

This was not very satisfactory to French, and as he tried to think out a programme, a well-known feeling began to take possession of him. Frustration! In how many cases which had started promisingly, had he been brought up against a blank wall upon which all his efforts could make no impression! How often had he looked defeat in the face! How often had he actually been defeated! On the other hand how often, as dawn follows darkness, had this ghastly frustration been the prelude to success! How often when things seemed at their worst had they taken a turn for the better!

Therefore because he could not see his way, he must not despair. The road to success was simple and it applied over the whole range of human activity. The old nursery jingle perhaps best expressed it: If at first you don't succeed, try, try, try again.

Next day was Sunday. He spent most of it in an excursion with Mrs French in which he resolutely kept his thoughts off the case, but after tea he settled himself in his most comfortable chair and once more producing Dulcie's typescript of the inquest, set himself to reread it. Carefully he reweighed every fact and stopped to think out and note its implications. For two hours he worked, and as he passed incident after incident and statement after statement without gaining a glimmer of fresh light, his forced optimism began to recede and black waves of frustration again rose round him.

Then suddenly he stopped and remained motionless gazing at a sentence in the script. The passage was concerned with the evidence of Arthur Boone, Sir Roland's personal attendant. French read it carefully once again.

CORONER: It is common knowledge that the deceased was always well dressed. Was he, in your opinion, particular about his clothes?

BOONE: That's correct, sir, he was most particular. He would consider carefully what suit to wear and what socks and tie should go with it. The trousers had always to be perfectly creased, and he would never allow any bulky or heavy object in the pocket, in case it dragged the cloth.

CORONER: And on last Tuesday morning? Did he make any remark?

BOONE: No, sir, except that he would wear his light grey. But there was nothing for him to remark about. If all had not been in order I should have pretty soon heard of it.

CORONER: Very well, when he was dressed, what happened?

BOONE: He went out to the sun trap. I gave him an arm and carried his books and his second stick and settled him with his rug in his lounge chair.

CORONER: Now have I got that right? He got up about half past ten, dressed, and went straight out? About what time did he reach the sun trap?

If, and French's excitement grew sharply, *if* Sir Roland was natty about his dress and had nothing heavy or bulky in his pockets, and *if* he went straight from his bedroom to the sun trap, i.e., without visiting the study, *who took out the pistol?*

French put down the manuscript and lay back in his chair. If this evidence of Boone's were true – and no one had cast doubt on it – Sir Roland had not taken it himself. Admittedly the pistol was small, but it had a fairly long barrel. French was satisfied that it would have been impossible for the old man to hide it from his valet in the thin and elegant summer clothes he was obviously wearing.

French now saw that the hitherto accepted theory presented a further difficulty. If Sir Roland had not decided to commit suicide until he had read the threatening letter, assumed to have been proved by his normality which he reached the sun trap and his distress when Boone a quarter of an hour later took him his soup, and if he had not left the sun trap between these two visits, which was established by the gardener, how had he obtained the pistol from the study?

Clearly he had not obtained it! Who had then? With a thrill French saw that there was but one answer!

So it was murder after all! And in view of the other facts he had learnt, could there be any doubt as to who that murderer was? The hunches of Dulcie and Lethbridge were certainly correct. However he had worked it, Roscoe was unquestionably the man!

But how was this to be proved? Well, there was the investigation into Roscoe's activities while at Jasmine Lodge. To have carried out such a murder, preparations must have been made. What were they?

French's idea had been that the inquiry itself should answer this question, but now he believed that without moving a finger he should be able to deduce at least a partial reply. How far could abstract reason help him?

Leaving aside the actual method of the murder, of which he was still ignorant, there were two items to be considered: first, the deceased's state of health, and second, the threatening letter. If Roscoe were the murderer, had he taken advantage of the existence of these, or could he have himself brought them about?

First then, Sir Roland's depression: what would be necessary to enable Roscoe to produce it? Surely only two things: knowledge of the required drugs and the drugs themselves. Could Roscoe have obtained either?

As he considered the question, French sat up sharply. Roscoe *did* know something of medicine. Admittedly he had not completed his university course, but at least he must have learnt how to gain the requisite knowledge from medical books.

But had he access to such? Suddenly French saw how he could not only have consulted the books, but obtained the drugs as well. The nature of the thefts at the university and the garage showed that the thief had used keys for the vital locks. Had Roscoe made himself keys for the Harley Street house? Burt, even though a surgeon, presumably had some drugs. If so, had Roscoe obtained what was needful from him?

French went further. Suppose Roscoe had done so, could he have administered it? French now saw that he already had sufficient information to enable him to answer this question also. Boone had said that in taking up Sir Roland's breakfast he customarily left the tray on the hall table while he went to the box on the hall door for the letters. French remembered the layout of the hall and the position of the table. To go to the door meant passing out of sight of the table, and while the letters were being obtained there would be ample time to put dope into the coffee.

Well content with his progress, French turned to the question of the letter. It was obvious that if Roscoe had gone to Town on the day before the murder, or had an accomplice there, he could have posted it. But this appeared to be the only way in which he could have got it to Sir Roland. Had he deposited it in the door box before Boone cleared it, or exchanged it on the tray while the man's back was turned, the cancellation date would have been wrong. It should be easy to find out whether Roscoe had gone to Town, though difficult to learn whether he had asked Dulcie to post it. This latter, however, French thought most unlikely, as it would be practically handing her proof of his guilt.

Then a revolutionary idea flashed into French's mind. The sudden distress had been used to account for the suicide. But there had been no suicide. It was an invention of the murderer's. Therefore could this also be true of the distress? *Had* Sir Roland been specially distressed before his death?

From this question another followed almost automatically. Had the old man received the letter at all? Had he known anything of the alleged prisoner? In other words, had Roscoe murdered him and then planted the letter on the body?

French twisted excitedly in his chair. It was obvious that this theory would clear up many difficulties. First, there was the contradiction between the deceased's character and that which the threatening letter postulated. Major Lethbridge's attempt to reconcile the inconsistencies was ingenious, but not convincing. The fact that the letter and envelope had been typed on different machines was also suggestive. But most striking of all, French now saw, was the matter of the previous letter. The whole case had been built on the assumption that there had been such, as if not, Sir Roland could not have recognised the second. But if a previous letter had come, its receipt must have gravely distressed him. Nothing of the kind had taken place! The depression had come on gradually. French now believed that the entire story had been devised simply to make the motive for suicide more plausible.

If so, was it not a typical criminal's error? If the man had not been so clever, he would have been a lot safer!

French went a step further. If Roscoe had planted the letter, how had he obtained the correctly-dated postmark? For a time this puzzled French, then he saw that it could have been done in the simplest way possible. When the old man had gone out with Boone, Roscoe could have examined the wastepaper basket in his bedroom. It was practically certain that at least one typed letter of the morning's delivery would have found its way there. All Roscoe would have to do would be to remove that letter and its envelope. He would destroy the letter, and after putting the initials SA on the envelope, would take it out and place it on the dead man's table. At the same time he would put his own letter in the deceased's pocket.

Then French sat up sharply. He was wrong! All this splendid theory was crashing about his head! In his eagerness he had for the moment forgotten Boone! Boone also had certified the existence of the letter and the deceased's sudden distress.

Was it possible after all that both men could have been involved? French systematically weighed the idea. He simply could not believe it. People only conspired to commit murder under the most exceptional circumstances.

It was inconceivable that the attendant and the secretary in their quite different walks of life, could have jointly undertaken such a crime.

For some moments French felt completely dashed, then habit resumed its sway and he continued his ruminations. Two things at least he could do. He glanced at his watch, then picking up his telephone, he spoke to Burt.

"I want some further information from you, sir, which I really think, may lead us to the truth. Would it be too much to ask you to come down to Harley Street now?"

Burt seemed surprised, but agreed. Taking an enlarged photograph of the letter typescript which Pardoe had given him, French set off to meet him.

"I want," French explained a few minutes later, "to test two theories. They may be false, but if either is true it will prove Roscoe guilty of murder. And here I feel it's only fair to tell you in confidence what we suspect," and he imparted to the astonished Burt what was in his mind. "I'd like first to find out if the letter was done on Miss Heath's typewriter, then I want to know if you have a drug which could produce depression, and if so, whether it has been tampered with?"

French's luck now seemed to have run out. The letter had not been done on either of the two typewriters in the building, and though Burt had a drug which would produce the required effect, he was unable to say whether or not his stock was diminished.

Considerably disgruntled, French apologised for the trouble he had given, and went despondently home.

– 17 –

THE OVERLOOKED CLUE

It was when he was lying awake that night, his thoughts still busy with the case, that the great fundamental idea which had so long eluded him leaped sharply into French's mind. He held his breath as he considered it. Yes, at last this was what he required! Here was the explanation of everything! Why, the murder was no mystery at all! Its method was simple and clear as day! How was it possible that he had not seen it the moment he had learned the circumstances? What had Lethbridge and his men been thinking about, that they had allowed it to puzzle them? Their mutual failure was something which he and they would be glad to forget.

Then his enthusiasm suffered a slight relapse. To see how everyone had been tricked was one thing: to prove it was quite another. Most of the rest of the night he spent worrying over the problem. By the morning he had worked out a possible line of inquiry. It was not promising, but it was the best he could think of.

He went down early to Staines and saw Superintendent Clements. "Just one question, if you please, Super," he said innocently. "I wonder if you could find out for me whether any unexplained shots were heard previous to Sir Roland's death? Probably at night, though that's not certain."

Clements looked at him curiously. "May I ask what put that into your head, Mr French?" he answered. "Shots were heard, and we never could find out who fired them."

"That's very satisfactory news," French replied, trying to keep the exultation out of his voice. "Tell me about them, please."

"Our own patrols heard them on several nights. They were faint, more like pistol shots than from a gun or rifle. They seemed to come from a disused sandpit. In each case the patrols searched the pit, but without finding anything. In the daytime also I had a man look round, but he could see nothing out of the common."

"I wish you'd let one of the men who heard the shots show me the pit. Excuse me, Super, for being mysterious for just a few hours. If I'm right in my suspicion it may help us quite a bit. In any case I'll tell you the whole thing when I get back."

Half an hour later under the direction of a young constable French was examining a corner of the great empty pit. "It was there it sounded, sir," the man pointed, "but of course I couldn't be sure of the exact place, for I was on the road which runs about thirty feet back from the edge."

"It's a good place for anyone who wished to indulge in secret pistol practice," French declared. "The flash couldn't be seen."

"That's right, sir, it couldn't except from the pit itself, and it's not likely anyone would be in this disused place after dark."

French agreed. He thanked the constable and got rid of him. Then in the corner specified he began one of the most meticulous searches of his career. His chief difficulty was that he did not know exactly what he was looking for, or rather what form the object he hoped to find would take. First he marked out an area of ground into squares, then making a mat of brushwood, he knelt down and minutely examined the surface of each.

At least he picked up a small object. It was like a scrap of stone or baked clay, broken from something about the size and shape of a tennis ball. He scraped it with a knife and to his delight satisfied himself that it was neither stone nor clay. He packed the fragment carefully into a small box and resumed his search.

Before he left he found two other pieces. They did not fit together, yet they clearly had come from either the same or a similar object.

French returned to the station. Rather to his relief Superintendent Clements had gone out. Pardoe however was there and French called him.

"Could you spare an hour or two helping me to look for something at Jasmine Lodge?" he asked. "I could do it myself, but I'd like a witness in case I'm lucky."

Pardoe was interested and gladly offered his services.

As they went along French drew out his little box. "I'm hoping to find something like that in the sun trap," he explained. "As you can imagine, it'll take a bit of searching for, because it's so like the soil. I'll tell you what I think it is," and he entered into explanations which left Pardoe gasping.

They walked along the riverbank and found their way unseen into the sun trap. There they repeated French's operations in the sandpit. For a long time they searched, crawling about on the ground and even sifting through their fingers the loose soil beneath the bushes. At last French gave a delighted chuckle. Here was a piece of the same kind of stuff! Fancifully he thought it like a scrap of bitten apple. He called Pardoe over.

"What about that?" he pointed.

Pardoe seemed almost overwhelmed. "It's a true bill, Mr French," he gasped. "You've got it!"

"*We've* got it," French amended.

Pardoe shook his head. "We thought it was suicide," he muttered.

"Bit of luck," French said easily. "I'd like to find some more pieces if I could," he went on, as watched by Pardoe he carefully marked his find and put it into another box.

Unhappily their combined researches produced no more of the mysterious fragments and French had to be content.

"What we have will do the trick," he said. "You'll be able to swear to it?"

"Of course, sir."

French nodded and went on: "Now I'd like to take a look over the workshop. I think we'll assume that your previous connection with the case gives you the right of entry and not worry about permission. Matter of fact, I don't want anyone to know we're here."

"Then if you carry on, I'll see that no one comes."

They withdrew from the sun trap as they had come, along the bank of the Thames. Then entering the little estate through a convenient gap in the hedge, they reached the workshop unseen. It was unlocked, and while Pardoe stood at the door, French began a rapid search.

It was not upon the tools or materials or boxes of nails and other items that he concentrated, but upon the bench and floor. With his lens and a fine bradawl he began clearing out the joints between planks and floorboards. Half an hour passed and then he grunted with satisfaction. Pardoe, inquisitive, went over to him.

"Another bit of luck," French said, glancing up. "Look here."

In the crack between two floorboards was some white powder. "Plaster of Paris, or I'm a Dutchman," went on French. "That's what he made those balls of. If we can trace his purchase it'll be a help."

"Hard to trace a sale of plaster of Paris; it's pretty common stuff. The colouring matter would be more unusual. What would you say it was, sir? Burnt umber?"

"I couldn't be sure. Some brown powder he mixed with the stuff to make it look like earth. I agree it would be useful to find it, but I haven't come on any trace. But our people at the Yard will tell us what it is and then we'll have a try for the sale." He paused, then continued: "Look here, Pardoe, here's something else I've found. That'll be useful too." He held in his palm some tiny metal shavings. "From the lathe. The point is that they're steel. That makes it much easier than if they were, say, gunmetal."

Pardoe stared. "I don't follow, sir."

"You will," said French grinning.

Guarding his treasures more carefully than if they had been rubies, French went back with Pardoe to the police station. Clements had returned and for the second time French told his story. The Super's obvious chagrin did not prevent him from handsomely congratulating French.

"If you could spare a man or two to help me to find those sales it would assist me, sir," French continued after acknowledgments. "And there's one other thing. I've an idea we might get some evidence out of the river. Could you find me a boat and a couple of men?"

"Of course. What's the idea?"

French told him and Clements was still more impressed.

"I agree," he said warmly, "but you'll need to keep your operations secret."

"I thought," French answered, "of doing the river at night?"

Clements was doubtful. "Could you manage in the dark?"

"It's not absolutely dark. There's a crescent moon: enough for us to work by, but not enough for anyone to see us from the shore."

"Very well, I'll arrange the boat. Tonight too soon?"

"No, I don't think so. I'll have to go to Town for some apparatus, but I can be back in time."

About one next morning a light skiff put out from Staines. French with a small suitcase sat in the stern, while a constable took the sculls and Pardoe kept a lookout in the bow.

The night was admirable for their purpose. Not a breath of wind stirred and the surface of the river was without a ripple. The banks were faintly visible, just enough to enable them to fix their position with accuracy.

"Now, Pardoe," said French as they approached Jasmine Lodge, "picture to yourself someone standing in the sun trap with a small metal object he wants to get rid of. What does he do?"

Pardoe made the obvious reply.

"That's what I'm building on," returned French. "Will you estimate the area into which it might fall and get your man to row backwards and forwards across it. While he's doing so I'll fish."

As he spoke French took from his suitcase a powerful permanent magnet attached to a length of light rope. When they had come within the critical area he lowered it to the bottom, and as the boat crept slowly backwards and forwards, he raised and lowered it so that it moved along the river bed. At short intervals he stopped the boat while he pulled the magnet up for inspection.

For three mortal hours they worked till all were sick of the job. Then just as French began to think they must leave off for the night, he obtained his crowning stroke of luck. Clinging to the magnet was a small cylindrical metal object.

"I told you it was well for us he used steel," he remarked. "This magnet was much the easiest method of search."

Pardoe swore comprehensively. As he and French gazed at the object by the light of a carefully screened torch, it seemed to both that at last the whole of the murderer's plan stood crystal clear. The object was an elaborate silencer of a size which would just fit the late Sir Roland's pistol.

Delighted beyond words, French during the morning tested this and a few other points and later that day called by appointment at the police station at Staines to make his report.

"I'm sorry, Mr French," Clements greeted him, "but the CC has been unavoidably detained in Town. He went up to some meeting. Will you carry on or would you rather wait until he comes back?"

"Carry on, if it's left to me. Which would the CC prefer?"

"He would rather you went on. He said so when he rang up."

French accordingly described his researches. "From what I found there can be no doubt at all as to what was done," he added. "The murderer first obtained the necessary drug and dosed Sir Roland at intervals, so as to bring about his depression and thus pave the way for the suicide theory. Then he prepared the letter which was to cap this theory, and arranged in the way we've already discussed that it should have an envelope with the correctly dated postmark. This letter and envelope he planted at the time of the murder."

"I'd be glad to see him hanged," Clements declared vindictively. "It wasn't enough to kill the old fellow, but he had to blacken his character also."

"His conduct certainly leaves something to be desired," French agreed, manfully repressing a smile. He realised the source of Clements' wrath.

"In the meantime," resumed French, "our worthy friend had been making other preparations. He had obtained some plaster of Paris to cast some small bombs and brown colouring matter so that when these were broken the pieces would look like clods of earth. The bombs had to fulfil two requirements; first, they had to sound like a pistol, similar to the deceased's, and second, they must not leave any recognisable trace."

"That last wouldn't be so easy."

"By no means. I've thought a lot about it, and I can see only one way in which it could have been done. The murderer would have begun by preparing two cords. The first would be for the fuse, and would consist of several strands of cotton twisted together and soaked in a solution of saltpetre. As you know, such a cord will smoulder slowly, and the rate of burning varies roughly as the strength of the saltpetre solution."

"I've done it myself when I was a boy."

"Then you know more about it than I. The second cord would be required to burn quickly, almost instantaneously. It would be made by soaking string in the saltpetre, then drying it and working into its fibres a paste of starch, water and gunpowder. When dry, this cord would almost flash into nothing. In addition to the second cord, some two or three inches at the end of the fuse would be treated in the same way."

Clements grinned. "I wish I had known that when I was young."

"Perhaps as well you didn't," French retorted. "The murderer then would have made his plaster of Paris bombs, something like a largish apple with a hollow core. He would have inserted the gunpowder-treated end of the fuse into the core, filled up with powder, probably taken from some of Sir Roland's cartridges, and blocked the hole with a plug of plaster. The fuse would smoulder for the calculated time, then flash through the plug and explode the bomb. Of course a number of experiments would be necessary to get everything right, and that's where your sandpit shots come in."

"Very thrilling, Mr French: don't stop. But look here, a bomb like that would leave traces of burning or blast on the grass or wherever it exploded."

"Yes, I know. I thought of that. But there's one place where that wouldn't occur. If the bomb were hung from a branch of the oak in mid-air clear of everything solid and over shrubs, not grass, it would disintegrate without trace. That's what the prepared string would be for. When the bomb went off, the string that supported it would flash away into dust."

"Also without trace!"

"Quite. Now for the actual crime. As I see it, the murderer chose a time at which witnesses were outside the sun trap, so that there should be proof that no one left it after the shot. He may have waited for several days, but on the occasion he finally selected there were not only the four tennis players on the west side of the trap, but the gardener on the north."

"In addition to Lady Chatterton and Boone."

French looked at him curiously. "Yes, that was a pretty bit of timing. But no doubt if they had been too early he would have found some excuse to delay them. Very well. He goes into the sun trap with the bomb, the letter, the pistol and the silencer, which latter he has made in the workshop. He shoots Sir Roland. The essence of his plan if that he does so in silence, at least he hopes that if a faint sound is heard, it will be taken for the thud of the ball on a tennis racquet. He throws the silencer into the river, presses the deceased's fingers on the pistol, and drops the latter under the open hand. Then he lays the envelope on the table and thrusts the letter into Sir Roland's coat pocket."

"It's all likely enough."

"He has then only to arrange for the shot. He probably has already passed a dark cord over the branch, and he ties the prepared string to this, draws it over the branch in its turn and makes it fast. Then he removes his dark cord, lights his fuse, and goes for Lady Chatterton. When he and his companions are on their way to the sun trap the bomb goes off, completely disappearing. Naturally it is taken for the shot."

"I'll hand it to you," Clements exclaimed again. "You've made as pretty a case as ever I've heard. The CC will be pleased. But," Clements smiled wryly, "he'll think we ought to have found it out."

"Just a bit of luck, Mr Clements. You know as well as I that you can do good work for a month, but it's the bit of luck at the end that gives you the result."

"I'll not argue that with you," Clements smiled. "Now we must consider an arrest?"

French hesitated. "I question if we're ready for that," he said slowly. "Whom would you arrest?"

Clements looked at him searchingly. "Well, I think we've a fairly good case. Roscoe had the character for it. He had access to the drug and the knowledge to administer it, for Burt's evidence was negative. He had the opportunity and skill to make the silencer. He had a strong motive and he was last with the deceased. Who else, Mr French?"

"What about Boone?"

"Well, what about him? So far as we know he had few of the necessary qualifications. You don't suspect him, do you?"

"Before we make an arrest I think we should be sure which of them it was. For the matter of that, how do we know they weren't both in it?"

"Well," Clements sat back. "I suppose that's theoretically possible. But I shouldn't have much hesitation myself. However, it's not for either of us to say. That'll be the CC's pigeon."

On this note of indubitable truth the conference came to an end. Thoroughly pleased with his exploits, French returned to the Yard. He was not so enthusiastic when that evening Pardoe rang him up to say that Major Lethbridge had decided on Roscoe's immediate arrest.

– 18 –

FRENCH THINKS AGAIN

When next morning Dulcie opened her paper and saw what had happened to Frank, her heart gave a leap. So he was guilty after all! Her hunch had been correct! The police certainly would not have arresmted him unless they were sure.

For a moment she felt only excitement, then as she realised what the sequel might be, a sick horror took possession of her mind. Surely, surely, this was not her doing? Surely, surely, it was not possible that her act had condemned Frank to a dreadful death? Frank, her Frank! Frank whom she had worked with, who had been her companion, who had loved her and whom she had loved!

Oh, *why* had she not left things alone? Now when it was too late she understood the truth. She still loved Frank. She had always loved him. She always would love him. Without Frank the world was empty. Without him she did not want to live. What hideous madness had taken possession of her? Her foul jealousy? Was that what had ruined both their lives?

What would she not give to undo her action! To get her chance over again! Even suppose Frank had loved the Chatterton girl. If he had married her he would have been

275

happy. To have Frank happy! That, she realised, was all she had ever wanted.

Now there would be no more happiness for any of them, neither for Frank nor Juliet Chatterton nor she herself. For herself there would be no more life. If Frank died through her action she could not live on. She would join him on the ghastly morning, if it came to that.

She sat motionless before her untasted breakfast, Harley Street and the day's work forgotten. Oh, was there anything that she could do? Was it really too late?

With no very clear idea in her mind, she put on her street things and went out. In a sort of dream she hurried along, and it was almost with a feeling of surprise that she found herself turning in through the gates of Scotland Yard. She asked the officer at the door for Superintendent French. She gave her name, but though she was incoherent about her business, after a searching glance, the man sent her up. French greeted her pleasantly. If he was surprised to see her, he gave no sign of it.

"My dear Miss Heath!" he exclaimed, glancing at her shrewdly. "What has happened? Can I help you?"

She stared at him dully. "What has happened?" she repeated. "You ask that? Haven't you arrested him?"

"The local police have," French answered. "I was not consulted. But you're very much upset. Did you not think him guilty?"

"*No!*" She almost shouted the word. "I was wrong! I was mad! Frank is not perfect, but he is not a murderer! No, no! He never did it!"

French glanced at her still more searchingly. "Sit down and let us talk this over," he invited, and his quiet matter-of-fact voice brought her comfort. "Have a cigarette?"

She smoked feverishly, and this also relieved her. "I'm in despair," she said presently in a more restrained tone. "I feel that what I said to Mr Liddell has brought about this ghastly mistake. For I was wrong! I see it now, I was...Well, I have to tell you: I was mad with jealousy. For the moment I thought I hated him. But I don't! I love him! Oh, tell me, is there any hope? Have I killed him and myself too?"

French looked at her steadily. "If it's any comfort to you," he said gravely, "I may tell you that I knew all this and it was considered in weighing the value of your statements. I know more. I know that even now you have not told me everything. You were jealous, yes, but you were also frightened. Why were you frightened, Miss Heath?"

A day earlier Dulcie would have listened to these words with a feeling of absolute panic. Now they made little impression on her. Remorse had submerged every other feeling. As she sat silently, trying to collect her thoughts, the urge to confess grew till it became irresistible.

"You're right!" she cried with a sudden gesture. "I have more to tell you. We've been robbing Mr Burt. Both of us at first, but when Frank went to Jasmine Lodge I carried on alone. There, you can put me in prison! I don't care any more what happens to me."

"I'm glad you told me that," French said more gently. "I knew all about that too. You were robbing, not Mr Burt, but his patients. I know just how much you've taken, and how much came from each."

In spite of her distress, this gave Dulcie one of the most terrible shocks of her life. She stared incredulously. This scheme that she had been carrying on so successfully and so secretly, of which she had been certain that no single person in the world suspected the existence, this scheme was known in all its details to the police! It was impossible!

How had she given herself away? She simply could not believe she had done so.

Presently she became dully conscious that French was speaking. "...need not answer anything I may ask you," he was saying, "or if you like you may have a solicitor present on your behalf before you do so. Also I have to warn you that anything you do say will be taken down and may be used in evidence."

He paused, looking at her questioningly. But Dulcie could make no reply and presently he went on. "Having given you this warning, I can honestly advise you, now that you've gone so far, to tell me everything. How did two honourable decent people like you and Roscoe come to do such a thing?"

Dulcie hesitated in her turn, and then the whole story came out in a flood of words: Frank's return in illness and poverty, his loss of his gratuity through blackmail because of an earlier fault, and his purchase of the incriminating document with money taken from Burt in a moment of sharp temptation. Then the scheme, intended at first only to enable that money to be paid back, and finally its continuance owing to its lure of ease and apparent security. She told everything exactly as it had happened and without attempting extenuations. A constable who had come in answer to a ring took down all she said.

"I'm glad you told me that," French repeated. "Now I'll have to ask you to wait here until your statement is typed, when you can read it over and if correct, sign it. Then you can go."

Once again on this day of shocks and surprises Dulcie stared open-mouthed. "Then you aren't going to arrest me?" she breathed.

"Not at the moment at all events," he answered. "I'll be quite candid with you and tell you it may come to that. If some of these people you've defrauded prosecute, we shall have to. But don't do anything silly. Even if we do so, your confession will count in your favour."

Once again her thoughts swung away from herself. "I don't care for anything but Frank," she declared. "Oh, tell me, Mr French, is there any hope for him?"

"Well, I can tell you my own motto," he answered, and his voice now sounded really kind. "Never give up hope and never believe that things are too bad to improve. What do you propose to do now?"

"Go and tell Mr Burt about it."

"Right," he declared almost warmly, "that's your plan! And if you take my advice you'll go at once, in case your resolution cools."

The unexpected kindness from such a source almost broke Dulcie down. She murmured her thanks, and having signed her statement, was shown out. Then she hurried to Harley Street, nerving herself for the terrifying interview which she faced.

French, left alone, put aside the files on which he had been working. He was uneasy, and when uneasy he could not concentrate on such dull routine matters as the sorting of old papers. The truth was that he was not convinced of Roscoe's guilt. In one way it was not his business. The decision to charge the man with the crime lay with Lethbridge, and French's opinion had not been asked. All the same he felt himself responsible. For the nth time he wondered was there no fact which he had failed to interpret, no deduction he had overlooked, which would establish the matter beyond question.

The affair had got on his mind and he could not drop it. For three solid hours he reread his notes and racked his brains to find some further clue. Then suddenly he swore. With a growing excitement he reconsidered some of the evidence at the inquest. Yes, there was something he had missed! A statement of one of the witnesses, an apparently ordinary commonplace remark, yet he now saw that upon it hung issues of life and death!

He drew a sheet of paper towards him and clarified his idea by putting it in writing. Then he rang up Clements.

"Sorry to butt in, Super, on a matter which in a way isn't my business, but I'd like to have a talk with you and perhaps the CC about the Jasmine Lodge case. I think there's some further evidence that you should know. Can you fix up a meeting?"

"Certainly, Mr French. We're having a conference tomorrow at ten. Can you join us?"

As French next day reached the police station Lethbridge's car drew up. "Good morning, Mr French," the CC called out cheerily. "You say you've some more information for us?"

"A point occurred to me last night, sir," French told him, "and I thought you ought to consider it. It struck me as important."

"Good. Come along in and we'll discuss it. 'Morning, Clements. Your room ready?"

When they were seated and had dealt with some technical points the CC turned to French. "Now, Mr French, we'll be glad to hear what you have to tell us."

"I should like to ask first, sir, whether Roscoe has made a statement since his arrest?"

"Yes, he asked to be allowed to do so. I have it here." The CC passed over some typed sheets. "It's not a very convincing document, but I daresay it's the best he could do."

French handed the sheets back. "Before I read this, sir, will you allow me to make a guess at what he has said?"

Lethbridge looked surprised. "But of course. We'll be interested to hear you, eh, Clements?"

"Very much so, sir," the Super answered. Both he and Pardoe looked as if they thought French was riding for a fall, and that they would not be too sorry to see him do it.

"I suggest then, sir, that he began by saying that part of his statement at the inquest was false, but that he now wished to tell the truth. Next he declared that his evidence about the question he wished to ask the deceased regarding his book was correct. He knew the old man was not very flourishing that morning, but he was held up until he got the answer and thought he might risk it."

French noticed with gratification that the three men were looking slightly startled. The CC glanced at Clements who said slowly, "Well, you've made a good beginning, Mr French. He said exactly that, but pointed out that the question was a simple one which the deceased could have answered in a word."

"Quite," said French, "it was one to which the answer was yes or no. Then I imagine he said that he had not known anything of the deceased being in a particularly distressed state, but expected to find him normal."

"Right again," Clements admitted heavily.

"When he entered the sun trap he was appalled to find Sir Roland shot. He saw at a glance that he was dead, and noticed the pistol on the ground and the envelope on the table."

All three officers were now staring at French, obviously much impressed. As none of them spoke, French went on.

"He saw that he must give the alarm at once and hurried out of the sun trap to do so. But at the entrance he met Boone. What he told you that Boone said I don't know, but I will try to invent the conversation. Boone probably began: 'Well, you see what's happened. I've just shot him. But if you give the alarm *you'll* be suspected.' Boone would give a reason for this. I can't say exactly what, but he might have discovered Roscoe's affair with Miss Chatterton, and if so, the motive would be the double one of avoiding the father's opposition to a marriage and getting the legacy for the daughter. 'Don't forget,' Boone might have gone on, 'that you were last in the sun trap. With the evidence I can invent, you won't have a dog's chance if you split.' "

Again there was a silence. At last Lethbridge murmured in a strangled voice, "Go on."

"Then, probably as they walked towards the house, Boone would tell him of his plan: how he had used a silencer, and how the bomb would soon go off and be taken for the shot, and how before that they must have reported Sir Roland's alleged distressed condition to Lady Chatterton. Roscoe was no fool. He would see his perilous position and conclude that to adopt Boone's plan would be safest. Both men would have plenty of time to agree on their statements to Pardoe."

The three Staines men exchanged glances and then the CC spoke. "I don't know how you reasoned it out, French, but I have to admit you're correct in your...you said guess, but somehow I don't think there was much guessing about it. Does this mean that you believe Roscoe to be innocent?"

Clements nodded heavily. "That's the point, sir. What do you say, Mr French?"

"Before we go on to that," French answered, "may I make a second guess? What Boone might say if you arrested him?"

"Go ahead." The CC's voice sounded almost like a groan.

"I suggest that he would tell very much the same story as Roscoe. He also would ask leave to make a statement and would begin by saying that his previous evidence was false and that he now wished to tell the truth. He would say, I think, that when he took Sir Roland the soup, the old man was normal except that he would not drink the soup, but told him to leave it. Boone would give some reason for going back to the sun trap: several suggest themselves. For example, he might say that it occurred to him to ask Sir Roland if he would prefer cocoa, which he sometimes took. In any case I do not think Boone would admit having seen Roscoe going in."

"Speculative, French, isn't it?" the CC murmured.

"It's what I called a guess, sir," French smiled. "I don't say I'm right."

"Well, it's very interesting at all events. Go ahead."

"He would say, I think, that when he reached the entrance to the sun trap he looked in and saw Sir Roland lying shot in the chair. He was about to rush in and investigate when Roscoe appeared coming out. Roscoe would realise that Boone knew and he might say: 'Yes, you see what's happened. I've just shot him. But if you give the alarm, *you'll* be suspected.' Roscoe would give a reason for this. I can't say exactly what, but probably that his evidence would be that he had gone into the sun trap to ask a question about the old man's book and had found him shot, and that Boone was the only person who could have done it. 'With the evidence I can invent,' he might add, 'you

283

won't have a dog's chance if you split.' Then he would explain his plan of the silencer and the bomb. Boone is not a fool any more than Roscoe. He would necessarily conclude Roscoe's plan was the safest for him, and back it up."

"Speculative," the CC repeated, "but you may be right."

"I would submit, sir, that it's no more speculative than my guess about Roscoe's statement."

"You've got me there," Lethbridge admitted ruefully. "But, French, your conclusion becomes more and more puzzling. As I understand you, your case is that both men were lying in their evidence and that either may be guilty?"

"I told you, sir," put in Clements, "that Mr French did not seem convinced of Roscoe's guilt."

"You did, but I wasn't anticipating this new exposition. Go on, French. Are you really in doubt as to which man is guilty?"

"I was, sir, until yesterday afternoon. Then I reread the evidence at the inquest and I suddenly saw that there was absolute proof which was our man. Boone had stated it unwittingly."

Lethbridge again glanced at his men. "This is most interesting. I've read the evidence and I confess I didn't see the point. What did you discover?"

French was diplomatic. "I also, sir, read it, not once but I suppose a hundred times, without seeing it. The proof hinges on a matter of time. Just let us make a calculation or two." He opened his notebook and spun over the pages. "First," he went on, "how long must it have taken the murderer to carry out his work in the sun trap? Just think again of what he had to do. To enter, walk to Sir Roland and shoot him. To take the silencer off the pistol and throw it in the river. To see that the pistol was clear of all prints except

Sir Roland's and to put Sir Roland's on it, not only in the shooting position, but as he might have handled it. Then to drop the gun on the ground and see that the hand swung above it. To put the envelope on the table, and crumple up the letter and push it into Sir Roland's pocket. To tie the suspending cord of the bomb to that already over the branch, haul the bomb up to five or six feet from the ground, make fast and remove the dark cord and put it in his pocket. Lastly, to light the fuse, making sure it had caught properly. How long for all that? What do you say, Mr Clements?"

"Five minutes?" Clements suggested and the CC nodded his agreement.

"I also made it five or six minutes," French declared. "Now in his statement Boone said he was in the sun trap for four or five minutes while arranging the old man in his chair. And we may note that he must necessarily have given approximately the correct time in his evidence, as he could have been seen going in and out by several people."

"That's true."

"Roscoe on the other hand said he was only in the sun trap for a minute or two, and the same argument as to the truth of this would apply."

Lethbridge moved uneasily. "I admit that seems right, and yet I don't find it very convincing. What about you, Clements?"

"It's not convincing," French interposed, "but I think this is. Boone stated at the inquest that he was walking from the sun trap towards the rear of the house when he saw Roscoe leave the front door and go down towards the river. He stated that he stopped and waited to see whether Roscoe would enter the sun trap, and when he saw that he had done so, he at once went back to the entrance, where he met Roscoe coming out. Now, sir, how long would it have taken Boone to walk that distance?"

"Ah," said the CC, "at last I begin to see," while Clements growled out a muffled but comprehensive oath. "He would have done it in less than a minute, eh, Clements?"

The Super moved his heavy bulk. "Mr French has got us this time, sir," he declared. "There's no doubt he's right. Roscoe could not possibly have done the thing while Boone was walking down the lawn. I'm afraid we've slipped up."

"Never mind," Lethbridge declared. "No real harm has been done. We'll have to release Roscoe and bring in Boone."

Then ensued a discussion of ways and means, including the points upon which further evidence might be obtainable. It may here be stated that intensified research established the following facts.

On two of the nights on which the explosions had been heard in the sandpit, Boone had been seen on the road, admittedly not near the pit, but between it and Jasmine Lodge. On one occasion it was before the shots were heard and he was then going towards the pit. On the other it was after the detonations and he was then walking away from it.

No information about the plaster of Paris or the steel was obtained, but at a big building supplies establishment in Victoria Street the purchase of the colouring matter was established. Boone had been so sure of himself that he had become careless. He had asked for a powder which would turn plaster of Paris to the colour of earth. The salesman's interest had been aroused by the unusual request, and he remembered his customer and picked out his photograph from a dozen others.

Further, before Boone had worked in the mental home, he had spent a couple of years as an apprentice in an engineering works. He was therefore capable, with the help of the excellent tools in Sir Roland's workshop, of making the silencer and bombs. Also it was proved that some two months earlier he had paid a visit to a former colleague in the mental home and had been alone while the colleague was being sought. During this time he could have abstracted a quantity of a debilitating drug, though admittedly it could not be proved that he had done so.

Finally, a motive was suggested, though here again absolute proof could not be obtained. The facts about Boone's desire to purchase the licensed house became known. From his mechanical skill and the fact that he had abstracted the pistol from the locked drawer, it was argued that he must have copied Sir Roland's keys. This indeed was to all intents and purposes proved, as a long and tedious inquiry established the fact that he had bought blanks of the correct sizes. These blanks included one for the safe, in which was a copy of Sir Roland's will. It seemed obvious therefore that Boone had read the will and knew that he was to have a legacy of £50 for each year he had served Sir Roland. This for his nine years would amount to £450 and with the £25 per year coming to Maggie Green from the same source – amounting to £100 – he would receive rather more than the sum he required to complete the purchase. Here also it may be added that all this evidence proved sufficient to convince the jury at the trial which followed, and Boone in due course paid the dreadful penalty of the law.

And what of Frank and Dulcie?

Though Frank's period of detention was short, he had time to think over his conduct, and the knowledge of what might lie in front of him jerked him sharply back to a saner outlook on life. He determined that if he could escape this horror, he would try to run straight. Unhappy and feeling terribly alone, he found that it was not Juliet Chatterton that he longed for. It was Dulcie, and now that it was possible he might never see her again, he realised how much he loved her.

Therefore it came about that when he was released and returned to Town, his frame of mind was much the same as hers. He told her at once how sorry he was for his treatment of her and that it was she only whom he loved. He was immensely relieved to learn that she had confessed the fraud, and insisted on going at once to Burt to admit that he had been the chief offender.

The bar to complete happiness was that neither she nor Frank knew what the result of their confessions would be. Only a small amount of the money brought in by the fraud had been spent – in getting Frank an outfit for the Jasmine Lodge post – and they were able to replace this as well as the original £200 from this sum, added to the savings they had been able to make from their respective salaries and Frank's legacy. The full amount taken by the scheme was therefore handed to Burt. He undertook to return it to his patients, but said that while under the circumstances he would not prosecute, some of them might. As it turned out, all of them were pleased to receive twenty or thirty unexpected guineas, and said that since the damage had been made good, they would let the matter drop. But to abstain from prosecution was Burt's extreme concession. He would not retain Dulcie in his employment, and she and Frank found themselves practically penniless and without jobs. But the shortage of labour stood them in good stead. Both obtained work, and soon they were able to marry and set up house in a tiny flat. Happier than they had ever been, they once again began to plan for a saner, if humbler, future.

In the meantime the completion of the case enabled French to snatch a little more time for the clearing of his files.

FREEMAN WILLS CROFTS

THE BOX OFFICE MURDERS

A girl employed in the box office of a London cinema falls into the power of a mysterious trio of crooks. A helpful solicitor sends her to Scotland Yard. There she tells Inspector French the story of the Purple Sickle. Her body is found floating in Southampton Water the next day. French discovers that similar murders have taken place. After gathering evidence he learns the trio's secret and runs them to ground.

THE HOG'S BACK MYSTERY

The Hog's Back is a ridge in Surrey and the setting for the disappearance of several locals. A doctor vanishes, followed by a nurse with whom he was acquainted, then a third person. Inspector French deduces murder, but there are no bodies. Eventually he is able to prove his theory and show that a fourth murder has been committed.

'As pretty a piece of work as Inspector French has done...on the level of Mr Crofts' very best; which is saying something.'

E C Bentley in the *Daily Telegraph*

Freeman Wills Crofts

Inspector French's Greatest Case

We are here introduced for the first time to the famous Inspector French. A head clerk's corpse is discovered beside the empty safe of a Hatton Garden diamond merchant. There are many suspects and many false clues to be followed before French is able to solve the crime.

Man Overboard!

In the course of a ship's passage from Belfast to Liverpool a man disappears. His body is picked up by Irish fishermen. Although the coroner's verdict is suicide, murder is suspected. Inspector French co-operates with Superintendent Rainey and Sergeant M'Clung once more to determine the truth.

Freeman Wills Crofts

Mystery in the Channel

The cross-channel steamer *Chichester* stops half way to France. A motionless yacht lies in her path. When a party clambers aboard they find a trail of blood and two dead men. Chief Constable Turnbull has to call on Inspector French for help in solving the mystery of the *Nymph*.

Mystery on Southampton Water

The Joymount Rapid Hardening Cement Manufacturing Company is in serious financial trouble. Two young company employees hatch a plot to break in to a rival works, Chayle on the Isle of Wight, to find out Chayle's secret for underselling them. But the scheme does not go according to plan. The death of the night watchman, theft and fire are the result. Inspector French is brought in to solve the mystery.

OTHER TITLES BY FREEMAN WILLS CROFTS AVAILABLE DIRECT FROM HOUSE OF STRATUS

Quantity	£	$(US)	$(CAN)	€
THE 12.30 FROM CROYDON	6.99	11.50	15.99	11.50
THE AFFAIR AT LITTLE WOKEHAM	6.99	11.50	15.99	11.50
ANYTHING TO DECLARE?	6.99	11.50	15.99	11.50
THE BOX OFFICE MURDERS	6.99	11.50	15.99	11.50
THE CASK	6.99	11.50	15.99	11.50
CRIME AT GUILDFORD	6.99	11.50	15.99	11.50
DEATH OF A TRAIN	6.99	11.50	15.99	11.50
DEATH ON THE WAY	6.99	11.50	15.99	11.50
ENEMY UNSEEN	6.99	11.50	15.99	11.50
THE END OF ANDREW HARRISON	6.99	11.50	15.99	11.50
FATAL VENTURE	6.99	11.50	15.99	11.50
FEAR COMES TO CHALFONT	6.99	11.50	15.99	11.50
FOUND FLOATING	6.99	11.50	15.99	11.50
FRENCH STRIKES OIL	6.99	11.50	15.99	11.50
GOLDEN ASHES	6.99	11.50	15.99	11.50
THE GROOTE PARK MURDER	6.99	11.50	15.99	11.50
THE HOG'S BACK MYSTERY	6.99	11.50	15.99	11.50
INSPECTOR FRENCH AND THE CHEYNE MYSTERY	6.99	11.50	15.99	11.50

ALL HOUSE OF STRATUS BOOKS ARE AVAILABLE FROM GOOD BOOKSHOPS OR DIRECT FROM THE PUBLISHER:

Internet: **www.houseofstratus.com** including author interviews, reviews, features.

Email: **sales@houseofstratus.com** please quote author, title and credit card details.

OTHER TITLES BY FREEMAN WILLS CROFTS AVAILABLE DIRECT FROM HOUSE OF STRATUS

Quantity		£	$(US)	$(CAN)	€
☐	INSPECTOR FRENCH AND THE STARVEL TRAGEDY	6.99	11.50	15.99	11.50
☐	INSPECTOR FRENCH'S GREATEST CASE	6.99	11.50	15.99	11.50
☐	JAMES TARRANT, ADVENTURER	6.99	11.50	15.99	11.50
☐	A LOSING GAME	6.99	11.50	15.99	11.50
☐	THE LOSS OF THE JANE VOSPER	6.99	11.50	15.99	11.50
☐	MAN OVERBOARD!	6.99	11.50	15.99	11.50
☐	MANY A SLIP	6.99	11.50	15.99	11.50
☐	MYSTERY IN THE CHANNEL	6.99	11.50	15.99	11.50
☐	MURDERERS MAKE MISTAKES	6.99	11.50	15.99	11.50
☐	MYSTERY OF THE SLEEPING CAR EXPRESS	6.99	11.50	15.99	11.50
☐	MYSTERY ON SOUTHAMPTON WATER	6.99	11.50	15.99	11.50
☐	THE PIT-PROP SYNDICATE	6.99	11.50	15.99	11.50
☐	THE PONSON CASE	6.99	11.50	15.99	11.50
☐	THE SEA MYSTERY	6.99	11.50	15.99	11.50
☐	SIR JOHN MAGILL'S LAST JOURNEY	6.99	11.50	15.99	11.50
☐	SUDDEN DEATH	6.99	11.50	15.99	11.50

ALL HOUSE OF STRATUS BOOKS ARE AVAILABLE FROM GOOD BOOKSHOPS OR DIRECT FROM THE PUBLISHER:

Hotline: UK ONLY: 0800 169 1780, please quote author, title and credit card details.
INTERNATIONAL: +44 (0) 20 7494 6400, please quote author, title, and credit card details.

Send to: House of Stratus
24c Old Burlington Street
London
W1X 1RL
UK

Please allow following carriage costs per ORDER
(For goods up to free carriage limits shown)

	£(Sterling)	$(US)	$(CAN)	€(Euros)
UK	1.95	3.20	4.29	3.00
Europe	2.95	4.99	6.49	5.00
North America	2.95	4.99	6.49	5.00
Rest of World	2.95	5.99	7.75	6.00
Free carriage for goods value over:	50	75	100	75

PLEASE SEND CHEQUE, POSTAL ORDER (STERLING ONLY), EUROCHEQUE, OR INTERNATIONAL MONEY ORDER (PLEASE CIRCLE METHOD OF PAYMENT YOU WISH TO USE)

MAKE PAYABLE TO: STRATUS HOLDINGS plc

Order total including postage:_____Please tick currency you wish to use and add total amount of order:

☐ £ (Sterling)   ☐ $ (US)   ☐ $ (CAN)   ☐ € (EUROS)

VISA, MASTERCARD, SWITCH, AMEX, SOLO, JCB:

☐☐☐☐☐☐☐☐☐☐☐☐☐☐☐☐☐☐☐☐☐☐

Issue number (Switch only):

☐☐☐

Start Date: Expiry Date:

☐☐ / ☐☐   ☐☐ / ☐☐

Signature: _____

NAME: _____

ADDRESS: _____

_____

POSTCODE: _____

Please allow 28 days for delivery.

Prices subject to change without notice.
Please tick box if you do not wish to receive any additional information. ☐

House of Stratus publishes many other titles in this genre; please check our website (**www.houseofstratus.com**) for more details